Greg faced Sara ac
a touch of his anger ou~ ~~
felt the blood pulsing through her neck.

'I need someone to manage this homestead,'
Greg said unexpectedly. 'And this family.'

Sara looked at him in surprise. There was a
bitter coldness in his voice. Then it was suddenly
tired. He sat down. He took up a paper knife,
then let it fall to the table. He took a cigarette
from the box and lit it. At last he lifted his eyes
to Sara. They were like marbles that had no
light in them.

'Would you consider marrying me, Sara?'

Available in Fontana
by the same author

Joyday for Jodi
Shining River
Six for Heaven
The Gone-Away Man
Home at Sundown
Come Home Dear
Wife to Order
The Other Girl
Follow Your Star
The Call of the Pines
The Man from Outback
The Moonshiner
Kingdom of the Heart

and many others

LUCY WALKER

Master of Ransome

Collins

FONTANA BOOKS

First published 1958
First issued in Fontana Books, 1966
Ninth Impression March 1973

© Lucy Walker 1958

Printed in Great Britain
Collins Clear-Type Press
London and Glasgow

CHAPTER ONE

Sara Brent stirred in her comfortable slung seat in the Dakota plane. The girl in front of her sat up to adjust her safety belt ready for landing, and once again Sara could see the neat golden curls in a pretty line under the other's close-fitting hat. Sara wished those golden curls didn't disturb her so much. They did, not so much from envy, though they were so neat and beautiful envy might well have been justified, but because Sara had met their owner before. She had met Julia Camden in the offices of the Camden Pastoral Company in Adelaide where Sara had lately been working as a typist to Clifford Camden, business manager of the Company which controlled several properties in the north of Australia.

Sara herself had come to Australia as a typist with a Trade Commission from the United Kingdom. With her parents' consent she had transferred to the Camden Pastoral Company to gain experience in the main occupation of the country.

Because of her position in this firm Sara could not help knowing that Miss Julia Camden, beautiful and sophisticated member of the big grazing family of Camden, was someone exceptionally selfish.

Now that Sara had been sent to work as a kind of organising secretary to the Camden family on their big station north of the twenty-sixth parallel she was disturbed to find Julia on the same plane as herself. If Julia was also bound for the station then life might prove just a little bit difficult.

To begin with, Sara was nervous of Julia's autocratic and condescending air, as she had sensed it when they had met for a brief moment in Clifford Camden's office in the city.

How big was a station homestead, Sara wondered? The property covered a million acres, she knew that. But did that mean the homestead was big enough to allow one to live at close quarters with Julia Camden . . . and be happy?

And ought she to make herself known to the other girl?

She decided not. If Julia could forget she had ever met Sara, then Sara could also have regrettable holes in her own memory.

She fingered the clasp of her safety belt as she felt the faint upsurge of stomach muscles and knew they were losing height preparatory to landing.

This is it, she thought, and closed her eyes. She knew the most dangerous moments in flying were at the times of taking-off and landing. She wished that graziers and station owners didn't do everything by air these days. If God had meant secretaries to fly he would have given them wings surely. Sara had only been in a plane once before and she was still not very brave about it.

The plane was running along the tarmac now and Sara heaved a sigh of relief. Oh, how good and kind and beloved was the earth! Even if it was brown sun-dried earth with nothing green about it except a few eucalyptus standing in forlorn clumps in the distance.

Sara undid her safety belt and stood up to take her case from the luggage rack.

'Good trip, wasn't it?' said the air hostess pleasantly.

Her smile took in both Julia Camden and the dark-haired girl behind her. Julia did not see the smile, or was not interested, so Sara returned it pleasantly. When Sara smiled her face showed a merry elfin quality. She didn't know it but quite a lot of people looked at her twice. She had shining dark hair with just a hint of natural wave. It curled to her cheek below her high cheek-bones. This and the wide-set eyes and small curled fringe gave her the elfin touch. These —and a hint of the retroussé about her nose. This latter feature Sara deeply regretted and longed for a nice Grecian nose like Julia's. Her mother and father who were in England had nice long aristocratic noses. Why, Sara wondered, had she taken after an aunt instead of her mother?

'You've made us very comfortable,' Sara said to the air hostess. 'Thank you.'

'Oh, don't thank me,' the hostess replied. 'You weren't any trouble. Quite an old hand at flying, I can see that.'

Sara smiled wanly.

'I like mother earth best,' she admitted. She didn't have any touch of the elf now. Her eyes were serious and immediately the merry quality gave way to one of earnest endeavour. Anyone interested in Sara as a personality would have marvelled at the way her firm little mouth and chin argued the point with her nose, her wide grey eyes and the pretty page-boy haircut.

She was twenty years old but only looked that when her

6

mouth and not her eyes was in control of the situation.

The hostess glanced at Sara's luggage label.

'You're going to Ransome station?' she said. She pointed through the window. 'There's the station wagon waiting for you the other side of the wire fence.' Her smile deepened. 'That's Andy Patterson at the wheel. You're about to begin the most hazardous part of your journey now.'

'Goodness me. Does he drive like that?' asked Sara.

'And how! Never mind, you'll get into the safety zone again when you get in the Camden plane. There's nothing you can hit in the air except a bird.'

'How far do we drive before we get the Camden plane?'

'It's about five miles out into the country. They use private land, out from the town.'

Julia Camden, in front, had got her case down from the luggage rack.

'Oh, look here,' she said, turning to the hostess. 'Give me a hand with this thing, will you? 'Pon my word, these spaces between seats are the limit. I don't know why you don't use a Convair or Constellation on these runs. . . .'

'We're waiting for a jet liner on this run,' the air hostess said agreeably. 'I don't suppose the Company could afford *both*.'

'Jet liner on this run?' said a young man waiting for both Sara and Julia to move out of the aisle. 'That'll be the day!'

Julia gave him a withering stare and the young man winked at the air hostess. Sara caught just the edge of it and could not help smiling.

'May I?' he said to Sara, lifting his hat with one hand and taking her case with the other.

'Oh, thank you so much. That is kind of you.'

He was a nice young man and Sara felt oddly surprised and pleased that he had taken her case and not Julia's.

'I think I go over to that station wagon . . .' Sara said uncertainly to her escort. 'I was told that was for the Ransome station plane.'

'You going out to Ransome? Well, well! We'd better introduce ourselves. I'm Jack Brownrigg and I'm a friend of Greg Camden's. He's the boss out there. . . . I suppose you know that? You come up for the big party and the muster?'

'Yes and no,' Sara said quietly. 'I'm the secretary. I believe it's going to be a very big party and a very big muster and the Company thought Mr Gregory should have a secretary while it's on.'

7

'Greg with a secretary!' Jack Brownrigg threw back his head and laughed. 'Wait till the other station owners hear about that. Mostly they do with their book-keepers and a jackaroo.'

A faint colour rose in Sara's cheeks.

'I gathered it was something new,' she said.

They had reached the wire fence and Jack Brownrigg passed her case between the wires and held them apart by putting his foot on the lower one and holding the upper two wires upwards with his hand.

'Climb through,' he said. 'Nobody ever uses gates if they don't have to.'

Sara climbed through and turned to thank him.

The young brown-faced man at the wheel of the car got out and came towards them.

'Here's your passenger, Andy,' Jack Brownrigg said. 'Tell Greg I rescued her.'

'Morning, Jack. Morning, Miss . . . er . . . Miss . . .'

'Brent,' Sara said. 'Sara Brent.'

'Sara Brent,' said Jack Brownrigg with a smile. 'I'll remember that when I come out to the party.'

'Where's my other passenger?' said Andy dryly. 'Guess she's turning the airport upside down looking for me.'

'She'll come in good time,' Jack said. 'Julia always turns up.'

Sara looked at him in surprise. He hadn't shown recognition of Julia in the plane.

Sara had noticed that when Julia left the plane she had disappeared inside the Air Office.

'Shouldn't I do something about my ticket?'

'You should have,' said Jack Brownrigg. 'I'm afraid you're in for serious trouble not checking out officially.'

'Had I better go back?' Sara asked anxiously.

The two men laughed.

'He's the boss cocky,' said Andy, pointing to the other with his thumb. 'He *is* the Air Office.'

'Oh!' said Sara in some bewilderment.

'Give me your papers. I'll see they don't arrest you,' said Jack Brownrigg, taking her ticket. 'I'll leave you with Andy now. Don't forget to tell Greg I saw you.'

He lifted his hat and walked rapidly back in the direction of the galvanised iron house that was the Air Office.

Andy Patterson, tall, lean and weathered in the face till he looked like leather, slung her case in the back of the station wagon and then held open the door for her. His wide-brimmed, incredibly shabby slouch hat was pushed well back on his head. He grinned down at Sara.

'You don't know anything yet, miss, but that fella owns half the air line. Air pilot in the Korean War. Only a kid then. Best pilot in the north these days. . . .'

'I would have thought he would have known Miss Camden. Miss Julia Camden, I mean. She was a passenger.'

'He'd have known her all right. But he wouldn't have been bothered, if you know what I mean. It's heavy going, with Julia. She's got too much money and too many airs for blokes like Jack Brownrigg. She probably said "Good day" when she got in the plane and turned her back on him. She's kinda like that. . . .'

'Oh, I'm sorry . . .' said Sara and tried hard to think of something by which to change the conversation. Andy changed it for her.

'Guess I'll amble over to the shed and pick her up,' he said. 'Might as well. . . .' Then smiling rather wickedly down at Sara, 'Not that she deserves it, mind you. I'll just do it for Greg's sake.'

'Greg's sake?'

'Well, she's kinda his girl in a way, even though they're cousins,' Andy said. 'Then Julia got flying high and broke it up. Guess they'll patch it up. She's always coming up here since the wool clip on the south run turned out worth half a million. And Greg . . . well, he's never looked at anyone else anyway.'

'She's very lovely,' Sara said, feeling she must say the right thing to this man. She couldn't imagine what his status on Ransome was. He looked like a cross between a hobo and a stockman.

He swung the car round and jolted over the rough ground at a great pace towards the iron building.

'Here she is,' said Andy, grinning. 'Make way for the great lady.' He braked sharply and said to Sara, 'You sit tight, miss. If she wants the seat you're in you just tell her to fly a kite. You're here first.'

Oh dear! Sara thought. What do I do now?

Julia, however, did not want the front seat beside the driver. She preferred the back seat and plenty of room to herself.

She greeted Andy Patterson with a perfunctory nod and Sara with the merest 'How do you do?' Sara said nothing

9

about having met before. Obviously Julia was not intent on conversation.

Sara looked away over the vast brown distances of semi-desert country so as not to let Andy wink at her.

While Andy drove . . . at a reckless pace . . . he whistled through his teeth and this prevented him from making conversation.

Sara thought that if others at Ransome felt like this about Julia, she, Sara, was not going to have an easy time of it.

Then she remembered what Andy had said about Gregory Camden . . . the boss. He was attached to Julia. Sara felt glad of that. She as a good secretary had always to be on the side of the 'Boss.' It would simplify her attitude to Julia. It would be 'Julia right or wrong.' Sara's position would be clear-cut . . . and that was important.

She had tried to please Clifford Camden at the city end of the big pastoral company. Mr Clifford had kept on breaking all the rules of office procedure. He made love in a mild kind of way to the typists, all of them, including Sara. Sara had been relieved when she had been posted to the station for six weeks. Mr Clifford's love-making had been innocuous, confined to an occasional touching of an arm and a sly way of commenting on any new dress or change of shade in make-up. But it had been there and was very bad taste. Sara hoped Gregory Camden was not of the same cut of cloth.

But no. Andy had said Greg had never looked at any girl other than Julia. She'd be safe with Greg. Besides, he ran the station very efficiently. Sara knew that from her inside position in the firm.

She remembered some of Gregory Camden's terse commands and the clean-cut directions that had come through the mail to the office. She had visualised him as being a strong man. A good administrator of a very intricately constructed property . . . one that included a number of members of a loosely knit family, some of whom were contentious. Julia had been one of the contentious ones. She was always spending money and demanding more. Each member of this family, some of whom were cousins and second cousins, held a share in Ransome station . . . and each seemed to feel he or she could run the station better than the manager.

Gregory dealt firmly with these shareholders . . . and he never wasted a word in so doing. Some of the demands that came from one or other of the Camdens were verging on the ridiculous. The very last one that had come into the office before Sara left was a request from a Louise Camden for Clifford to buy an ocean-going yacht and have it equipped and ready to sail out of Townsville for the Barrier Reef in three months. Louise Camden had written that she owed such a lot of people hospitality she thought it quickest to buy a yacht and take them all for a fortnight's trip to the Great Barrier Reef.

Clifford has tossed the letter across to Sara and said, 'Wait till Greg hears about that one.'

That was the day Julia had come into the office, looking like a million dollars and smelling faintly of Chanel Five.

'I want some money, Cliff,' she had said. 'I haven't a rag to my back.'

Clifford had said, 'Poor Julia. You really do look down and out. I'll ask Greg what the cattle are likely to fetch this season.'

'Coward,' Julia had said scornfully. 'You always fall back on Greg, don't you?'

'If Greg didn't save your skin for you the others would fall on you like a pack of wolves,' Clifford had said with a smile. 'Actually, my sweet coz, Greg's the best friend you ever had.'

Julia had tapped her long gloved fingers on the polished jarrah table and looked thoughtfully at her cousin.

'M'm . . .' she said at length. 'I think I under-estimated Greg in the old days.'

'Or under-estimated the value of that southern run and its subsequent wool cheque?'

This might have been insolent of Clifford if he hadn't spoken with a smile.

'You never were a good business man, Cliff. Greg has other charms besides his managerial interest in Ransome.'

'Since when have the scales fallen from your eyes?'

'Since I've been around,' said Julia. 'And I have been around, you know. Quite a lot.'

'So your bank balance . . . or rather the absence of it . . . tells me.'

Sara had not quite understood the references to Greg and his charms but now Andy Patterson had enlightened her. Greg had once been in love with Julia . . . and she had turned him down. He was still her best friend . . . according

11

to Clifford . . . and that might mean anything.

Andy Patterson stopped whistling and looked down at her. 'Homesick already?' he asked.

'Oh, no,' Sara said hastily. 'I suppose I'm just a little tired.'

'Well, take a look at that lake over there. That'll take your mind off your sorrows.'

Sara looked away to the north, and across the brown and grey stubbly undergrowth she could see a great expanse of shining blue water. She could even see the blurred outline of clumps of trees on the far side.

'Oh,' she said. 'Why didn't I notice it before?'

'Because it wasn't there before. It's just got there in the last five minutes.'

Sara looked at him puzzled.

'It's a mirage,' he said with a grin. 'Want me to drive into it to prove it?'

'You drive straight on, Andy,' said Julia sharply from the back seat. 'Miss Brent will see plenty of mirages before she leaves Ransome and I don't want to be all day getting there. I'm sure Miss Brent is quite as tired as I am.'

'But it's marvellous,' said Sara wonderingly. 'One could *swim* in it, it's so real.'

'It's real in a way, I guess,' said Andy. 'It'll probably be a sky reflection of Dampier Lake . . . that's about fifty miles away. You get Greg to take you out some day while you're at Ransome. Or maybe I'll take you myself.'

'Really, Andy,' said Julia from the back seat. 'Is that all you have to do with your time? No wonder things on Ransome want shaking up.'

'They'll certainly shake up with you there, Julia,' he said. 'I can see the whole place getting a face lift.'

'I'm certainly going round the bores this time and see for myself just what you are mustering out at those grass patches. Have you ever really taken a complete count of the stock on Ransome?'

'Nobody could ever do that, Julia. You know that. There's always cattle in the scrub that never get caught in a muster. And now that the sheep down south are paying the way they do the cattle get away more than ever. Remember the day when you fought 'em single-handed to keep the sheep off the place, Julia? That was the day! I bet you've eaten those words many a time since.'

'I was merely putting Greg on his mettle,' said Julia

12

haughtily. 'A little opposition galvanises Greg into activity.'

'M'm,' said Andy meaningly. 'Well, there's the old plane over there, Miss Brent. How does she look after the Dakota?'

Sara had already had it drummed into her that the Dakota was very utilitarian compared with the big liners, but this funny thing to her untutored eyes looked more like a handful of tin cans soldered together. She tried not to feel anxious.

'What is it?' she asked.

'Anson,' said Andy. 'Backbone of the north. Without the good old Ansons north of twenty-six we'd be marooned.'

Julia, who had complained of the Dakota, oddly enough did not find anything wrong with the Anson. She got into it and settled herself down on one of the narrow seats as if she were getting into a car. Sara half expected her to say 'Home, James' any minute.

Sara in her ignorance was appalled at the dilapidated interior and the exposed cockpit. There was no controls board. Just a mass of knobs and wires.

Andy Patterson handed the station wagon over to a black driver and got into the plane and sat in the cockpit with the pilot. The pilot was a second Andy . . . tall, thin, laconic, dressed in open-necked shirt and brown drill trousers. He wore nothing at all on his head.

What a crazy crew, thought Sara and shut her eyes and hoped for the best as the plane took off. She kept them shut for the next three-quarters of an hour until she felt the plane come down, strike the bumpy ground and seem to ricochet off it. A few more bumps and the engine was silent. Then they were at a standstill.

They were at Ransome. She was alive.

In the paddock was another station wagon, half a dozen barking dogs racing towards them, followed by a host of little black piccaninnies.

Beyond the brown stubbly paddock was a garden green with shrubs and trees. Between them was a glimpse of a white painted roof and behind that three tanks standing up like spires in the air. Away to the sides of this oasis, and to the rear, were a host of buildings, some brilliantly covered with bougainvillæa.

It was like a small township set down in the middle of a seeming desert. Only in the distance was there green of timber and blue of hill and valley.

This was Sara's first view of Ransome . . . a homestead

set in the middle of a million acres of cattle country. The home of the Camdens. She was in the north now. The place of fascination and mystery; of crocodiles, pandanus, floods and droughts. The place where, a hundred years ago, they said white men could not live and stay sane.

CHAPTER TWO

Julia Camden and Sara had been met on the wide veranda in front of the open front door by a young girl in shorts with a very gay blouse, very fair somewhat tousled hair and sleepy but curious eyes. She was sane enough . . . that was certain.

She kissed Julia and said, 'What have you come for so early, Ju Ju? Didn't expect you till the eve of the party. Not that you're not welcome.'

'I'm sure of that,' said Julia. 'Where's aunt?'

'Still having her siesta, I think.' She turned to Sara and held out her hand. 'You're Miss Brent? I'm Marion Camden, Greg's sister. I'm the one who's having the party all the fuss is about.' She grinned mischievously. 'Anyhow it's got us a secretary, which is really setting the bush telegraph humming. Hope you don't mind organising parties, do you?'

'I'm anxious to try,' Sara said with a smile. 'A house-party of sixty people is quite a big thing, isn't it?'

'Not to mention another sixty men and stockmen outside,' said Marion. 'Oh well . . . we'll manage. Oh, here's Mrs Whittle.'

A middle-aged woman dressed in a severe dark blue cotton dress had come through the front door.

'Welcome home, Miss Julia,' she said formally and the two shook hands perfunctorily.

'This is Miss Brent,' said Marion. 'Mrs Whittle is our housekeeper. I should say bodyguard and house guard too,' she added with an ironic grin. 'Nothing gets past Mrs Whittle, so don't try, will you, Sara? You don't mind my calling you Sara, do you? You'll have to call me Marion and Julia, Julia. Nobody in the outback calls anyone by anything but their Christian name. Even the stockmen will do it . . . so be prepared.'

'I've never got used to it,' said Mrs Whittle. 'In your

father's time it was not like this. No one has ever called me anything but Mrs Whittle.'

'Nor ever will, Witty darling,' said Marion. 'Come on, let's carry Sara's case for her. I'll get Nellie to bring in the big one.'

Julia had disappeared a few minutes earlier through the front door. From a passage entering the hallway from the left she now emerged with a look of annoyance on her otherwise lovely face.

'Where's Greg?' she asked irritably. 'He isn't in his office.'

'Ju Ju darling, if he'd been in his office he wouldn't have been out counting his cattle for you. Either way you'd be bound to be disappointed,' said Marion.

'He's down at the yards, Miss Julia,' Mrs Whittle said placatingly. 'He'll be up presently for a cup of tea. You go and have a wash and a rest. You'll see enough of him before your visit's out.'

'Which room do I have? The usual one?'

'Of course,' said Mrs Whittle. 'The green veranda one on the south side. You'll find everything ready . . . and Nellie will bring you some tea. I'll just show Miss Sara to her room.'

'I'll leave you to Mrs Whittle,' Marion said. 'I'm going to get under the shower before everyone else starts a run on it. Come out on the side veranda when you feel like it . . . that's where we all sit most of the time.'

A fat jolly-looking lubra with pretty, dark curly hair and a flashing set of teeth who had been hovering in the background took Sara's case from Marion and followed Sara and Mrs Whittle down a passage that opened off the hall. All the doors of the rooms were open, and Sara caught sight of a billiard room and two bedrooms before Mrs Whittle stopped at a door and said, 'This is your room. There's a shower next door, it's just been built in since we got the new engine. Would you like a shower first, or some tea?'

'A shower . . . I think,' said Sara.

'I bring 'um you,' said the lubra, smiling happily.

'Thank you very much,' Sara smiled back.

'I think you've got everything,' said Mrs Whittle, looking round the room professionally.

'It looks very nice. And I like those windows opening out like doors on to the veranda.'

'All the doors do that in this house,' said Mrs Whittle. 'It's built square and on a quadrangle for that reason. One has to have air in this climate. Except for the front veranda it's all fly-screened, as you can see. We never leave a veranda fly-door open.'

'I shall be careful about that,' Sara said, feeling that Mrs Whittle was giving her a polite instruction.

'I'll leave you now. Have a cup of tea and a rest. We have dinner at seven. The triangle sounds at six . . . that's for the men down at the quarters, but at that time most of the inside people go into the billiard room. They have a drink or a cigarette or something before dinner. They'll be expecting you.'

'Thank you,' Sara said gravely. She felt Mrs Whittle was being tactful and helpful. The woman was a little severe but Sara thought she might be going to like her. Intuitively she guessed that as far as the inside of the homestead was concerned Mrs Whittle was the power behind the throne. If so, Sara would have to work with her in the organising of the big house-party.

Mrs Whittle went out and shut the door softly behind her. The passage was so thickly carpeted Sara did not hear her footsteps receding.

Sara's room was plainly but comfortably furnished. The bed was wide and covered with a blue cover that matched the small arm-chair over by the veranda door. The other pieces of furniture, a dressing-table and wardrobe, a small bedside table and another chair, were made of a light red wood. It looked very old furniture . . . but very good. Brought here, Sara thought, by the first Camdens who had brought their own furniture out from England. Probably a hundred and twenty years ago. The curtains were gay and light.

Sara's first impression of Ransome became her lasting one. It was furnished in a good and comfortable way and there was something solid and dignified about it in spite of its white roof, its fly-screen like a netting all round it and its flanking of small galvanised iron buildings. The first Camdens had built the homestead solidly of mud brick and stone in an age when most pioneer graziers had had to build of wood and iron. They had planted trees and creepers on this place where they had found water, and somehow a hundred years had added to the solidity of the whole building rather than produced signs of wear.

She had showered and changed into a light dressing-gown by the time Nellie, the lubra, brought her her tea.

'You like 'um plenty good, plenty hot?' said Nellie, smiling happily.

'Yes, thank you. This is very nice. Just what I wanted, Nellie.'

'You drink 'um up plenty soon. I see you'm bye-'m-bye,' said Nellie.

At six o'clock Sara heard the triangle being struck outside and she got up from her bed, creamed and made up her face and brushed her hair. She slipped on a plain but pretty dark pink silk frock and a pair of open-toed light shoes. She had been given an extra travelling and dress allowance by the firm because of the necessity for tropical clothes. She looked at herself in the mirror and wondered if she did justice to that dress allowance.

I don't look like Julia, she thought. But I ought to do.

Somehow it was a very nervous moment to appear before the household for the first time. Sara had to screw up her courage before she opened her door and stepped into the passage. She could hear laughter and voices, male and female, coming from the open door of the billiard room farther down the passage. She drew in a deep breath and walked steadily towards the door.

I do hope I'll do, she thought, and wondered if her dress and shoes were either too elaborate—or under-elaborate. She wished she *knew*, really *knew*, what was the right thing for a secretary to wear for dinner on a far north station.

She paused in the doorway of the billiard room.

'Here goes!' she breathed.

She took a step inside, and then hesitated.

She was in a very big room. On the far side two french windows, wide open, gave on to the veranda. A young man was just coming through. He held a glass in one hand and turned to a table which was almost weighed down with decanters, jugs of frosty water and glasses and a variety of bottles. There were two other men at the table with their backs to Sara. She supposed she saw them first because they were so big.

Then, looking across the acre of billiard table she could see another man. He, too, was tall and he was standing in front of the other window, one foot raised to rest on the edge of a chair. Sara could only partly see him because Julia was talking to him. And Julia had her back to the door. Sara was just conscious of the fact that this man, dark and bronzed, was tall, perhaps thirty years of age or more, and that he looked down as he listened to Julia.

Sara blinked. Then she was aware of the group sitting

in wide cane chairs at the end of the room, and of Mrs Whittle, dressed now in a dark grey silk dress, coming towards her.

'Oh, there you are, Miss Sara,' she said. 'You must come down and be introduced to Mrs Camden.'

She led the way towards this group in cane chairs and Sara quite literally walked 'down' the room. It was like parading a ballroom. She was aware that the three men by the table under the window turned round and looked at her. She was also aware . . . though she never knew why . . . that Julia Camden and the tall bronzed man to whom she was talking did *not* turn or lift up a head. They took no notice of her at all.

As Sara came towards the group at the end of the room, Marion, who was sitting in one of the cane chairs, smiled at her affably. For a moment Sara could not see Marion's companion. She was buried deep in her chair and its back was towards the door.

Sara and Mrs Whittle walked round the chair and the introduction was more in the nature of a presentation.

'Miss Brent, Mrs Camden,' Mrs Whittle said formally.

'So here you are,' Mrs Camden said, holding up a soft white powdered be-ringed hand.

Sara bent a little to shake hands.

Mrs Camden smiled happily.

'Sit down, my dear. Marion, pull up a chair. Mrs Whittle, get her a drink. What do you drink, my dear? Whisky? Gin? Anything you like, dear. It's all over there.'

She waved her hand towards the table. Mrs Whittle had not waited to ascertain Sara's choice. She had simply gone to the table and one of the men was pouring something from a tall frosty jug.

'Don't be silly, Mother,' Marion Camden said. 'As if Sara drinks whisky at this hour. You don't, do you?'

Sara shook her head.

'I'd rather have a lemon drink or something like that just now.'

'That's just what Witty'll bring you,' said Marion with a grin.

Sara sat down in the chair Marion indicated. It was between Marion and her mother, and she could just see Julia and the dark bronzed man out of the corner of her eye. But she did not look at them. Instead she looked at Mrs Camden.

'Well . . . tell me how you got here, dear,' said Mrs Camden.

Sara could not help reflecting that here was a plump, very coddled woman, but pretty in her own way and certainly very kind and friendly.

'I came on the mail plane . . .' began Sara.

'Wonderful plane,' said Mrs Camden, interrupting her. 'What would we do without it! Of course, my father, and the children's father, used bullock wagons. Here's your drink, dear. Marion, tell those boys to come over and meet Sara. Boys always like to meet a pretty girl.'

'In a minute, Mother. Let Sara have her drink. Besides, the boys are shy too.'

Sara glanced round at the three men by the window. One she might have called a boy. He wouldn't be more than nineteen or twenty, but the other two were big, thick-set men well in their forties.

She wondered if Mrs Camden included the man talking to Julia amongst the 'boys.' Sara looked at him. He was still looking down. One eyebrow might have been just a little cocked as if he was listening to Julia. Sara wondered who he was. There was an air of quiet authority about him. And his shoes were of beautiful polished fine leather. No wonder he liked looking at them.

Sara didn't have to pay much attention to Mrs Camden. Her hostess kept up a running commentary of conversation that was half questions . . . the answers to which she did not wait for . . . and statements about things and people to Marion . . . to which Marion did not reply.

Mrs Whittle had gone over to speak to the man by the window, the man talking to Julia.

For the first time he looked up and Sara could see all his face. It was very bronzed. His eyes were blue and he looked at Mrs Whittle with a kind of unflinching gaze as if he was paying great attention to her. Yet still he said nothing. Then quite sharply Julia lifted up her right elbow and leaned it on the man's shoulder. She looked right up into his face as she spoke to him.

For the first time his smile widened a little as he looked at Julia and Sara could see the quick flash of his teeth. The two made a conversation piece that might have been called 'Possession and Tolerance.' Or was it something more than tolerance?

Sara could not help a mild feeling of sadness that everyone in the room had noticed her . . . that a stranger had come amongst them . . . except these two by the window.

She did not expect courtesy from Julia but she could not help but wonder that the man had made no move at all. After all, they were on a lonely cattle station a hundred miles from the nearest neighbour. It must be something to have a stranger in the house!

Mrs Camden was chattering on, rather like the brook, and Marion interspersed it with, 'Don't be silly, Mother,' or 'All right, Mother, in a minute.'

Sara had only to sit, smile and occasionally say 'Yes' or 'No.' It was soon apparent there was no possible way of communicating with Mrs Camden. She did not wait for answers or comments.

While Sara listened to Mrs Camden with politeness she could not help but take in the room and all who were in it.

She was dressed right. Thank God for that. Mrs Camden and Marion were both in gay floral dresses of pure silk. Sara could almost feel the lovely quality in the gentle light of the sheen. Julia, like herself, wore a plain dress, but it was beautifully cut.

The men were dressed much alike. The three by the window wore immaculate white shirts with long sleeves and soft silk ties. They had on some kind of loose-legged cotton drill trousers. Only the man talking to Julia was a little different. He had a loose cotton coat over his white shirt. His tie was dark and long and straight. His trousers were a fawn-coloured gaberdine and like his shoes were of beautiful fine well-cut quality.

Mrs Whittle left the group and came down the long room towards them.

'Here comes Witty,' said Marion with a grin. 'I guess she's going to introduce you to Greg now. The other poor darlings have had to wait.'

Sara felt something like a shock go through her.

So that was Gregory Camden! She was to be his secretary. How odd that he did not come and greet her himself! Odder still that he hadn't even looked up to see what kind of a secretary he had!

And that Mrs Camden hadn't made introductions! And that everybody had hung back, waiting . . .

Maybe he was some kind of a harsh taskmaster. Sara remembered the terseness and brevity of his business letters.

Yet his face wasn't harsh.

Sara thought all this as she walked back up the room, this time on the window side of the billiard table, with Mrs Whittle. She could look at his face because he had ceased to look at Julia now and was looking down again at the toe of his shoe. It still rested on the edge of the chair. He hadn't once changed his position.

His face wasn't harsh. His face was rather a nice face except that, now he wasn't smiling, it looked grave, as if it was in thoughtful repose.

His features were even and strong. He had far and away more personality than anyone else in that room.

Was that really true? Or did she read it in him because he had a million acres and 15,000 head of cattle strung round his neck? Not to mention 10,000 sheep on the south run below the twenty-sixth parallel?

Sara could not help a little thrill of anticipation as Mrs Whittle brought her towards the two by the window.

Yes . . . he had a good face. He'd be all right to work for.

'Miss Sara Brent, Mr Greg,' Mrs Whittle said.

Sara began to lift her hand and then it wavered in mid-air and fell to her side. Her smile faltered.

Gregory Camden had looked up from his shoe at last.

His eyes were a dark blue. They were grave and appraising. In addition there was a cold, forbidding antagonism in them.

'But why?' Sara asked herself. 'Why? Why? Why?'

He said 'How do you do?' in a soft voice that came between barely opened lips.

'Quite well, thank you.'

He did not drop his gaze but went on looking at her with that look of cold, reflective dislike in his eyes.

'Oh, so you're here,' Julia said with some insolence.

It was Sara's turn to look at the speaker gravely.

The customer is always right, she remembered, and secretaries cannot answer back.

She did not attempt to answer Julia but turned and looked inquiringly at Mrs Whittle.

'Now come and meet Mr Benson; he's the book-keeper. Jim Smith's the overseer and Dave is one of our jackaroos.'

CHAPTER THREE

Dinner was served in a style that Sara had thought to belong to another age.

They all sat down to a long wide table in a big room nearly as big as the billiard room. Greg Camden sat at the head of the table and carved. His mother sat on his right hand and Julia on his left. It was Mrs Whittle who did the honours with the vegetables at the other end of the table. Three other quite young men had come in at the sound of the dinner bell, and Sara, at Mrs Whittle's request, had taken a seat half-way down the table between one of these young men and Mr Benson, the book-keeper. Sara noticed with a smile that her seat was neither above nor below the salt. She was exactly halfway to the hierarchy at the top of the table.

Marion Camden sat next to Julia so she had evidently moved down one to make place for Julia. Two jackaroos were ranged between her and Mrs Whittle.

The men on either side of Sara were talkative and friendly. Both the jackaroos on the other side of the table, young Englishmen sent out to learn the business of cattle-raising, were shy of Sara but not of her neighbours.

At the top of the table Mrs Camden kept up her stream of happy innocuous chatter. Occasionally Greg Camden spoke to Julia or Marion, but mostly he concentrated on the business of the administration of a big meal to a big family.

It was Marion who seemed to concern herself most with Sara's welfare. When there was a lull in the conversation she spoke down the table to Sara.

'Do you type and do shorthand? Both?' she asked. 'Can you type on an old chaff-cutting machine, because that's all we've got in the office? You'll have to cadge off Mr Benson if you want something modern and well-oiled.'

Mr Benson was the stout and kindly book-keeper.

'Mr Benson has the best of everything,' Mr Benson said. 'A labourer is worthy of his tools.'

'Labourer!' one of the jackaroos scoffed. 'Sitting in the cool of a bough shade all day! You and Miss Brent have the best end of a day's work on a cattle station.'

'If we didn't, you wouldn't get your bust-cheque when

you shoot through,' said Mr Benson happily. 'Someone's got to sign on the dotted line.'

'Sara won't have anything to do with cheques, will she, Greg?' Mrs Camden sounded puzzled, 'She's going to write all my letters for me, isn't she? All those cards. That's what Clifford sent her for. . . .'

'Nothing of the kind, Mother,' interrupted Marion. 'You're not to monopolise Sara.' She looked down the table at Sara and the slightly ironic smile deepened. 'Clifford sent you up to help Greg. At least that is what he *said*.'

Sara was conscious of a sudden silence round the table. It wasn't as if they were waiting for her to say something so much as that they *knew* something in advance and were waiting to hear her views.

'My instructions from the Camden Pastoral Company,' Sara said carefully and with a smile, for she felt she was skating on thin ice, 'were that I was to be secretary to Mr Gregory Camden for six weeks.' She let her smile broaden and her eyes shone. 'With a verbal rider to make myself useful all round.'

There was a ripple of laughter all round the table. Greg Camden did not drop his eyes from her face, and Julia leaned forward and helped herself to a piece of bread.

'Useful all round for Clifford,' she said with a drawl. 'The girls Clifford sends up here seem to be so busy being useful to him nobody on Ransome ever sees them except for meals.'

There was another silence and all the men were suddenly busy with something on their plates. Greg dropped his eyes and went on eating. Only Marion remained looked at Sara.

What did they mean by *all Clifford's girls*? No other girls had been sent up from the office as far as Sara knew. And hadn't that man at the airfield . . . Jack Brownrigg . . . said something about it being quite unique Greg Camden having a secretary?

'Clifford's girls!' said Mrs Camden suddenly as she had just caught up with the conversation. 'There was that girl with the red hair. What was her name? Well, it doesn't matter. She was a sweet little thing. Used to put flowers in my bedroom every day.'

'Now, Mother,' said Marion. 'We don't have flowers every day of the year on Ransome.'

'Was she here a whole year? Dear me, I had forgotten.'

'One month,' said Marion.

Mrs Camden turned to her son.

'Sara is going to help me, isn't she, Greg? And there's that business about the yacht. I'm sure I could get one and there'll be all the invitations . . .'

So Mrs Camden was the Louise Camden who had wanted the company to buy her a yacht!

She shot Sara a sudden quick look under her eyelids and Sara realised she wasn't quite as simple and innocuous as she pretended to be.

But what did they mean about Clifford's girls? Were they confusing Clifford's guests with his employees?

'I'm employed by the Company,' Sara said gently. 'Not a friend. . . .'

Greg Camden looked up at her quickly, then turned and spoke to the lubra who had been serving the meal.

'Nellie will put the tea and coffee in the billiard room,' he said. 'Miss Brent, perhaps you could give me a few minutes in the office.'

Sara sighed with relief. So he was going to notice her in her capacity of secretary at last!

'If you're going to shut yourself in for the night, Greg,' the overseer said, 'do you want those horses out in the morning? I'll get Blue-Bag to yard them.'

Greg Camden had risen. He turned and looked down at Julia.

'You want that early morning ride, Julia?' he asked. His voice was suddenly quite kind, and Sara thought his manner visibly softened.

'Of course I do. I want to ride and I want to talk to you *not* in the middle of a crowd.'

'Don't do it, Greg,' said Marion. 'She only wants to talk to you about dollars.'

Julia stretched across the table and took a sultana.

'That's all you know,' she said. 'Clifford's not the only Camden who gets courted on his home territory.'

Sara felt as if her heart missed a beat. What were they trying to say? What were they implying?

She could not help her gaze going quickly to Greg Camden's face. But he was looking at Julia, the little tight smile playing round his lips.

'Sun-up in the saddling yard!' he said. 'I think that's about five-ten, to-morrow.'

He stood aside at the door for his mother and Marion

to go through. Mrs Whittle was obviously remaining behind to oversee the lubra clearing away the meal.

Sara hesitated.

Greg looked at her and raised his eyebrows.

'Miss Brent?' he said, indicating the door. Sara went through it quickly. 'The office is the middle room in the passage on the left of the main hall. I'll join you in a minute.'

Sara had no difficulty in finding the office. It was a medium-sized square room with a large table behind which was a swivel desk chair. Behind the table was a long sash window and doors leading into the room to the right and the left of the room. A bookcase stood in front of one of these doors. The wall behind the door through which Sara entered was lined with shelves which were packed with the folders and files of years. The desk was heavily piled with papers too but they did appear to be stacked in orderly arrays. There were too many shelves and bookcases for pictures, but on a table in the far corner stood a transceiver set, and beside it, on a smaller table, the 'chaff-cutting machine' that would pass for a typewriter.

Sara sat down and waited.

She looked around. The room was neither tidy nor untidy. It was the office of a business man who had too much to do. Greg Camden was evidently orderly and efficient in his office management but the volume of correspondence had overtaken him.

Sara had left the door open behind her, and because the passage outside was thickly carpeted she did not hear Greg coming until he entered the room.

She half rose.

'Sit down, Miss Brent, please.'

His manner was authoritative and there was an edge of sharpness in his voice. He closed the door behind him and walked quickly round his table and picked up a bundle of mail that had probably come in with the plane that afternoon.

Sara looked at his hands rather than at his face. His movements and the movements of his hands were quicker than she had expected. There was something lithe and tigerish in them.

He dropped the bundle of mail unopened and looked at the girl sitting correctly but easily in the chair the other side of the desk.

'Do you think you can understand all this sort of thing?' he asked, waving his hand over the desk.

His eyes were inquiring but still hostile. Sara wondered if he had had a secretary foisted on him by the Company and if he was just one of those station owners, conservative and reactionary, who would not accept change.

Yet that couldn't be the true explanation. She knew from the town end of the station management that Ransome had always been very advanced as far as the ordering and installation of plant were concerned. In fact, this had been one of the toughest bones of contention with other members of the family who were shareholders. Greg, they had constantly claimed, was spending a fortune . . . their fortune . . . buying every new-fangled idea and piece of mechanism that came on the market.

Sara hesitated before she answered. She wanted to give confidence so she chose her words carefully.

'I don't think there'll be any difficulty about that, Mr Camden. I have handled all the station's correspondence for the last year. Perhaps if you would give me a day to do some sorting I will be able to help you.'

'How do you propose to begin?' he asked. He was still standing and the hand that had held the mail was now holding a paper knife. He waited . . . questioning and unconvinced . . . on her answer.

'From my instructions, Mr Camden, I understand you are about to organise two big events on Ransome. If I could reduce your current correspondence to an "in" and an "out" tray and answer your "yes-no" letters for you, we could . . .' she faltered. Then, swallowing, she went on firmly. 'You would then know what you would wish me to do. You would be able to instruct me.'

Greg Camden pulled his chair up and sat down. He rested the palms of both his hands on the table and sat looking at them thoughtfully.

He hasn't any confidence in me, Sara thought. I wonder why. I must have been well recommended.

'Have you an idea what organising a big gathering and a muster in the Far North is like?' he asked.

'No,' said Sara simply. 'But I can find out. I think I'll be able to help you, Mr Camden.'

He got up abruptly and walked backwards and forwards across the room. He thrust his hands in his pockets and stared

26

at the floor. Then he halted in front of the desk again.

'I suppose we've got to give it a trial now we're landed with one another,' he said, stopping suddenly and facing her across the desk.

Sara allowed herself a very small and friendly smile.

'Perhaps we may surprise the Company and do it quite efficiently,' she said.

'I always do things efficiently,' he said abruptly.

'Yes, Mr Camden. I'm the one who has to prove myself, I think. If I'm not able to help you I would like you to say so.'

He was silent again, looking at her thoughtfully.

'All right,' he said at length. He waved his hand over the table. 'I'll be out on the run all day to-morrow. See what you can do.'

Sara felt dismissed so she stood up.

'You understand that my mother and Mrs Whittle must be consulted?'

'Of course. I will take no responsibility without reference, Mr Camden.'

'Very well then. I will tell Mrs Whittle to make arrangements to make the office available to you to-morrow.'

He pulled a scribbling pad towards him and began to jot something on it with a pencil. He tore off the leaf and began to write on the second page. Sara could see his writing was big and bold and the memos contained no more than a few words.

At that moment there was a firm tap on the door.

'Come in!' His voice was staccato and commanding.

The door opened and Mrs Whittle came in.

He looked up and pushed both the memos across the table in her direction.

'I was just sending you a note,' he said. 'Will you arrange for Miss Brent to have what meals she wants and when she wants them? In the office, if necessary. Dinner, of course, we all have together. The other note is to authorise Benson to let Miss Brent go to the store for any materials she needs in the office.'

'Very well, Mr Greg. Do you want to see the menu for dinner to-morrow?'

'Yes. Thank you.' He took a small card from Mrs Whittle and glanced down it.

'That's all right,' he said. 'I don't suppose Julia has any special dislikes at the moment. If she has, we'll no doubt hear about them in the fullness of time. Are the drinks put away, Mrs Whittle?'

'Yes, except the fruit drink in the dining-room refrigerator, and there's a fresh bottle of port wine in the decanter.'

'Good. Thank you.' He turned to Sara. 'There's usually tea in the dining-room about half past nine. Or port wine and a biscuit if you prefer it. We're early risers so the homestead closes down early.'

'All except you, Mr Greg,' Mrs Whittle said severely. 'I hope that now Miss Brent is here you won't do so much office work late at night.'

He did not answer her.

'Good night, Mr Camden,' Sara said as she went to the door.

'Good night! Mrs Whittle, just wait one moment, will you, please?'

Sara was dismissed in more senses than one and she closed the door quietly behind her. She met Marion on her way down the opposite passage leading to the billiard room and the bedrooms beyond.

'Well, how did you get on with Greg?' Marion asked. 'Did he throw you out or did you walk out on your own steam?'

'He didn't throw me out,' Sara said with a smile. 'Why should he?'

'He put up a first-class battle against you before you came. Poor old Greg. Sometimes the family takes the big stick out of his hand and waves it for him. He doesn't like it.'

'A secretary *can* be helpful,' Sara said quietly.

'That's what Clifford says. But then one never knows with Clifford. He's always got an ulterior motive.'

Marion's smile was nothing but amused irony now.

Sara kept a firm control on her smile. At that moment Julia came out of the billiard room. As she walked towards the two girls down the carpeted passage-way Sara thought, again with reluctant admiration, that she had a superb figure. Julia moved soundlessly, like the shadow of a ballerina.

'Where's Greg?' she asked. It was a pity that her voice was so arrogant, because it was a good voice.

'In his office . . . if you want to help him burn the midnight oil?' said Marion slyly. 'But Witty's with him right now.'

'Mrs Whittle does not alarm *me*,' said Julia. 'And I'll soon get rid of her.'

She moved on, silently, beautifully, except there was the

faintest wriggle of her back contours.

'I bet she will too,' said Marion. 'No work for Greg to-night.' She turned to Sara. 'You going to bed? Don't blame you. It's a long journey. Oh well . . . sweet dreams. I guess Clifford will write to you on the next mail. Anyhow he'll be here in a fortnight, so don't feel too homesick.'

'I shan't,' said Sara. 'Good night.'

A letter from Clifford! So that's what they thought!

CHAPTER FOUR

Sara woke on the following morning to the sound of horses galloping across the plain beyond the garden.

Her veranda doors were wide open and already the heat was striking into the room. She raised herself on one elbow and looked out through the palms and paw-paws to the endless stretch of browned grasses and hummocky grey bush where she could see the riders now wheeling in towards the saddling paddock. Julia, hatless and her fair hair shining like gold in the early sunlight, was unmistakable. Greg might have been any of the several tall slim bronzed Australians on the station, but Sara knew that it was he. Unlike Julia, he wore a hat, pulled down on his brow. He wore an open-necked shirt and tight-fitting trousers.

The riders wheeled at a canter around the corner of the house and Sara could see them no more. She wondered why the sight had given her a sense of sadness. Perhaps because it had been a fleet moving picture of the life people might live if they had leisure, money and wide-open spaces.

That, she thought, was hardly fair to Greg Camden. He had wide-open spaces, a great deal of money, but Sara was fairly certain he had very little leisure.

She hadn't had time to think about her strange situation in the household before she went to bed. She had had a shower, brushed her teeth and hair, creamed her face and crawled into bed. She remembered slipping in between the cool linen sheets and that the pillow had been soft and invit-ing and that was all. She had slept the sleep of the just and the exhausted, and known no more until galloping horses had awakened her.

Why hadn't Julia been equally exhausted? She'd made the same day-long air trip, boarding the plane at three in the morning, just as Sara had done. Maybe it was something to do with being used to air travel and not being afraid of aeroplanes.

Sara got out of bed, stretched herself and padded in her pyjamas in bare feet into the shower alcove that had been so recently built . . . a pill-box of concrete . . . leading off her room and jutting on to the veranda.

By the time Sara was out of the shower Nellie the lubra was at her door with a small round tray holding a teapot, cup and saucer and a plate of the thinnest bread and butter Sara had ever seen.

She looked at it and smiled at Nellie.

'You make?' she asked.

'No me.' The black girl giggled as if it was the funniest joke she had ever heard. 'Kitchen Mary make 'um, plenty,' she said.

Sara was to learn that for laughter and smiles there was nothing to equal the lubras.

She sat on the edge of her bed and enjoyed her tea and the wafers of bread and butter. She began to think now that the cold shower had cleared the cobwebs from her brain.

Clearly Gregory Camden had not wanted her. She had been foisted on him. Secondly he had no way of knowing whether she was going to be worth the trouble or worthy of what Mr Benson would doubtless have called her 'bust-cheque' . . . the money she would receive at the end of her labours and before she 'shot through.'

This did not disconcert Sara. She knew that in her secretarial capacity she could be of great use to Mr Camden. The thing was to win his confidence in that respect. One could always do a great deal more for a boss who *knew* you could do the work and passed it over.

The other thing . . . the business about Clifford Camden! That was more difficult because it was unpleasant. No girl likes the kind of suggestion that was in the air about herself and Clifford Camden if there was no truth in it. Not all the acres of Ransome could make her like Clifford as a man. He was all right as a director of a station property and he was a shrewd man with finance. But his sleek smile! His way of looking at a girl's new dress! His assumption that his gallantries were flattering!

Sara made a face at herself in the looking-glass.

However did he come to be related to a man like Gregory Camden, she wondered? The other was hard, reserved, terse. Sara thought he might possibly be even a little ruthless. Well, she hoped he'd be ruthless about Julia's dollar hunt. Sara knew enough about the Camden affairs to know just how unfair was the spending allocation of Ransome money. Every partner . . . even those who never set foot on Ransome except to see what was going on . . . got an equal amount. Gregory got an extra share in payment for his management and Clifford got a salary in addition for his management of the affairs at the city end. Yet these two appeared to be the only two of the nine family shareholders who did a thing about wringing the wealth out of the cattle run.

The heat was already so great that Sara had no compunction about putting on a sleeveless cotton dress and a pair of white sandal-type shoes.

She made her bed and tidied her room and then went down the long passage across the hall into the dining-room. Would the others have breakfasted? It was seven-thirty by her wrist-watch and the big clock on the dining-room mantelshelf, but there was no one in sight.

The table was set at one end, and though there were no used dishes in sight there were evidences of others having been before her. There were two empty unused places and in the middle of the table a glass crock holding breakfast cereal.

Sara's footsteps had brought the lubra padding into the room.

'What you like?' Nellie asked, all smiles. She went to a small cupboard door let into the panelling in the walls and opened it. It was a refrigerator. On several glass dishes were cut grapefruits sprinkled with ginger and nuts. Nellie brought her one of these dishes and it was icy cold.

'You eat 'um that fella,' Nellie said. 'I bring some more 'nother time.'

Sara didn't quite know what that meant but she was very pleased to engage on the lovely juicy tangy fruit.

She had barely finished when Nellie came back with a dish of grilled tomatoes and bacon. Nellie pushed the crock of cereal towards Sara.

'You have this one time?' she asked. Then putting the hot dish on the table, 'This fella 'nother time.'

But Sara shook her head to the cereal. Grapefruit and

31

grilled tomatoes and bacon were enough for a tropical breakfast for her. Nellie drew boiling water from a vacuum urn into a teapot.

'You make this fella some time you want 'um,' she said. Sara smiled and nodded.

'Any time of the day, I suppose?'

'All-a same you have 'um any time. All-a same daytime, night.'

Sara understood. There was a running fount of tea on Ransome for any time of the day or night.

Sara finished her breakfast and in spite of the heat felt fit for anything. She walked out of the hall and down to the office.

Greg had said he would be out on the run all day so she did not think to knock on the office door. She simply turned the handle and walked in. She felt confused when she came face to face with her new boss. He had evidently been about to leave the room and the thick carpeting of the passage had prevented his hearing her footsteps. She nearly bumped into him.

Sara flushed with embarrassment.

'I beg your pardon,' she said. 'I should have knocked.'

'There is no need to knock at the office door,' he said politely. And then with a harder note in his voice, 'It is your domain now.'

Sara spoke quietly. 'I haven't proved myself yet, have I?'

There might have been a plea in those words for Greg Camden's manner changed. He looked at her closely but there was more of inquiry in his gaze than hostility now. Perhaps it occurred to him that if this girl was genuine he was giving her a rather tough reception.

He turned now and walked back towards the table. Then he moved over to the window and stood gazing silently out of it. Sara waited. She knew that Greg Camden was making up his mind about something. When he turned round, his face seemed quite altered. The hard, stern quality had gone out of it. In fact, if Sara hadn't thought it impossible for a man of his personality, she would have thought there was a hint of a plea in *his* words.

'Well, there it all is . . .' he gestured round the room. 'Make what you can of it.'

He walked thoughtfully back towards the door. He paused as he passed Sara.

'Marion will help you, I think, if you are in difficulties.

32

Of course she knows nothing of the office business. But in the house . . .'

Sara smiled.

'Thank you,' she said. 'I rather thought she might be a port in a storm if I made any mistakes in navigation.'

There was something in his eyes that was actually a fleeting grin but it was gone as quickly as it came.

'I'm going out with the overseer,' he said. 'We should be at Number Two Bore at midday. I've told Dave James . . . he'll be around the homestead most of the day. He's helping Blue-Bag with the horses.'

The next moment he had gone and the door closed quietly behind him.

Sara sat down in Greg's chair behind the table and surveyed the neatly stacked piles of circulars, letters and pamphlets that took up the greater part of its area.

'He's neat and methodical,' she thought. 'He just hasn't time to clear it.' She leafed through one pile of circulars. 'Begging letters,' she said, shaking her head. 'Things he doesn't say "no" to or he would have thrown them in the basket as fast as they arrived.'

Appeals for the blind, for spastic children, for the Red Cross, for Missions to Seamen, for Maimed and Limbless Soldiers.

Sara had a flair for knowing 'yes' from 'no' and it was one of the qualities that made her a good secretary.

She picked up a pencil and wrote on the page of each of a chosen batch, 'How much?' When she had completed the pile she clipped them together and added a memo: 'Do I apply to Mr Benson for cheques?' and left enough space at the end of the line for Greg to write *yes* or *no*.

'This,' she said to herself, 'is only tinkering. I think I'll have to have a "think" before I really start work.'

She got up, pushed the sash window higher, and walked out on to the veranda.

On this side of the house the garden was more thickly planted, more tropical. The palms, the paw-paws and the pandanus on the outside fringe almost screened the violent harshness of the plain beyond the garden confines.

Sara walked through the garden. It was cool and damp. At that moment Andy Patterson came round the corner of the house.

'What-ho!' he said, lifting his shabby, broad-brimmed hat high. 'Come into the garden, Maud! Well, what do you think of the old camp?'

'I think it's very wonderful because I know it's man-made.'

'Oh, God was good too,' said Andy, hands on hips, and surveying the garden. 'When He dried out the desert He kindly overlooked a mighty deep water-hole right here. Goes right through to Brazil, so they say. Fact is there's a race on with the other side of the world to see who can drain the flaming thing dry first.'

Sara laughed.

'Is that why you cut it off at eight-thirty in the morning? To give the Brazilians a chance?'

'No . . . that's so friend Sol doesn't get more than his share. Greedy fellow that. Dries it off faster than we run it through. Seen the vegetables? They're round the other side.'

Sara shook her head.

'Then don't go near 'em till Hoh says you can . . . and conducts you personally. He's got a fiercer blast than old Sol if he gets angry. Ever seen an angry Chinaman?'

Sara shook her head again.

'You will. You will.' Andy turned his head towards the front of the homestead. 'And look what the South Pole's blown in just to gladden our hearts!'

It was Julia, if not as cold as the South Pole at least as cool as a cucumber. Sara couldn't help feeling that no one had any right to look as calm and immaculate at eight-thirty in the morning after she'd had a twenty-hour day the day before and an early morning ride this day.

Andy put her thoughts into words.

'How . . . does . . . she . . . do . . . it?' he drawled.

Julia was fitting a cigarette into a long amber holder. She arrived in front of Andy in time to have him light it.

'Not working, you two?' she said as she exhaled the first puff of smoke.

'Nobody ever works on Ransome, Julia,' Andy said with a grin. 'Remember? You said it last time they had a big muster and brought in six hundred stragglers from the range.'

'Seems what I said two years ago holds good for to-day.'

'How 'bout you getting a nice mountain brumby and doing a cattle hunt with the boys next week?'

'That's just what I intend to do. But not on a brumby. I'm having that roan I tried out this morning.'

'Phew!' Andy pushed his hat on the back of his head, stuck his thumbs in his snake belt and bent his head sideways to look searchingly at Julia.

'There's an awful lot to think about in what you just said, Julia. First, what's come over Greg he's letting that roan out to anyone but himself. Got round him already, hey? Second . . . and worse for the boys . . . women on a cattle camp's going to be a terrible awful ordeal.'

'You'll survive it,' Julia said coolly. She looked at Sara. 'Don't you bang a typewriter, or something?'

'Marion called it a chaff-cutting machine. I'm just about to go and try it out.'

'Sara,' said Andy firmly, again removing his hat to a different position, this time wedged well down on his brows, 'if women are going with the cattle, then by crikey you see you come too. No letting Julia get away with everything.'

Sara smiled at him non-committally. How she would love to go out to a cattle camp! But that wasn't what she'd come to Ransome for and in a minute Julia would say so. Sara didn't wait for Julia's views on the subject.

'I think the chaff-cutting machine calls,' she said. 'You'll have to excuse me.'

She smiled politely at Julia and returned to the office by way of the veranda and the sash window.

How she would like to go out to a cattle camp! She could hardly invite herself if the work in the office was heavy . . . and possibly she might not be wanted by anyone but Andy. She had a little private prayer that if Julia and perhaps Marion were to go, Andy would remember to mention Sara herself to Greg.

By noon Sara had decided the chaff-cutting machine was all but unusable for neat and orderly type. Sara had a pride in the appearance of her work and a pride in the appearance of work that went out over her boss's signature. Any boss.

She went down to her room, found a shady straw hat and made her way across the garden where the oleanders, the hibiscus and the magnolias were already drooping in the blast of midday heat. The ground looked as if it had never known the early morning water.

Which of the medley of buildings constituting the station village was the book-keeper's office? Some were obviously garages, machinery buildings, stables, saddleries. Down the line was a mud brick square building with a galvanised iron room. Its walls were covered with flaming bougainvillæa and hoisted on top of it was a sprinkler spraying water continuously over the roof. When she came up to it she perceived the next building, a little bigger, was similar and similarly kept cool by the flow of water over the roof.

One will be the book-keeper's office, Sara thought, and one will be the store.

She was right about the first. The door stood wide open except for the fly-screen and Mr Benson could be seen bending in front of a big Chubb safe.

Sara tapped on the door.

'Come in. Saw you coming down the line. What's the trouble? Knew you'd be here before the day was out.'

He turned round with an affable grin.

Sara entered his office and looked round inquiringly. She saw at once what she wanted. On a long narrow table along the side wall were two typewriters. They were neatly covered and from the look of the covers were not of very ancient vintage.

She smiled at Mr Benson and the elf quality danced in her eyes.

'One guess?' she said.

'You sit down and tell me.'

Sara sat down on a heavy wooden chair that was meant to stand up to bushmen who never sat in this kind of chair without tilting it back.

Sara looked towards the two typewriters. She could read their makes printed on the covers.

'That one,' she said, pointing to the Royal.

'Ho ho! Got an eye for a good thing, hey? What makes you think I'm going to part with any typewriter? Much less my Royal?'

Sara sat quite still for a moment and looked at him thoughtfully. Mr Benson continued to smile, but he began to look with greater interest at the girl. She had character in her face. He wondered vaguely if she was 'one of Clifford's girls' or if, by some stroke of luck, she was genuine.

'I've never sent out bad work for Ransome Pastoral Company, Mr Benson,' Sara said. 'Apart from that, I think Mr Greg Camden deserves something better than the chaff-cutting machine.' There was a reproach in her eyes if not in her voice, and the book-keeper was taken aback.

'Listen, young 'un,' he said. 'Nobody's ever called me Mr Benson in the back country. Barring Mrs Whittle, that is, and she doesn't count. Sam's the name and you'll have to use it if you want to get on round here. Same as you'll have to be Sara . . . like it nor not. No "Misters," no "Bosses" in the outback. Even the black stockboys call Greg, Greg. And he *is* the boss. Don't you muddle that up with anything Clifford Camden or that city bunch might have told you.'

'I won't, Sam,' Sara said.

The book-keeper slapped his dusty brown cotton trousers with his hand.

'That's the girl. Now we can talk business. What was that you were saying about the typewriter?'

Sara told him. She put her case quietly and firmly, the smile gone.

All the time she talked, Sam's wary eyes were watching her. After ten minutes Sam agreed to her having one of the typewriters . . . but it wasn't to be his own beloved Royal . . . and he shouted for a black boy to come and carry it up to the homestead.

'Now mark you, young 'un,' said Sam. 'The minute that crowd coming up to Ransome's gone, and the cattle muster's over, that typewriter comes right back here. I can spare it because whichever jackaroo's on the book-keeping business has to be out on the run for the big chivoo.'

'If you sent down to the Company office in the city Mr Clifford Camden would see that a machine was sent up right away.'

The quizzical light came back into Sam's eyes. He scratched his rotund and middle-aged abdomen with the stem of his pipe.

'So Clifford's the white-haired boy and will do anything for the young 'un, hey?'

Sara remained serious.

'I've worked for Mr Clifford for two years, Sam. I've never known him not to be very prompt about necessary requirements for the station.'

'For the station or for Sara?'

For a moment Sara's lips were a narrow thin line. Sam, through half closed eyes, noted it.

'I think as Mr *Greg* Camden's secretary of the moment, a typewriter for the inside office is necessary.'

'Okay, Sara. We'll call a truce. You have it and when Clifford flies in in a few weeks' time *you* ask him for another. Let's see if you got the same winning ways with Clifford you seem to have with me.'

Suddenly he relaxed and laughed.

'Come on,' he said, getting up and reaching for a bunch of keys from one of the shelves in the open safe. 'I'll show you something. Everyone likes to see the station store. Not too hot outside for you?'

Sara shook her head.

'I don't mind the heat, and I'd love to see the store.'

Sam clapped a wide-brimmed, shabby straw hat on his balding head and led her out of the office and towards the next building.

'Would you like to know something, Sam?' Sara was looking at him sideways and with her eyes suddenly lit up with merriment. 'I had two bets with myself as I came down here. One bet was that which of these two buildings wasn't the office, was the store. . . .'

'And the other?'

'That you'd let me have a typewriter, if there was one.' Sam stopped dead in the doorway of the store and stared at her.

'Now just what made you so sure of yourself? Don't you know I'm the toughest nut to crack north of twenty-six?'

'Yes . . . I think perhaps you are . . .' said Sara. 'Even so, you put a premium on efficiency. I made a bet on that too.'

'Did you now? Well, I'll tell you what I think of your efficiency in about six weeks' time. Seems like efficiency goes by the board when Clifford Camden gets up here and he's got a girl on the line. . . .'

The enthralling sight of the station store, which was exactly like a shop . . . counter, shelves, cabinets and all . . . was lost to Sara for a minute.

'I happen at the moment,' she said severely, 'to be Mr *Greg* Camden's secretary. What are all those bolts of cloth for, Sam? Don't tell me Marion and Mrs Camden will wear all that pink and red gingham.'

'No. That's for the lubras. Look over this side. Sweets, tobacco, cigarettes. See in through there . . . flour, sugar, kitchen groceries. Bigger shop than you see in Alice Springs, heh?'

Sam proudly showed the station store, and as they emerged from its cool shade and he locked it up the triangle was sounded in the men's quarters for the midday meal.

'Can you find your way home, young 'un? I eat in my own office and the men all eat down at the quarters midday. Mrs Whittle'll have something for you up top. Don't know where the family is, but look hard and you'll find them.'

Sara thanked Sam for his kindness and walked back up the avenue of buildings towards the homestead garden.

CHAPTER FIVE

Within two days Sara had reduced Greg's correspondence to recognisable order. Moreover, she had wrung a large number of manila folders from Sam and had managed to file all the current 'In' letters and the carbon copies of the 'Out' letters. She longed to file the back-log of years in proper steel cabinets with a card-index to it.

Tentatively she broached the idea to Gregory Camden.

'A card-index system would relieve you of the necessity of secretarial assistance, Mr Camden,' she said. 'I feel perhaps . . .'

Greg Camden lifted his head and looked at her across his table.

'The same type of cabinet that Sam's got?'

'Yes. It's very simple really when the key card has been worked out. I could do that. I did it for the office down south.'

He was silent and Sara already knew him well enough not to push her case by speech. When Greg was silent he was thinking.

'You could do it in the time?' he asked shortly.

Sara might have allowed herself a wry smile in anyone else's presence. Evidently Greg didn't want to have her foisted on his hands for longer than the arranged period. She wished she wasn't such an embarrassment to him as a person. Never mind! She had a job of work to do and there was a time limit to it. She would do her best.

'Yes,' she answered simply.

'Very well. I'll order them by wire. I'll have them air-freighted up. You might let me have the particulars and I'll send them over the Flying Doctor Service when the air's open to-night.'

This was something Sara did like very much about Greg Camden. When he had made up his mind he was immediate and final in putting things into operation. In this instance it again demonstrated his confidence in Sara as a secretary. It all seemed as if, having finally made up his mind that she was efficient, he accepted all that side of her without question. His aloofness was for herself as a person.

Sara was just an efficient secretary, that was all. Thus

she saw herself in the shadow of Camden history.

Greg now spoke unexpectedly.

'I hope a plane load of expensive office equipment arrives before the rest of the Camden family,' he said. There was a sudden flicker of a smile in his eyes. 'I'm afraid there'll be another outcry at my expensive habits if they see it before it accumulates some age. Do you think you could allow some office dust to settle about the place before the families all arrive?'

Sara smiled, and her eyes sparkled but she didn't know it.

'I could put a scratch or two on it . . . even on the new typewriter . . . though it would hurt me very much to do so.'

'The new typewriter?'

'I was going to ask you . . .'

'Sam spoke to me about it.' His manner was again thoughtful.

'I think it would help you, Mr Camden. Sam insists on this machine going back to the book-keeper's office.'

Greg Camden sometimes had a disconcerting way of looking at her thoughtfully. It made Sara want to drop her eyes but pride in the rightness of her requests made her hold his gaze. It seemed to go on for such a long time that Sara could not help some bewilderment creeping into her own eyes.

Why did he look at her like that? Was there some lack of confidence after all?

'You seem to have found a soft spot with Sam,' Greg said. He looked away from Sara and let his gaze wander around the office, out of the window, then back momentarily to Sara.

'I'm afraid . . .' There was a touch of embarrassment, an unexpected shyness in him now. He ran his hand through his hair, looked down at the table, and then back at Sara.

'I'm afraid you'll have to call me "Greg,"' he said. 'It's all Christian names here. A sort of convention . . . I'm sorry!'

Sara looked away towards the window too.

'Yes, I know. I understand.' She looked back at him and smiled. 'I might just forget now and again, at first . . .'

'Yes, of course. It's just to keep things normal.' This time he actually smiled. 'Somehow "Mr Camden" and "Miss Brent" sounds a lot more pretentious than . . . than Christian names.'

'I think so too.'

'I'll order the typewriter, though heaven knows who'll use it when you go.'

'You will,' said Sara. 'You'll type on it with two fingers. They all do, once they get one.'

Greg straightened his back and looked at her with considerable surprise.

'Is that so?' he said.

'I'm afraid so,' said Sara, nodding her head seriously. Then they both laughed.

There was a knock at the half open door. It was Mrs Whittle.

'Mrs Camden has sent her list of guests, Mr Greg,' she said. 'I'm afraid it's very long.'

Greg stood up. He took the pages of closely written paper from the housekeeper.

'That's all right. I'll be vetoing three-quarters of them anyway.'

'Miss Marion's is shorter.'

'Well . . . it's her party.'

He glanced down the page which indicated Marion's guest list.

'Some of these people . . .!' he said, shaking his head. 'They'll have to come, I suppose. It's her party.'

Sara could not help a feeling of both wonder and irritation that Greg and Mrs Whittle had to arrange and do everything for Mrs Camden and Marion . . . even to running the homestead. Sara knew already that Mrs Whittle was the power behind the throne and that she ran the homestead. Sara guessed, rather than knew, that Greg's part was nominal and more to keep the last say in his hands in the case of differences or complaint.

But he shouldn't have to do it, she thought.

'Miss Julia wants to order some special clothes for the muster. She's bent on chasing the cattle, Mr Greg. I suppose her order could go by wire over the transceiver to-night?'

Sara saw there was a complete change of expression on Greg's face now. He and Mrs Whittle exchanged a smile.

'We must have Julia looking the part, Mrs Whittle. Anything but Julia at her best would be a loss for us all.'

Mrs Whittle appeared to nod approval.

'I'll get her to give you the particulars.'

Again Sara felt irritation. Why couldn't Julia look after her own wardrobe instead of loading Greg up with silly domestic requirements. And why did he do it? And obviously he expected Julia to fulfil her promise that she was going out to the cattle camps for the muster!

Sara's heart dropped a little. Not because Julia was going . . . but because she would like to go herself and did not see its possibility.

What would the homestead be like with them all gone except Mrs Whittle and Mrs Camden?

Well, if the cabinets arrived express she could get on with the key card and the filing. That would keep her busy. Perhaps while they were all away she could have an occasional ride at sundown, as Marion did. Sara didn't know how to ride but she longed to try. She wondered if she dared mention it to Andy.

She looked now at Greg where he had resumed his seat and was crossing out name after name on Mrs Camden's list of guests. He looked cold and remote again.

Greg threw his pencil down on the table.

'Will you send invitations to the names I've left in,' he said. 'Leave Marion's list as it stands.'

Sara understood the challenge in his manner. She knew well enough that he and Mrs Whittle had to manage Mrs Camden's affairs for her with a minimum of reference to her. But he did not wish to discuss this with his secretary. Nor did Sara wish to discuss it with him. She simply accepted his instructions without comment.

'Yes, Mr Camden . . . er . . . er . . . Greg.'

For a moment she lost her poise and actually blushed. Greg looked away quickly.

'Clifford will be here on the twenty-fourth,' he said. 'We got a radio message last night. He wants to know if you have anything you wish him to bring up for you?'

'No, thank you. I think I've everything. . . .' Sara wondered if that would have been her answer if she had been going out to the cattle camp or even riding modestly in the early shadows of evening. She had no jodhpurs . . . only blue drill jeans. Well . . . if she did manage a ride in the absence of the others, the jeans would do. There would be nobody to see except Sam, an elderly retired stockman, and the black people.

Greg pushed back his chair, stood up and reached for his hat.

'I'll be down at the stockyards for the rest of the day. I'm breaking-in a blood colt!'

Without looking at her again he left the room.

Two minutes later Julia came in without knocking.

'Oh! So you're alone. Where's Greg?'

Sara went quietly on with her work as she replied, 'He said he would be at the stockyards all day.'

'Well . . . he didn't tell me.'

Julia dropped into a chair, took a cigarette from the box on Greg's table and reached in her blouse pocket for the amber holder. She watched Sara out of half closed eyes.

'Not very communicative this morning, are you?' she said.

Sara wondered if Julia knew how arrogant and insolent her voice and manner were. Hardly . . . because she used them thus with everyone. She wondered what Julia had in her to recommend her as a person, other than her fine sculptured looks and her one-ninth share in Ransome station. Well . . . something. Because everyone on Ransome treated Julia with an air of tolerance and humour. There was something more in Greg's manner than that. His face had softened and a really very nice smile had shone through at Mrs Whittle when he had been confronted with Julia's request for a wardrobe for the cattle camp.

Greg and Mrs Whittle understood one another on the subject of Julia . . . that was certain.

'Too busy to talk?' Julia said again.

'I'm sorry,' Sara said. 'I was thinking out a sentence. No, I'm not too busy to talk. In fact I'd quite like to talk a little. Greg is not very communicative, you know, when he is in the office . . . which is seldom.'

'So? We've got around to calling him Greg, have we?'

Sara looked at Julia and hoped her eyes were as cold as she intended them to be.

'One doesn't seem to have any option about Christian names on Ransome,' she said. 'To use the surname seems an intolerable affectation.'

'Well, don't let's fight . . . *Sara*. If that's the way you like it.'

Sara didn't want to fight with anyone on Ransome so she thought she'd better follow everyone else's example and treat Julia with friendly tolerance. She smiled now.

'I do like *Sara*,' she said. 'Most people don't like their own Christian names. Always think somebody else's is better. But I like mine. It is my mother's.'

'So you've got a mother?'

43

'In England,' said Sara quietly.

'Oh, I see. Well, that's not what I came to talk about. . . .'

'I thought perhaps you came to see Mr . . . Greg.'

'You can give me the information. You're his secretary so I suppose you have all the information necessary. It's the mob of sheep down south. Who financed . . . and with what money . . . the base flock down there two years ago?'

'I really couldn't say.' Sara hoped the words sounded as if they meant she really couldn't *tell*.

Sara knew very well that Greg Camden had financed the base flock from his own personal account and had then turned the thing into the general Ransome account. She also knew the fantastic difficulties he had with his fellow-shareholders in keeping Ransome together and in one piece.

'I am handling Greg's personal correspondence in relation to the people coming on to the station for Marion's party and the muster,' she added quickly. 'Sam would be the one to give you any information about station accounts. I do not touch them.'

Julia stood up, stretched herself gracefully, shook her ash on to the ash-tray on the table and moved towards the door.

'I thought you might have arrived at the *confidential* stage with Greg,' she said coolly. 'My advice is . . . *don't*. The Camdens as a family are as prickly as hedgehogs.'

Sara made no reply, partly because Julia did not wait for one and partly because she, Sara, was too angry to trust herself to words. Julia's words held an under-current of warning. And it wasn't altogether to do with Ransome business affairs. Julia wanted Sara to know that she, Julia, had a proprietorial interest in Greg . . . and Sarah was to keep out.

Keep out? As if she wanted to do anything different. She knew just what was the role of secretary and employer. What did these people think she, Sara, was made of?

Being a modern miss, Sara said quietly, firmly, 'Damn them!' She banged the typewriter very loudly and at great length until she had calmed down.

By the time she went into the dining-room to take her solitary lunch . . . the family lunched very much later than Sara . . . she was ready to laugh at herself and laugh at the Camdens.

'It'll all be the same in a hundred years,' she reflected. 'And I'll be away from Ransome in five weeks' time.'

More because her spirits were not to be dampened than for any other reason, Sara put on a very pretty new blue dress for dinner that evening. It was of fine polished poplin, had a flared skirt, with a square framed neckline. The neckline showed off the soft contours of her throat and face, and the colour gave a hint of blue to the colour of her eyes.

There were some times in life, Sara reflected, when a secretary had to become a person just to prove to herself she sometimes was a person and not always a machine.

When she went into the billiard room for the before-dinner drinks Sam Benson was the first to pay her a compliment.

'My!' he said. 'Where've you been hiding that pretty dress, young 'un? Not keeping it for the boy-friend when he comes up?'

Sara shook her head.

'Sam,' she said. 'I haven't got a boy-friend. And sometimes I haven't got a sense of humour about being teased.' She looked at him seriously. 'As my best friend on Ransome, would you not make that not-very-funny joke again? You see, *both* Mr Camdens are my bosses. I have to work with them, and this kind of teasing could be an embarrassment.'

Sam cocked one eyebrow inquiringly. Seeing the girl was really very serious he conceded her point.

'All right. Subject's closed. Let's talk about the weather. How you standing up to the heat?'

'I like it, but whether I would like it so much if I stayed here for the whole of the Dry I don't know.'

'It's better than the Wet, you take my word for it. Turkish bath weather. Knocks most of 'em to pieces.'

Mrs Camden, endlessly crocheting lace, called Sara over. As usual Marion sat with her mother and favoured Sara with her half friendly, half ironic smile as she balanced a cocktail with one hand and waved a cigarette in the other.

'My! My! Pretty dress!' Marion said. 'Any more tucked away like that?'

'I've got a nice dress for your party, Marion. I suppose I will be able to see something of the party?'

Marion threw back her head and laughed.

'You haven't been to a house-party on a station before? Why, it's everywhere. You couldn't keep out of it if you wanted to. Nowhere to hide from people who aren't partying all over the place. Even the blacks down by the river have a party. You'll need more than one dress.'

'Sara can wear the one she's got on,' Mrs Camden said with her more than sweet smile. 'You do look pretty, dear. It reminds me of when I was young. I always wore blue when the young men were around. You ought to talk to the jackaroos, dear. They'd like to have a nice girl like you. . . .'

'They can't all have her, Mother,' Marion said. 'It's a monogamous world . . . even north of twenty-six.'

'I was going to ask you something,' Mrs Camden went on. 'Now, whatever was it? That pretty dress sent it right out of my mind.'

'You were going to ask Sara about the yacht.'

'Oh yes.' Mrs Camden put down her lace-work and looked at Sara with as winning a smile as she could conjure up. 'You must be awfully close to Greg, dear, being his secretary. I want you to win him over for me. When the families all get here and have a meeting I'm going to put the idea of my yacht to them . . . and I want Greg to help me. You fix it for me, will you, dear? Wear that pretty dress. Any girl could get anything from him in a dress like that.'

Sara couldn't help smiling at the ingenuousness of Mrs Camden's words. Obviously she had no idea that her son was as tough a business man, as well as station manager, as he was. Also he was very honourable and upright. Even Julia's lovely clothes and superb appearance did not move Greg on station matters. Perhaps Julia might move him in other matters, matters of the heart, but not in station affairs. Sara was sure of that. And for some inscrutable reason she was sorry if Julia could affect Greg's heart.

While Mrs Camden was prattling on about her yacht and the wonders of the Great Barrier Reef, Greg came into the room. He had just showered and his hair was polished down on his head, smooth and still wet. He walked across the room to the men at the table by the window and Sara could not help marvelling at the firm, agile way in which he carried himself and the freshness of his whole appearance. No one looking at this man, and not being informed, would dream he had been up before sun-up . . . five o'clock . . . and been more or less in the saddle or down at the yards in the blazing heat all day.

He must have great reserves of physical strength, Sara reflected. She felt a tenderness of pride in her new boss.

But where was Julia?

Sara had passed her in the passage and Julia had raised supercilious eyebrows at the blue dress, but so far she hadn't put in an appearance for a before-dinner drink.

'And so, dear, we'll be able to do lots of things together,' Mrs Camden was saying. 'With the whole homestead to ourselves we'll be able to go into all our plans about what we'll tell the families when they come up. You will help me, won't you, dear?'

Sara looked at Mrs Camden, startled. She hadn't been listening.

'It will be quite easy, dear. You and I will be able to tell Mrs Whittle about the food we'll have. Sucking pigs, lobsters, Pavlova cakes . . . all the lovely food the young people like. Then, of course, I must go through some accounts with you. Then there's all my letters . . .'

'When . . . when did you say, Mrs Camden?' Sara asked.

'Marion! This wretched Marion of mine is deserting me to go out to the cattle camps with the boys! It'll ruin her complexion for the party, I keep telling her. And there are two MacKensies coming from Turra Station. She really ought to try and marry one of them. Three-quarters of a million acres!'

Dinner was announced, and at that moment Julia made her entrance. Her blue dress outshone Sara's. It was the same colour, but so beautifully made, the rhinestones decorating the bodice glittered and the tight swathed skirt proclaimed that Julia's arithmetic was 33-23-33. The perfect figure.

Greg Camden turned round from the window and when he saw Julia he smiled.

There was the kind of silence that a properly timed entrance is expected to make.

'Why, Julie,' Sam Benson said, 'you look as if you've never done a day's work in your life in that outfit.'

'I wasn't born to work,' said Julia, taking a cigarette from Greg. 'I'll have a gin and lemon, thanks, Dave.' This to the jackaroo who raised a bottle and one questioning eyebrow.

Greg lit Julia's cigarette for her and Sara could not help noticing the hint of a smile he had on his lips.

'What would the menfolk do without the decorations of the day,' he said. 'It's not for women to work. Only to look beautiful.'

'If I had a million dollars I'd give it all to my wife to wear,' Sam said. 'But mind you, she'd have to look like it. Don't you reckon, Greg?'

'I think it would be worth it.'

Sara, the other side of the room, took a cigarette from Marion and lit it. She wanted to do something to ease her anger. She was feminist enough to resent that men should think of women as either ornaments or chattels. Yet, in fairness to Greg Camden, how else could he think of them? Probably he had spent all his life, except his schooldays, on Ransome station and quite clearly the womenfolk there fitted exactly into these two categories. Mrs Camden, Marion and Julia were the decorations. Mrs Whittle and herself the chattels. Herself not wanted . . . to begin with, anyway.

That, Sara supposed, is what bothered Greg about herself when she first arrived. Was she going to be an ornament . . . Clifford's ornament . . . or a chattel?

She had turned out to be a chattel and that was what had eased his manner. She would be useful after all. Good! But it was the Julias and the Marions of the world he admitted to his intimate circle and treated as equals.

Women were meant to look beautiful . . . irrespective of their character qualities!

If Sara hadn't had such a high opinion of Greg Camden she would have thought that his possible fate at Julia's hands served him right. As it was, she felt both saddened and angry.

CHAPTER SIX

After dinner the following evening Sam Benson played billiards with one of the jackaroos while Mrs Camden, Marion and Sara sat in a group at the end of the room talking to one of the other young Englishmen. Neither Julia nor Greg had appeared since dinner.

Marion was asking the jackaroo about the colt Greg had been breaking-in the last two days.

'Is this one of Greg's long jobs or short ones?' she asked. 'I meant to go down to the yards this morning to see how far he'd got.'

'He's going to be a little beauty,' the jackaroo said of the horse. 'Full of intelligence. Any other breaker in the north would have him in hand in two days. But not Greg. Greg never works that way.'

'Greg never breaks a horse,' Mrs Camden said unexpectedly. 'He makes them.'

'Wins them,' said Marion.

'I wouldn't even put it that way, Marion,' said the jackaroo. 'I think he just puts the whole thing to the colt as an intellectual discussion.'

Everyone, including Sara, laughed.

'I mean that.' The young jackaroo spoke with some vehemence. 'I'll swear it's an approach to horse sense. What do you think, Sara?'

'I don't know. I've never seen a horse broken in.'

'You come down in the morning and watch Greg handle this one. It's an education in itself.'

'I'd like to . . .' Sara hesitated. 'But I'm a working woman, you know.'

'We're all working on Ransome,' the jackaroo said, 'but I don't know anyone who doesn't stop off to watch Greg handling blood stock in the yard. Hey, Sam!' he called across the room. 'How about Sara coming down to the yards in the morning? She's never seen a young horse broken in.'

Sam, squinting down his stick, hesitated, decided to chalk it and then looked over the table at Sara.

'You come down, young 'un. You're missing a treat sitting up here maltreating my typewriter while everyone else is holding up the fence at the yards.'

Sara hesitated. Everyone else seemed to take it for granted she not only should but could go.

'I'll ask Greg . . .' she began.

'Ask Greg be blowed,' said Marion. 'He didn't expect you to do much work before you ever arrived here. He must have been getting the shock of his life the last few days.'

'Nearly every girl who comes to Ransome comes to have a good time,' Mrs Camden said. 'You must have a good time too, dear.'

Well, at least Mrs Camden didn't want Sara to miss all the treats!

'I'll try and be there,' was all the answer she allowed herself. Her training was too deeply ingrained in her system for her to walk out on a prescribed job without permission.

In the morning she tentatively asked Greg if she could some time go down to the yards.

He looked surprised.

'Haven't you been down there yet?' he asked.

'No. I haven't been beyond the store.'

'Good heavens, you don't even know what the place looks like? The homestead's no criterion of station life, you know.'

Sara was only human and could not help some slight disappointment in man's selfishness to a secretary's labours. Sara had heard of men in the city, who, being out at work all day, insisted that their women at home were doing nothing . . . just because the man wasn't there to see the work done.

Greg looked thoughtful.

'You'd better see something of the place before you go home,' he said abruptly.

Sara hoped this meant permission. Greg got up from his chair and went over to the window. He stood, his back to Sara, looking out. Sara stole glances at him from between the fringes of her eyelids.

He wore the tight-fitting pants he usually wore when he went out riding first thing in the morning, and for the first time she noticed that his tight-fitting boots, under the short leggings, had higher heels than usual.

'Well, I'll see you later,' he said, suddenly turning, and with a quick gesture picked up his hat . . . it was an old one . . . and left the room.

'I guess that means permission,' Sara said to herself.

She put the cover on the typewriter and walked to the window where Greg had lately been standing. She saw him come round the side of the house and speak to Andy Patterson, who had been bending over some of the reticulation pipes leading from the pump-house into the garden. Then Greg went rapidly through the garden, and as he went through the gate a black boy appeared riding a horse and leading another. Sara saw Greg spring up in the saddle and the two of them jog-trot away through the outbuildings that flanked this side of the house.

Sara longed to be able to ride. The way Greg went up into the saddle was something that filled her heart with envy. It was so light and yet there was so much strength implicit in the movement. She supposed he was born in the saddle.

'Morning, Sara,' said Andy, raising his cabbage hat high in the air. 'What you doing out here at this hour? You haven't had breakfast yet.'

'Oh, yes I have. I have mine at half past six like everyone else now. It was only on my first day I was a laggard.'

'Hum. Soon learned that life begins and ends with the rising and the setting of the sun once you're over the twenty-sixth parallel, hey?'

'I'm learning a lot and very fast, Andy. What I want to learn to-day is how a man breaks a horse. Where do I go down to the yards and how can I get there . . . and be there without being seen or heard?'

'It's only half a mile down. I'll get you a hoss. You go and put some right things on instead of that billowy skirt.'

Sara looked sadly at Andy.

'I'd love a "hoss,"' she said. 'But, Andy, I can't ride.' She felt as if she was admitting she hadn't been baptised.

'That's nothing,' he said cheerfully. 'Half of them that comes up here can't ride. Always have to have a dozen hacks kicking around for the city folks that have ambitions. You go and do what I said and I'll get you the kind of hoss that doesn't know how to throw a baby, let alone a lady.'

'Oh, Andy, thank you. You are a darling.'

'Here! Save that for Clifford. I'm not looking for any fights with Clifford once he comes rampaging up here.'

'Clifford is no concern of mine,' Sara said tartly, but she softened it with a smile as she turned and went back into the homestead.

The jeans would have to do. Well, who's going to look at me, anyhow, she thought. No one while Julia is around.

Within twenty minutes Sara was back at the garden gate, looking much sprucer than she herself thought in a shining white cotton shirt blouse, sleeves rolled up in a professional style, and the dark blue jeans and sun hat in their right places.

Andy was coming round the outside paddock on horseback and leading another.

He threw his leg over the saddle and slid off.

'Up you go,' he said. 'Get the ball of your foot on the stirrup . . . so. Now, hand on the pommel. Woof . . . she's up.'

Sara was elated. She was up on the horse and found it comfortable and she was able to take an elevated view of mankind.

'Oh, it's lovely, Andy. What happens next? Don't let him gallop away with me, will you?'

'It's a *her* and her name is Gentle Annie. Better shorten the stirrups for you. Teach you to ride English fashion. You're not likely to need the good old Aussie's jog-trot. Straight back, now press with the knees. Hold the reins so . . . Good! Press on the balls of your feet and rise gently off the saddle when she comes up, and you won't get the bumps. We'll go slow.'

Andy mounted his own horse and they walked them together away from the homestead.

'Feeling okay?' he asked with a grin.

'Absolutely okay!' said Sara joyously.

'Right. Well, now we'll trot. Take it gently and with rhythm. Off we go!'

Sara bumped a little at first but almost immediately got into the rise and fall of the trot.

'You're doing fine,' Andy shouted. 'We'll do a mild canter now. Stick firm in the saddle and give with the horse.'

The canter, mild though it was, brought them up to the yards.

'Well, how was that?'

'Lovely!' said Sara. 'I want to keep on doing it all day. Only I want to watch Greg break-in in the horse too.'

'You'll be sore enough after that little stretch. You'd better join the gallery on the fence and give a certain part of your anatomy a rest. Now wait till I show you how to get off.'

Within a few minutes Sara was on the ground feeling, some odd way, that she was several inches shorter than she really was.

'Hitch up this way,' said Andy, completing his lesson. 'Now for an inch on the fence. . . .'

He moved in his rolling gait towards the considerable crowd taking up every inch of sitting room on the rails.

'Move along for a lady.'

There were grunts of assent as several stockmen squeezed themselves together but their eyes were on the hard, too intent on what was going on there to take any notice of Sara. Andy hoisted Sara up on the rails, and as there was no room for him he left her.

Sara had never felt so happy in her life. She took in the long, lean, sunburned men around her. She looked at the wide-brimmed hats, as dusty as the desert itself, wedged down on their brows or pushed on the backs of their heads; the black boys laughing, their pearl white teeth gleaming like half moons in their ebony faces; the small cluster of lean, burned white women who must be the stockmen's wives and Julia . . . cool, immaculate in pale primrose jodhpurs and soft silk shirt.

Julia sat on a part of the fence that was shaded by the

52

high rails of the in-yard with the homestead jackaroos on either side of her.

Sara remembered Julia's earlier comment. 'Doesn't anyone work on Ransome?'

Evidently the breaking of a blood horse by Greg Camden was something that called for a gallery. Otherwise Sara could not see the overseer calling a halt in the day's work.

In the yard was a very young horse. It stood in the middle, its forefeet together, its ears back, the whites of its eyes showing. Greg Camden was quietly walking along the inside of the far fence rhythmically swinging a halter.

'No broncho jumping?' Sara asked the stockman alongside her.

He gave a short laugh.

'Not with Greg Camden and this kind of hoss. You won't see no jumps and you won't hear no barracking from the rails this go, lady. You keep your eyes on Greg now. He got the halter on the colt yesterday. To-day he'll make a friend of him.'

Greg was quietly walking to the horse now. The horse, terrified but curious, stood still. In a minute, almost imperceptibly, Greg had the halter on and had moved back. Then began the prettiest picture Sara had ever seen. Greg stood so still. There seemed a steel strength in him, yet his movements of the body and the hands were fluid as molten silver. The hands moved up the halter rope ever nearer the horse's nose.

At a point they stopped. The horse, legs braced, ears back, stared hypnotised at them. It, too, was a picture of fluid strength . . . of an animal torn between the opposite desires, to flee or to stay and inquire.

Everything in and around the yard was silent with concentration. It was like the moment before an electric storm broke. You could almost feel the gallery holding its concerted breath. Would the colt make a break for it?

Only Greg was easy. Easy and confident yet compelling. His eyes were on the eyes of the horse. He did not waver his gaze, and though one was conscious of compelling command there was so much kindness in it one felt the horse just had to understand it.

For five minutes nothing moved. Then gently, imperceptibly the horse lifted its head the fraction of an inch. It was smelling the air. Still there was silence. Greg did not move. His hands invited. His eyes invited. Then delicately, nervously the horse

53

stretched its neck towards the hands on the rope. It pulled back. Nothing happened. Greg was saying something so softly no one but the horse could hear. Its head went forward again and then the sensitive nose was touching the hands. Greg did not move. The horse tried again and Greg's fingers gently, tenderly stroked its nose.

That was all. Greg slipped the halter and quietly walked away to the opposite fence. He took a lighted cigarette from one of the jackaroos and smoked it. The horse, still frightened, raced back into a corner of the yard. The gallery remained silent.

Greg handed the rope to the jackaroo, stubbed out his cigarette and walked back into the centre of the yard. His movements were full of an unconscious strength and grace. Then he stood still and held out his hand. It was five minutes before the horse came gingerly, nervously, but compelled, towards that hand. It was a hand that invited and commanded but offered infinite love and care.

Greg fondled the horse a moment, speaking very softly and then walked away to the rails. He hoisted himself up between Julia and one of the jackaroos. He pushed his hat on the back of his head and lit a cigarette. His was the first voice that broke the silence.

'All right, Blue-Bag. Let him through the slip rail.'

A black boy dropped from the fence, lowered a slip rail, and in a minute the horse was out in a grassed paddock.

'*Smoko*!' someone said from the rails, and there was a general breaking of the silence. Figures began to slip from the rails and comments about the horse were flying in all directions.

'He's a little beaut!'

Sara remained sitting on the rails, unaware that those beside her were already on the ground and she sat alone. She had been deeply moved by the scene. It had touched a chord in her and she was trying to fathom it all out. She could not imagine any picture of action, of battle or of endurance that could have conveyed so much of compulsion and strength as Greg's stillness had conveyed in that moment before the horse touched him.

One of the jackaroos had come across the yard to her.

'Billy tea in the stables, Sara,' he said. 'Coming?'

Sara blinked her eyes and shook herself.

'Thank you . . . yes. I'd love some tea.'

The jackaroo was laughing at her as he helped her down from the fence.

'You wouldn't read about it in a book, would you?' he said.

'I thought it was a wonderful sight.'

'You won't see it anywhere else but at Ransome. There's no one north of the twenty-sixth can do it quite the way Greg does it.'

'I thought there'd be broncho-jumping.'

'Sometimes there is too. You ought to see some of the black boys at it. There's other ways of breaking horse, but that's Greg's way. Mind you, that colt was pretty flighty the first day Greg had him in the yard.'

Sara walked with the jackaroo to the group on the far fence. Julia was talking about horses and she gave no sign of recognising Sara's presence. The men all smiled, however, and Greg nodded his head. She found it difficult not to stare at him too hard. She wanted to read for herself what it was he had in his eyes, in the firm set of his jaw and the fine lines of his face that commanded so much authority.

'Tea, Greg?' It was one of the stockmen shouting from the entrance to the stables.

'Right.'

'Two ladies coming up,' the jackaroo shouted a warning.

'We got Wedgwood china for them.'

There was a shout of laughter.

Greg put out his hand and Julia took it as she jumped lightly from the fence. She brushed her primrose jodhpurs with her fingers, walked the few paces that put herself between Sara and Greg and proceeded to walk towards the slip rails with him. Julia went through first, and when the men stood aside for Sara to follow, the two girls found themselves side by side. As the men had to come through on the right of the girls Sara found Greg walking at her side.

'I enjoyed watching that very much,' Sara said. She knew her words were inadequate but there was too much constraint in her feelings for her to have spoken what was in her mind.

'You rode down from the homestead?' Greg inquired politely. 'Did they give you a good mount?'

'It was Gentle Annie. Andy promised she wouldn't throw me. I'm a beginner at riding.'

Greg looked at her with some surprise.

'I hadn't realised that,' he said. 'You'd better get Andy

to give you a few lessons.'

Sara's eyes brightened.

'Oh, I would like that.'

'I'll speak to Andy.'

They were in the shadow of the stables and there were boxes scattered about on which a great medley of stockmen and rouseabouts were sitting with their tin mugs of tea in front of them. Sara could not thank Greg because he moved away from her and ordered one of the rouseabouts to collect a 'decent clean' box or two for the ladies. He left the jackaroo to fetch the two newest-looking mugs . . . the Wedgwood china . . . for Sara and Julia. By the time Sara was seated and someone had put a mug of boiling black tea in her hand Greg was some distance away. He was standing, mug in hand and one foot up resting on the box, talking to the overseer and one of the stockmen. Sara noticed his attitude was the same as when she had first seen him in the billiard room at the homestead. He had one foot up and often he seemed to concentrate his gaze on the toe of that boot. Now and again he would look up and far away. Sara wondered what the distances did for his thinking powers, he was so often gazing thoughtfully into them.

On this occasion he was not being talked to. He was doing the talking and the other two men were paying great attention.

Andy came over to Sara.

'I suppose you need that police escort home, young lady.'

Sara was about to say, 'Yes, please,' when she changed her mind.

'I think I'll ride up to the homestead alone. Are you game to let me try, Andy?'

'Takes no courage on my part.' He grinned but Sara could see he was pleased with her.

Julia had stood up as if to depart. Greg suddenly looked up.

'You going up, Julia?'

'I'm certainly not going to sit here all day watching you all wasting time,' Julia said. 'I can waste my own time much more effectively and conveniently elsewhere.'

Julia's words brought a laugh from the men and a lopsided grin from the overseer. Greg smiled quietly and his glance flickered to Sara. Sara stayed put and looked into her mug as if she had yet more tea to drink. She was not going up to the homestead with Julia. She wouldn't be able to ride, even Gentle Annie, if Julia went galloping by on a thoroughbred.

It was Andy who came to Sara's rescue.

'You come out and look at that wee hoss kicking up his heels in the paddock now. He's had time to think about it and has decided being in with the humans is not going to be such a bad go after all.'

Sara walked with Andy around the stables and stood a few minutes watching the young horse she had so lately seen with Greg in the yard.

She felt grateful to the kindly stockman beside her but she didn't know how to convey it.

'She's gone,' Andy said after peering round the corner of the stables. 'If you'd ridden up with Julia she'd have ridden the guts out of Annie at the quarter-mile mark.'

Sara looked soberly at Andy.

'What makes Julia like that?' Sara asked.

'Too much money when she was too young. Too much spoiling and too many good looks. She hasn't had a fair go.'

Sara admitted the fairness of Andy's summing up. Everyone on Ransome treated Julia with the tolerance of one dealing with a spoilt child. Only Greg seemed to regard her with greater seriousness. Maybe it was because he had once been in love with her. Maybe it was because whatever he had found lovable in her might still be worth salvaging if he could win her away from her preoccupation with herself, and with the Ransome earning capacity. Maybe that pretty face and that lovely form brought nostalgic yearnings for a time past when Julia must have had some of the effervescence of youth. Maybe it was all just too much for any man's better judgment. Maybe he was so used to a certain grasping indolence in his womenfolk that he took it for granted as part of feminine nature.

Andy had untethered Gentle Annie and brought her round to Sara. He had just helped her mount when Greg came round under the shade of the coolibah.

'You going up with Sara, Andy?' he asked.

'She wants to go up on her own. Best way to learn.'

Greg looked at Sara thoughtfully.

'You think you'll be all right?' he asked.

'Quite,' said Sara.

Greg came close to her and began to examine the stirrup. 'Better make it longer, Andy,' he said. 'I don't think

Sara will be riding a hunter over the fences.'

'Better to teach her that style,' said Andy. 'She's not going to spend her life riding round the boundaries of a cattle station.'

'She might have some long rides while she's still here. And I never heard of any of my stockmen who couldn't clear a fence as well as any of the pink coats. Teach her a stockman's way to ride, Andy.'

Greg said all this pleasantly yet there was no further argument for Andy began at once to lengthen the stirrup.

'Ease off your knees, Sara,' he said. 'You won't need 'em any more riding this way. Use the ball of your foot and the calves of your legs. Well, ready?'

'I hope so. Good-bye.'

She gave a quick wave to the two men. With them both as onlookers she was determined to rise in the saddle from the first trot. With Gentle Annie's co-operation she managed it. She was delighted with herself and half turned and waved again. The last glimpse she had of the two men before the stable out-houses hid them was of them standing side by side, their thumbs stuck in their belts, and Greg's grin was as wide as Andy's.

Sara laughed. Perhaps he thought even chattels could supply entertainment on occasions.

She didn't feel quite so hurt any more. The morning's events had salved her wounds.

CHAPTER SEVEN

Sara was grateful to Greg for having given her the opportunity to ride. For several evenings she went out with Andy and when she proved a good pupil he handed her over without misgiving to Marion. He saw that she was mounted on a good but thoroughly reliable horse.

'You've outgrown Gentle Annie already,' he said. 'But I'm taking no risks. You take Trash from now on. She'll take you anywhere like the lady she is and she'll do it lady-like fashion. Plenty of speed but no nonsense.'

Sara was happier than she had ever been, and Marion appeared quite pleased to have Sara's company on her sundown ride. For the first time she saw something of the immediate environs of Ransome homestead.

She saw the river with its nearby cluster of blacks' quarters, she saw the grove of coolibahs and several great banyan trees. She reached the foothills of the range and skirted the timbered country. Even more interesting, she rode along the desert track stretching thousands of miles south over parched and treeless plains. In all Marion was good company in that she was never much inclined to talk. She was pleasant to Sara, greeting Sara's enthusiasm with her usual enigmatic smile, and left the girl to get her own experience as a rider.

During the day Sara worked carefully and methodically at her office work.

The invitations had all gone out. Orders to caterers and delivery contractors had gone forward. The station carpenter and his staff were put to work making partitions along two verandas and putting up the framework of innumerable camps on the upper billabong of the river.

Everything went as effortlessly as Sara and Mrs Whittle could achieve. Meantime Mrs Camden went on endlessly chattering as she sat, perfumed and ringed, making her lace. Marion sat about, read books, lacquered her finger-nails and got ready her clothes for the cattle camp and the party.

Julia pleased herself what she did and when she did it. Sometimes she went down to talk to the stockmen. Sometimes she rode out to one or two of the nearest bores. Often she went out with Greg. Sara had the impression that Julia really thought she was contributing to the management of Ransome affairs.

Well, Sara reflected with a sigh, she had a share in the place. She was entitled to do what she did. When all was said and done she had probably as much right to Ransome station and Ransome homestead as Mrs Camden and Marion.

What a pickle Greg would have if the rest of the Camdens showed this same overseeing, questing but critical interest that Julia did! Sara's sympathy was all with Greg and so she worked harder and more self-effacingly to keep things running smoothly for him.

When the replies to the invitations began coming in with the air-mail he asked Sara would she work back in the office with him on more than one night.

'Take to-morrow off,' he said on the second night. 'I'll be out on the run all day now. Everything on this place has got to be in order by the twenty-ninth. We'll have the first round-up over a bare week before the party . . . prime cattle to make a good show!' He paused. 'You know, Sara,' he said quietly, 'families are sometimes the most difficult of all shareholders to please.'

'I know,' said Sara.

She could say no more. It would not be in good taste to give Greg a hint of what she thought of his family.

One night he startled her by pushing back his chair, leaving the office and returning a few minutes later with two glasses, a jug of iced water, a lemon squeezer and a bottle of gin.

'I think we deserve a drink,' he said. 'Pure lemon or a dash of gin, Sara?' He was putting the jug and glasses in the middle of the table.

'What are you going to do for lemons, Greg?'

'They're in my pocket,' he said.

He plunged his hands and brought out three from each side pocket. Sara thought there was something happily domestic about Greg tumbling lemons out of his pocket, unsheathing his knife . . . like a sailor, a station man always carried a knife . . . and bisecting lemons on the blotting pad.

In silence he made Sara her lemon drink and added the merest dash of gin to it. In silence he returned to his seat on the far side of the table, lit himself a cigarette and sipped his drink. Sara didn't know whether there was something ominous or anticipatory in his silence.

'You know, Sara,' Greg said suddenly. He was tipping the ash from his cigarette into the ash-tray and did not look up as he spoke. He paused, and then went on, his face serious. 'You must realise you've made a considerable difference to affairs here. . . .'

He paused again, and Sara felt a glow of warmth at being appreciated.

'I'm inclined to think we need you on Ransome.' He looked up quickly and his blue eyes interrogated her. 'Do you think you could stay on with us?'

This invitation came with the shock of surprise. Sara had not realised Greg had so quickly outgrown his first doubts and suspicions. She was pleased her worth was acknowledged and that she was needed. But the invitation had overwhelming implications. In the first instance, for how long would she be needed on Ransome and how much would a long sojourn there jeopardise her job with the company in the city? If Clifford Camden were not agreeable to her remaining on Ransome could or would she afford to throw over her permanent and interesting work in the main offices?

If she stayed she would have no difficulties with Marion or Mrs Camden. But Mrs Whittle? She got on very well with Mrs Whittle so far, but Mrs Whittle had never really unbent. Whenever the Camdens, any one of them, was wrong Mrs Whittle had never admitted it. Her devotion to them was implacable and almost religious. How much would a permanent connection affect her relationship with Mrs Whittle?

Lastly, though she would love to stay on Ransome for some length of time, would she like to live there for ever like a shadowy and junior Mrs Whittle?

All these thoughts rushed pell-mell together through Sara's head and she could not sort out one from the other. She felt overwhelmed with the proposition and all it implied.

Her face must have shown how disturbed she felt for Greg got up, walked again to the window and stood looking out. All that he would see would be moon-washed paddocks through the veil of garden trees, but it was his characteristic way of having a 'think.'

Sara did not answer him, because she could not. She wanted to thank him for the compliment and the invitation but was too confused to find adequate words. She was incapable of giving a definite reply at the moment.

Like every girl in the world she would like one day to marry. Would living on Ransome for a period of years deprive her of that chance? Sara did not put this question to herself but it was an undercurrent of motive in her hesitation.

'Perhaps you would prefer to consult Clifford? He'll be here early next week.'

Greg had turned round and was looking at her with that direct and unwavering gaze that had disconcerted Sara once before. Her own eyes were held and she could not drop her gaze. Why did he look at her like that? Was he trying to read something deep inside her? Was he perhaps waiting to see her reaction to his mentioning of Clifford's name?

'Yes, please. I think perhaps I should. He is . . . he is my employer. . . .'

'The Ransome Pastoral Company is your employer, Sara. If, however, you feel you have special loyalties to Clifford, then, of course, you would wish to honour them.'

He sat down again, lit another cigarette and drew his glass towards him. He looked as if he might say something more . . . then changed his mind.

'Finish your drink, Sara,' he said instead. 'Then perhaps you might leave me to get on with this stuff alone. I suppose you've got something to think about.'

'Yes, I do want to think about it,' Sara said. 'It is a very kind offer, Greg, and I thank you for it.'

'You don't feel like accepting it?'

'I'd love to accept it. I just don't know whether it is the best thing . . . for us all.'

He stood up as she went to leave the room.

'It would be the best thing for Ransome. And for me,' he said unexpectedly.

It was a very bewildered Sara who found her way into the dining-room to make herself a cup of tea. She certainly did not feel like joining the others in the billiard room.

She made her tea and carried it down to her room. She put the saucer over the cup to keep the tea hot while she stripped off and had a quick shower. She put on a light cotton house-gown and sat down to drink her tea. She found a packet of cigarettes on the table by her bed and lit a cigarette.

'Now I know why thinkers always smoke,' she reflected. A cigarette and a cup of tea! Were these the things that helped resolve the perplexities of everybody's own little world?

She wished now that Greg's request had not been so unexpected and that she had had the power to see quickly and concisely all the details of the situation. A cooler person, she thought, would have been able to ask the necessary questions.

She assumed she would be paid her present salary. But perhaps not. After all, she was getting her living at Ransome. Perhaps some allowance would have to be made for that. Then there was the security of her post with the Company in the city. She could not very well have said to Greg that her only loyalties to Clifford were the normal loyalties of a girl employed in a secretarial capacity to her employer. She could not say to Greg that if she fulfilled his evident anticipations she might become indispensable at Ransome . . . and become a sort of old maid family retainer. If she didn't fulfil them how difficult might life become, marooned thousands of miles from anywhere and the prospects of her city job lost?

Oddly enough, more than anything else, she felt that Julia and Mrs Whittle were the real complications. Why she worried about Julia she could not say. Perhaps it was because there was in Julia's manner an undercurrent of suspicion. It did not often show itself on the surface because Sara's stay was expected to be so short. Hadn't Julia warned her not to get too familiar with the Camdens? 'As a family they're as prickly as hedgehogs,' Julia had said.

Sara finished her cup of tea and her cigarette. She drew aside the curtains from her wide-open window, climbed into bed and switched off her light.

One half of her . . . the romantic, adventurous half . . . said 'Stay!' The other half said, 'You know what you're giving up, but you don't know what you're taking on.' Then she realised with a shock she had put that through to herself in a way that implied the decision was already made.

'But it's *not*,' she said rebelliously. 'It's *not*. I want something more. Something *more*.'

The tears were smarting behind her eyes. Something more than a millionaire life on a million acre property?

Yes. She wanted love and warmth and happiness. Mrs Whittle's life must be very good, but it wasn't good enough. Sara saw herself on Ransome as a second Mrs Whittle. It wasn't good enough.

For the next two or three days work went on at Ransome as if no dilemma had appeared in Sara's life. Greg did not mention the subject again. She presumed he was waiting for her to discuss it with Clifford.

What had Greg meant when he had added that last remark: 'It would be the best thing for Ransome. *And for me.*'

On and off Sara worried about the meaning of these two cryptic statements. For there were two statements inherent in that remark. Something for Ransome, and something for himself. But *what*?

She began to feel angry with Greg. He had disturbed her deeply. He should have been more explicit. He should have put the whole business proposition to her in a business-like fashion. He should have told her what he would expect of her if she stayed . . . where her place would be in the family life and in what particulars she would be a good thing for him.

Of course, she knew very well she had been of great assistance to him. What she hadn't known was that he had either noticed or appreciated it. Sara began to think he might at least have said so earlier instead of leaving her to feel that she had been 'foist' on him.

He might have done and said a lot of things.

What things?

At last she boiled all her feelings down to one important one. 'He might have made me feel *welcome* as well as *needed*.'

Sara, on the horns of a dilemma, showed her worry more than she thought. She was preoccupied when she sat with the family in the billiard room. She was silent when she went riding with Marion. And her face, usually so content and sometimes merry, had a touch of sadness about it. She did not realise that others about her were watching her covertly.

Supplies had come up from the south. Julia had her new wardrobe and the filing cabinets were installed in the office. Sara spent long hours there working out the key card.

There was great activity in the environs of the homestead as more than one plant left for the mustering points miles away at the bores or water-holes scattered over the thousand square miles of Ransome grazing country.

More than once Sara had ridden down to the bottom of the homestead paddock at sundown to watch a fleet of trucks and jeeps laden with stores going out to the first staging camp. More stirring was the sight of stockmen and blacks geared and mounted on their cattle horses and leading strings of other alternative mounts and swag horses. Sundown or the small hours of the morning were the times for the plants to move out from the homestead. That allowed them time to travel far in the coolest part of the twenty-four-hour day.

The homestead party, including Marion and Julia, two of the jackaroos and Greg, left for their particular camp at four in the morning.

Sara and Mrs Whittle were left in charge of all the final arrangements for the arrival of the clan.

The object of the mustering of the cattle into a number of camps before the party were so that those who came up to Ransome for the occasion would see as much of the cattle at key points as was possible. Actually, mustering . . . the combing again and again of rough, almost untraversable country . . . had been going on since the Wet had lifted.

Greg gave Sara *carte blanche* to make any decisions necessary which might arise in his absence. In a sense this pleased Sara because it corroborated his former statement that she had done a lot for him and that he now had implicit confidence in her.

Only Julia had left her barb behind.

It was the evening of the departure of the homestead party for the cattle camp. The family had been sitting in the billiard room before making an early retirement. Greg was working with the book-keeper and overseer in his office. The jackaroos were already out at the cattle camps or were about to leave in the morning with the homestead party.

They were talking about the imminent arrival of Clifford Camden.

'You'll have him to yourself, Sara,' Marion said with a sly smile. 'You, Clifford, and the whole of Ransome! Have fun but don't get into mischief.'

'I'm quite sure the first thing Mr Clifford will want to do is to go out to the cattle,' Sara said.

'He'll have Jack Brownrigg with him,' Mrs Camden said suddenly. 'Now that's a nice young man. Sara ought to get friendly with him instead of anyone as unsatisfactory as Clifford. Clifford has too many girls. . . .'

'And a lot of acres,' Julia added meaningly. 'However, if Sara has the kind of weather eye for the main chance a shrewd girl ought to have, Jack Brownrigg ought to be her mark. He happens to be a nice fellow and not being a Camden, is not so slippery a fish.'

Mrs Camden put down her lace work.

'Really, Julia, you do talk in a puzzling way. What Camdens are slippery fish? Of course Sara would take a liking to Jack. He's a very nice young man . . . and much better-looking than Clifford. . . .'

'Oh, Clifford's got looks enough,' said Julia airily as she waved her amber cigarette-holder in the direction of the cigarette stand. 'But he plays around. I'm sure Sara would see that for herself. But if he ever marries he will do what the other Camdens have all done. Marry in the interests of property and the Camdens.'

She knocked the burnt-out cigarette butt from her holder, stood up, yawned and said, 'Well, bed for me. We've a long ride to-morrow.'

All the time Julia had been speaking Marion had been watching Sara with a quiet knowing smile. It occurred to Sara that Marion meant nothing by it except a mild curiosity to see how the other girl took these sallies. Marion always remained a little outside affairs and events. Sara had no possible way of knowing that there had been peace between Marion and Julia only because of her, Sara's, presence.

Sara kept her anger at Julia's remarks under cover. She showed no sign of what she felt.

'Jack Brownrigg?' she said. 'That name sounds familiar.'

'He travelled on the mail plane with you. Is a part-owner in the air company.' Julia was still standing and had not yet moved away. She was evidently determined to draw some kind of a retort from Sara. 'Preferred to carry your case than mine.'

'Jack Brownrigg's just one person who is left stone cold by your particular variety of beauty, Julia,' Marion said, now switching her curiosity and her quiet smile in Julia's direction.

'I am at the present moment *not* preoccupied with Jack Brownrigg,' said Julia coldly.

'Only with Greg and fifteen thousand head of cattle,' said Marion suavely.

'Very perspicacious of you, Marion! Well, good night all.'

Sara's opinion of Jack Brownrigg went even higher than it had been when she met him on the plane.

She hoped he might be a pleasant companion if he was going to be several days at the homestead. Moreover, she hoped he would keep Clifford preoccupied. If she had to get rid of the prevalent idea that she had her cap set at Clifford she might well be able to do it by showing a preference for Jack Brownrigg's company.

At that moment Greg came into the room.

'Sara,' he said, 'I wonder if you would give me a moment. There are some letters here I want to explain.'

'I'll come at once,' Sara replied.

He stood aside to let her go through the door. She felt very conscious of him walking along the carpeted passage behind her.

If it was Julia, she wondered, would he notice that undulation? The idea suddenly broke the solemnity of several days. There was a real twinkle in her eyes when she entered the office.

The book-keeper and the overseer had gone.

Greg looked at her in surprise. Then he quickly bent over the table and began to explain the kind of replies he wanted her to send out to two letters lying open on the table.

'Yes, I'll do that in the morning and see they go on

the outgoing plane.'

'By the way, you know that Clifford and Jack Brownrigg will be coming in with the plane?'

'Yes. They were talking about it in the billiard room to-night.'

'You might perhaps talk over that matter with Clifford? I mean the possibility of your remaining on Ransome for some time.'

Sara looked troubled again.

'Do you mean for some indefinite time, Greg? Or were you thinking of a special period?'

This question in turn troubled him. He stood by the table, tapping it with a pencil.

'That, Sara, would be up to you.'

It was all too unsatisfactory. How was she to explain to him she did not wish to throw over permanent security in a good firm for the sake of staying a period . . . long or short . . . on Ransome?

'Sit down, Sara. I want to talk to you,' he said suddenly.

Sara sat down and Greg walked round the table to his own chair. He leaned both hands on the table.

'I don't have to tell you we're always on the brink of trouble here. You see that for yourself? For some reason or other . . . and it must be something in you, Sara . . . we've had peace ever since you came. I haven't had peace from warring family personalities for a long time. I rather value it now. I'm offering you a job purely in my own interests. That's all. There's no obligation on your part, however, to bother your head about me.'

This brought a flush to Sara's cheeks.

'But I do, Greg. I would like to be of service to you. . . .'

'If you didn't feel it was your first duty to be of service to Clifford?'

Sara's mouth set in a line and her shoulders sagged a little. She shook her head.

'It isn't loyalty to Clifford as a person,' she said. 'Though there must be some loyalty to him as an employer. It was loyalty to myself I was thinking about.'

'Oh! Then you haven't made up your mind?'

'I . . . I just don't know. . . .'

'Very well.' Greg's manner was taut and conclusive. 'I'll see you when I come in about a week hence. You will defer to Mrs Whittle on purely housekeeping matters, won't you?'

'Yes, of course.'

She felt dismissed and stood up and went to the door. 'Good night,' she said quietly.

'Good night,' he said abruptly but he did not look up.

Sara went out and quietly closed the door behind her. She did not see Greg Camden sit down and pass his hand slowly over his face.

CHAPTER EIGHT

In the morning came Clifford Camden and Jack Brownrigg. Sara heard the plane come in low over the homestead and land far down the outside paddock. A utility rushed out from the garages to pick up the mail and passengers. As usual there was great commotion amongst the lubras, piccaninnies and few aged blacks left at the homestead while all the youths and older men had gone out to the various cattle camps.

They all knew that Clifford Camden was coming, and Clifford generally meant extra rations of tobacco, sweets and gee-gaws from Woolworths. Of all the presents brought to them the lubras treasured most the tiny plastic or coloured tin containers bought in the chain stores for a few pence.

Sara was relieved as well as pleased to hear the plane go overhead. She had had an uncomfortable hour with Mrs Camden in the office.

Mrs Camden had used Greg's absence to try and get information, mostly concerning Ransome Company affairs which were not Sara's province but rather that of the book-keeper. Sara had had to stall off Mrs Camden politely and try gently to persuade her she was quite unable to help her.

'You know, Sara dear,' Mrs Camden said. 'I *own* Ransome. It is my home. I must really stir myself and not let things get out of hand. I have to account to my brother and my nephews and nieces. They will want to know what I have been doing with their money and their property.'

This was pathetic to Sara. It had been quite clear to her that Mrs Camden wouldn't be able to account for the housekeeping, let alone capital values and cattle sales.

Sara nodded her head sympathetically for she did really feel sympathy for this woman who would so dearly like to believe she directed Ransome but who was incapable of doing anything more than direct her own toilette and the making of lace.

'I wish I could help you, Mrs Camden. I'm afraid I cannot. Sam Benson has all these affairs in his hands. You must see him. I shouldn't worry in the meantime. I know that Greg is very capably managing things.'

'Yes, I know, dear. He's a wonderful son. Always so nice to me. Never goes to bed without saying good night to me . . . and always brings me back such beautiful presents when he goes south.' She leaned her head forward and dropped her voice to something like a confidential whisper. 'I notice much more what's going on that you'd think. Or than *they* think. I mean Julia and Greg. . . .'

Sara found herself flushing.

'I think perhaps they would not care for me to discuss their relationship . . .'

'It isn't what you think, dear. Oh no! It's Julia. She's always got an overdraft. Once she could have had Greg, when he was a lot younger.' She tossed her head. 'Now she really wants him because he's quite rich now. The wool clip down there on the Ashburton made a big difference to Ransome. But it isn't just the *money*. Because Greg is so soft with her she's come to think she could *run* him, and Ransome, if she had him. Do you think Greg would tell Julia things he doesn't tell his own mother?'

It was at this point Sara heard the plane go over the homestead.

'There's the mail,' she said with relief. 'It should bring Mr Clifford with it. You must ask him all these questions, Mrs Camden. He would know the answers . . . and I just don't. I'm so sorry.'

Mrs Camden tapped her hand.

'I'm disappointed in you, Sara. I wanted you to stay at the homestead while they were all away. I arranged it. I was sure you would help me. . . .'

Fortunately at that moment Mrs Whittle appeared in the doorway. She gave Sara a quick, almost antagonistic glance. Sara could interpret Mrs Whittle's feelings. She neither wanted Mrs Camden to suffer any indignity at Sara's hands nor did she want Sara to discuss family affairs or betray Greg. As nothing was said Sara could not reassure her on these matters.

'I have set tea in the drawing-room, Mrs Camden,' she said. 'I know you always like to receive members of the family this way. The presentation silver service is on the round table. It looks very beautiful now the girls have given it a birthday polish. I've used the lace cloth too. It is the first time it has been used since you finished it.'

Mrs Camden gathered together her bag, her lace, her crochet hook and her handkerchief in her beautiful ringed hands, and stood up hastily. Her necklaces chattered together.

'Yes, I must come at once. Clifford must see everything at its best. Mind you . . .' she was saying to Mrs Whittle as they left the room, 'when Clifford sees how splendidly we've got everything here he'll probably think we're very much more expensive than we are. I must remember to tell him the tea service is *mine*. And that *I* made the lace.'

Sara sighed. What a family.

She walked to the open window and out on to the veranda to watch the utility go down to the plane.

It was overcast to-day. The air was hot and humid and she could smell the overpowering magnolias in the garden. Away on a distant horizon was a cloud of dust and she knew it was Blue-Bag bringing in a mob of horses to be grassed and quietened down for the invasion of the family.

There was a touch of the south-easterly trade winds in the sky for even as Sara watched a breath of cool air stole over the plain, dispelling some of the humidity.

It was rather a wonderful thing to reflect that for a thousand square miles around men were hunting Ransome cattle out of the hills, the timbered country, the scrub and the remoter water-holes. Here and there in all that vast territory Ransome stockmen were galloping, wheeling, swinging stock-whips, throwing themselves from their horses to swing on to the tail of a bull or bullock and throw it to the ground. Ears were being nicked with the Ransome marking, and branding-irons were smoking by isolated camp-fires.

The only reason Sara had had to miss all this was because Mrs Camden had wanted to get information from Sara!

Sara swallowed her disappointment. Pity to come so far and not see it all. Perhaps if she accepted Greg's invitation to stay she might see other musters. Sara was sure she would love station life. She saw herself galloping on the wings of great cattle mobs and sitting round the camp-fire at night listening to the mouth organ and the cattle songs. And when the stars were brilliant in a purple sky and the songs had died away, to the yarns, old and new, that came out of every cattle camp.

The utility was coming up the slope in a cloud of dust. Sara shook herself. She went back into the house to her

70

room and powdered her nose and added some fresh lipstick.

'And that's for Jack Brownrigg . . . and not Clifford Camden!' she said.

By the time she had come out into the hall she heard sounds of the men coming up the garden path. Mrs Whittle appeared from the kitchen regions and proceeded in her usual regal way to the front door. She passed Sara without a word. Sara realised, just in time, it was not advisable to join Mrs Whittle in a welcoming party at the front door. Sara was not a Camden and Mrs Whittle would not permit her to step out of place. So instead of going to the door Sara went to the drawing-room.

It was undoubtedly a beautiful room, and as Mrs Whittle had said, the great gleaming silver tea service looked magnificent set out on the delicate lace cloth on the dark round table. Mrs Camden, erect in her chair, her face carefully made up, her hair piled prettily on top of her head, was making lace.

'Sit down, Sara,' she said. 'The young men will be here presently.'

She looked at Sara very coldly and Sara's heart sank. In her refusal to help the other she had perhaps not only lost a friend but made an enemy. Mrs Camden's manner was one of aloof annoyance.

'I can't understand why all young girls are so idle,' she said. 'Why haven't you something in your hands, Sara? Even Marion *knits*. She is too clumsy by far for lace-making, of course. But take Julia! All that Julia ever has in her hand is a gin and lemon or that dreadful cigarette-holder of hers. Of course, it's all done to impress Greg. . . .' She paused. 'I shall certainly warn Clifford about *that*.'

At that moment Clifford Camden and Jack Brownrigg came into the room. They were both carrying their coats over their arms.

'Don't have to wear that thing in here, do I, Aunt Louise?' said Clifford, throwing his coat on to a chair. 'Why didn't we have tea on the veranda? There's more air outside.'

Mrs Camden pursed her lips.

'We have tea where my mother had it, Clifford.'

Then she unbent and used her rather sweet smile on Jack Brownrigg. She held out her hand in the manner of royalty and Sara thought it looked as if she expected Jack to bend and kiss it. He was taller, leaner and browner than Sara had remembered, and though he did not kiss Mrs Camden's hand at least he bent over it in a friendly manner as he shook it.

Clifford, who had barely pecked his aunt's cheek, came across the room to Sara.

'Well? And how's our Miss Brent?'

His eyes indulged his old habit of flicking over her in a manner that suggested familiarity. Sara gathered her professional air about her like a cloak.

'Very well, thank you, Mr Camden.' She then looked past him and smiled at Jack Brownrigg. 'Do you remember me, Mr Brownrigg? The girl who didn't give up her air tickets?'

'I remember you all right,' he said with a grin. 'But not for that reason.'

'Hey! Steady on with the compliments,' said Clifford. 'This is my territory.'

'I think I will leave you to a family conclave, Mrs Camden,' Sara said. 'If you will excuse me, please.'

Jack Brownrigg looked disappointed as Sara got up and moved to the door.

'Yes. Get something to do, my dear,' Mrs Camden said. 'It doesn't do for girls to sit around idle.'

Sara passed Mrs Whittle in the hall.

'I won't have tea this morning, thank you, Mrs Whittle,' Sara said. 'I'm going for a ride.'

Let who liked call her idle!

Sara put on her jeans and a straw hat and found her way down to the stables. She paused by Andy Patterson where he was unloading the utility by the garages.

'I thought you'd gone out to the cattle camp, Andy,' Sara said.

'To-morrow night. Had to go in with the station plane to the Airways to meet Clifford and Jack. Looks like I'm going to have company too. Clifford and Jack reckon they're coming out to the camp.'

'Oh!' Sara's disappointment was unmistakable.

'What's the "Oh!" for, Sara?'

'I hardly know myself, except that the homestead seems so empty with everyone away.'

'Why don't you come too?'

Sara was silent a minute.

'I think I was expected to stay and keep Mrs Camden company. It's rather hard on her to be left alone.'

'Mrs Whittle has been company enough for her in times past. Anyhow she won't be needing any company up at the homestead after to-morrow morning. Kitchen Mary came down five minutes ago with a message that Mrs Camden was to be taken out to the plane to-morrow morning. She's going to the coast.'

'The coast!' said Sara, astonished.

'No one ever goes as far from Ransome without remembering that another twelve hours'll get 'em to Perth. Nothing surprising in that, Sara. Mrs Camden often does it.'

'But I was with her an hour ago. There was no talk then of her going away.'

'Maybe you didn't turn out such good company after all. Better come out to the cattle camp with me and the boys. You'll sure be appreciated out there.'

'Oh, Andy . . . I would like to. But perhaps I'd better not. Greg expected me to stay in case Mrs Camden or Mrs Whittle needed me.'

'I'll fix Mrs Whittle.'

'No, Andy, you'd better not. Thanks for the thought anyway. Is there someone in the stable can catch Trash for me? I'm going for a ride.'

'Then don't go out of sight of the river or the homestead. You can get lost and never found on Ransome.'

'I can well believe that.'

Andy shouted for a black boy, and in no time Trash was in the stable and the boy had helped Sara to saddle up.

'You plenty good this time. Nother time you catch 'um this fella too,' the boy said with a grin.

'I think I'll try.'

She exchanged smiles with the boy and felt rather proud of herself as she mounted the horse unaided. She did not know Andy had been watching till she heard him give a whoop.

'Attagirl!' he said.

Once over the rise and amongst the cadgebutt trees she was in the grasslands . . . those lovely pastures still lush from the lifting of the Wet. In another month they, too, would be harsh and brown.

The breeze that had come in with the movement of air from the south-east rippled the grasses in silver, brown and green waves. Sara rode a mile or two up the creek and then turned Trash's head to walk back along the bank. Only once did she have an uneasy moment at riding alone and that was when Trash suddenly shied to the side.

'What's worrying you, Trash? Is it a snake?'

73

Sara could see nothing in her path to frighten the horse but she decided to rest on the mare's judgment. She turned her head a little to the south and some yards farther away from the river bank. At that moment one of the many logs that were left lying about by the floods and storms plunged into the river and disappeared.

'My goodness! A crocodile!'

Sara gave Trash her head and did not ease the gallop till she came into the stable yards. Andy was just coming down from the direction of Sam Benson's office.

'Whacko!' he said, both surprised and pleased. 'Who taught you to ride like that? Next thing is we'll have you mounted on a mountain brumby.'

'The best teacher in the world. Necessity.'

'Necessity? What? Frightened of the camp blacks?'

'No. A crocodile.'

'Get down off that horse and tell me just where you been riding.'

'Along the river bank.'

'All right. Now you know not to do it again without me or a gun alongside.'

'Yes, I do know. But now I'm not frightened to gallop madly any more. I can really ride, can't I, Andy?'

'You can ride all right. I hope you have nightmares to-night . . . just to teach you not to play with crocodiles. By the way, Clifford says it's a good idea for you to come out to the camp to-morrow night. Now go and have nice dreams instead.'

Sara was on the ground now and Andy was helping her to remove Trash's saddle.

'I would like to go . . .' she said dubiously.

'Isn't Clifford your boss? Well, you just take your orders from him.'

'I think I'm Greg's possession just now.'

'Oh, Greg won't mind. He and Clifford get on like a house on fire. Besides, he won't even notice you're there. Not with Julia around. Cut your hair and blacken your face and you can come out as my rouseabout.'

Sara laughed.

'That's the girl. You know what, Sara? When you laugh you got the nicest teeth in the north. And as for those eyes . . .!'

'Thanks very much, Andy. I'll take it all as said. And maybe . . . just maybe . . . I'll come. I think I'll consult

Mrs Whittle first.'

'I'll fix her,' Andy said under his breath.

Sara's feelings were very mixed as she walked back to the homestead gardens. She would love to go to the camp. Would Greg mind? Would Mrs Whittle mind? Would she be leaving undone anything she should have done? And moreover, how and when was she going to consult Clifford about remaining on Ransome?

It was in the billiard room before dinner that Sara saw Clifford and Jack Brownrigg again. She had kept out of their way all day . . . not a hard feat since they had spent most of their time cracking a bottle of whisky down at the main office with Sam Benson.

'Ah! Our Miss Brent!' Clifford said as Sara came into the room. 'Heard you played handies with a crocodile . . .'

'I was at least fifty yards away from it, and it was much more frightened of Trash and me than we were of it . . .'

'Never heard of a crocodile frightened of a plump girl before.'

'What will you have, Miss Brent?' Jack Brownrigg asked, waving a glass at her.

'Just a lemon drink to-night, thank you.'

'Well, how you getting on with Greg, *our* Miss Brent?' Clifford asked with a sly grin. 'First time me and Greg's ever shared a woman.'

Sara passed over the last part of his remark.

'I think we get on very well. . . .' Then, taking the bull by the horns, she added quickly, 'He would like me to stay on for some time.'

'Oh, he would, would he?'

'He suggested I consult you.'

'I think you ought to consult *me*,' Jack Brownrigg said. 'I'd answer in the affirmative at once. I'll bring you roses every time one of my pilots brings a plane up from the south.'

'What? Once a day? I can see the Airways sporting that one,' said Clifford. Then, turning to Sara, 'How long does Greg want you for?'

'He didn't say. I thought perhaps he ought to discuss it with you first. If you're going out to-morrow night you could perhaps mention it to him.'

'We're taking you when we go out. We've fixed that one up. I think we'll look this proposition over first. What do you think, Jack? Would you hand over a nice sweet young thing like our Miss Brent to Greg just for the asking?'

'I wouldn't,' said Jack chivalrously. 'But then I'd want your Miss Brent to be my Miss Brent.'

Sam had been pushing half a dozen billiard balls into pockets on the table and he now came and joined the group.

'Our Miss Brent and your Miss Brent is everybody's Sara,' said Sam. 'And she's my particular young 'un. So the majority will keep her. That means she stays on Ransome.'

Sara laughed and the elf came back and sat in her eyes. She was beginning to like her company to-night.

In the evening of the following day Sara rode out of the homestead paddock with Andy, Clifford, Jack and a black boy. They would reach the first staging camp by ten o'clock. Then if the moon was high and she, Sara, was not too tired they would ride on to the main camp, which they should reach about twelve midnight.

Clifford and Andy laid bets that Sara would not make the distance, but Andy, who had seen her galloping away from a crocodile, decided he'd take whatever odds they liked to make it. As betting was a serious business between men in the Far North, they settled down to steady and silent riding.

'You keep behind me, Sara,' Andy said. 'I'll pick the pad so it'll be good and easy. I'm going to win twenty pounds on you before the moon wanes.'

'I hope you do, Andy.'

Pride and her liking for Andy made her determined to ride the whole distance to the far camp.

They made the first stage in good and easy time, and when they slid off their horses to have billy tea by the stockman's camp she would not admit even to herself she was tired.

'I'll get there if you have to tie me in the saddle,' she promised Andy.

'That won't be the first time that's happened on Ransome,' said Andy.

Some distance away from the fire a mob of cattle had been quietened down for the night. Every now and again Sara could see the black silhouette of a stockman against the white, moon-washed sky as he rode round and round the mob telling them tales and occasionally singing them a song.

'What does he say to the cattle?' Sara asked.

'Not fit for ladies' ears,' a stockman said. 'Anyhow you wouldn't understand it, miss. It's all swear words. That's the only thing cattle understands . . . and it keeps 'em quiet.'

As they mounted again Andy explained that stockmen always sang and talked to the cattle in the night watch.

They were riding single file along the cattle pad now, so there was no chance for conversation. Every now and again Andy in the lead would turn round and shout a word of advice. Coming into a clear he would advise a gallop, or turning into a twisted and humpy part of the trail he would slow them all down to a trot or a jog. Every now and again, out of consideration for Sara, he would ease into a walk and the men would light cigarettes.

Faithful to schedule, they trotted quietly into camp within five minutes of midnight.

Someone had heard them coming, for already there were boots kicking the camp-fire into glowing coals and the rattle of billycans as they were set to boil.

'I heard you coming so I rolled me swag,' one of the stockmen said. 'Greg's gone down to the drovers' camp. He'll be back any time.'

The men were tumbling from their saddles, but Sara sat still and silent. Movement was beyond her. She ached in every muscle and she was falling asleep from weariness where she sat.

It was Jack Brownrigg who lifted her down, and it was thus Greg Camden came on Sara being carried to the camp-fire in someone's arms.

'Who in . . .?' he began to ask.

'Miss Brent. Sara. She's all in.'

'What in the great snake's name is she doing here? What made you bring her? She couldn't make that raking distance on horseback?'

Sara had never heard Greg in explosive anger before. She had seen him distant and ominously cold, and that she had thought was his way of showing displeasure. Now she knew a more fiery side of him.

She was too tired, almost unconscious with weariness, to worry. She sat where Jack Brownrigg put her, her back against a tree with some rugs piled hastily around her.

She closed her eyes and thought, Somehow I knew he wouldn't want me to come. . . .

'Andy's idea,' said Clifford carelessly. 'It broke his soft heart to leave her all alone in the homestead. Aunt Louise has gone to the coast.'

Greg was silent a minute. He kicked a log into the fire and then spoke sharply to one of the rouseabouts.

'Get cracking with that tea, Simes. You'd better see if there's a usable swag under the fly net with Marion. She'll have to sleep somewhere, and I hope you fellows told her there were no mattresses and pillows along with the cattle.'

They talked about Sara as if she were somewhere else. In point of fact she was. She could hear what they said but she could not feel it. It was as if she was listening while partly under an anæsthetic.

She heard Greg turn savagely to Andy.

'Why didn't you let her come in a jeep . . . if you had to bring her?'

Andy's voice was reassuring as if he had often heard Greg angry and knew it would not last, so long as no one added tinder to the fire.

'She can ride a darn sight better than you know, Greg. She's tired, that's all. In the morning she'll be sore but right as a cucumber for salad on a hot day. Come out in a jeep? She's no softy!'

'Well, this is a nice welcome for our Miss Brent,' said Clifford, reaching for a billy which was already on the boil. 'And I say "our" advisedly. Seems you want to share her, Greg.'

Jack Brownrigg brought a mug of tea over to Sara.

'Now you know what a cattle camp's like,' he said. There was a laugh in his voice. 'No hospitality . . . not treating ladies as if they were anything but stockmen. It's a tough life . . . Sara.'

It was the first time he had called her Sara and she felt grateful to him for his kindness. She was still too tired to say anything more than 'Thank you.' Vaguely she hoped Greg's displeasure wouldn't mean she'd lose both jobs . . . the one on Ransome and the one with the Company down south.

The noise round the camp-fire had brought Marion out of her swag. With eyes that would hardly stay open, Sara noticed Marion was in rumpled blouse and shorts. No night attire on cattle camps evidently.

'For crying out loud!' said Marion, leaning over Sara. 'Couldn't you even leave her for five minutes, Clifford?'

At this Sara stirred herself.

'If I can manage to sleep somewhere to-night,' she said,

'I'll go back with the first stockman going that way in the morning.'

There was silence from Greg but a sudden protest in unison from the others.

'Don't be silly, Sara,' Marion said. 'Everyone in camp is crabby at midnight. Matter of fact, I was against leaving you at the homestead in the first place. A week of Mama and Mrs Whittle would drive anyone to desperation.'

'You're all right, Sara,' said Jack Brownrigg. 'Everyone's just worrying for fear the trip was too much for you. Matter of fact, I had a conscience about it myself.'

'Andy reckoned she could ride the distance,' Clifford said defensively.

'So she could, and did,' said Andy calmly. 'I'll thank you two boys for ten quid each. And I'll take it before we turn in. You might clear out with the cattle if I leave it till morning.'

The tea had revived Sara somewhat and she sat upright and opened her eyes wide. To her astonishment Clifford and Jack were both taking out their wallets and counting out pound notes into Andy's hand.

Greg turned away from them and came over to where Sara was sitting.

'Would you like some more tea, Sara?' His manner had unbent a little. 'I was concerned that you had been in the saddle for over six hours.'

That was nice of him, Sara thought, but it didn't account for the extra remark he had made to Andy . . . *if you had to bring her at all.*

But he gave her a hand up as she rose stiffly to follow Marion to the nets where Julia was now lying awake, one hand under her head and the other waving a cigarette in the long amber holder.

'I wondered what the din was about,' said Julia. 'Did you bring your typewriter?'

To-morrow, thought Sara, as she crawled painfully into a swag, I'll find time to cry.

CHAPTER NINE

Nevertheless on the morrow Sara did not cry. When she awoke she was so stiff she could hardly move, but Marion showed a softer side of her nature by giving her a good rubbing down.

'Stay there for half an hour,' she advised, 'and then get up and move about. Keep moving all day. Otherwise you'll stiffen out flat like a plank of wood.'

Sara took Marion's advice, and after she had been to the water-hole for a wash and bent over the now smouldering fire to retrieve her own breakfast damper and chop, she began to feel some resilience coming back into her body.

Greg had given her a quick look, had said 'Good morning' and then walked away to the wooden uprights of the yard built some distance from the camping spot. He stood talking there to Clifford and Jack Brownrigg for some minutes. He then shouted for two of the stockmen and Sara could see him pointing to the distances. She supposed he was giving orders for the day.

When the man came back to the tea billies Clifford had something of a grin on his face.

'No riding for you to-day, Miss Brent,' he said. 'Greg says you can have a saddle to-morrow. Andy's been sent to Hell Hole and I'm going out to the overseer's camp with Greg. Jack will be around on the wing of the mob with the girls all day, so you'll be all right.'

'Where's Hell Hole?' Sara asked Marion. What a name! She wondered if the place was as bad as it sounded.

'Same thing as Coventry this morning,' Marion said with a grin. 'Greg's hopping mad with Andy. It's the toughest place to hunt cattle round this end of the run. Broken wild country and it's always tough bringing in stragglers.'

'Is that because Andy brought me?'

Marion shook her head.

'Greg doesn't mind you being here, Sara. My guess is he's rather relieved. He didn't like leaving you to Mama's mercy either. But he's wild that they had a bet over you. Even though Jack's a visitor he got the rough edge of Greg's tongue earlier on.'

'It was my fault,' said Sara contritely. 'I encouraged them

. . . really to help myself stick it out.'

'That won't help them out with Greg. Men in the north bet on anything from a thoroughbred race to a drinking contest. But they never bet on women. It's an absolute law. I guess Greg will keep you on Ransome now . . . if you want to stay, Sara. He wouldn't think Clifford fit to exchange typewritten letters over an office table . . . with any woman.'

Sara listened to this with astonishment. Not that it astonished her that Greg would have principles about betting on women but that he might still want her to stay on Ransome. She thought his displeasure the night before had been so keen he would regret his invitation.

For three days Sara enjoyed all the novelty and thrills of a cattle camp. After her first day of rest she rode out every day with either Marion and Julia, or Jack Brownrigg. Clifford and Greg had left the camp to join the overseer somewhere the other side of the timbered spur, and the girls were left to their own devices under the watchful eye of the head stockman and with Jack Brownrigg in attendance.

Of all the sights Sara loved best to see the stockmen racing round a wild bunch of stragglers, stockwhips swinging through the air, and bunching them in with the coachers and finally rounding up and embedding them in the heart of the main mob.

After one or two more teasing remarks about Clifford Camden, Sara was determined that she would rid them of that plaguey suspicion once and for all. She not only evinced no interest in where Clifford was or how soon he would return to the main camp but she spent as much time as possible with Jack Brownrigg. He was a nice young man and likeable. His company was easy without being inspiring, and Sara thought by staying with him she was demonstrating she could enjoy the company of more than one man and therefore did not hanker after the company of one in particular.

The life on the run was enough to settle Sara's own mind about staying. She thought it was the happiest experience she had ever had. She was absolutely confident on a horse now. She loved the chivalrous but unorthodox treatment of herself by the stockmen. She was intrigued and full of admiration for the open, brusque, totally uninhibited way they spoke to one another and of the overseer and Greg, yet for all their freedom of speech showing respect and obedience to them. This last she realised was because they respected them as men and not just as bosses.

The only thing she failed to notice was that Jack Brownrigg was responding to her friendliness and seeking out her company to the point of satirical comment from Marion and Julia. The latter two were still puzzling out what all this meant and had not yet started on a teasing campaign of Sara. So Sara failed to notice what was in the air.

On the fourth day Greg and Clifford rode back into camp.

As they sat around the fire that evening the head stockman looked up from his whittling of a peg and spoke across the fire to Greg.

'What's doing to-morrow, Greg? We've just about cleared out the river-bed and the gully of stragglers. Might pick up a few more later in the season when the Dry drives the rest of 'em round the permanent water-holes.

'I think we'll get the drovers moving this lot along the Wyndham track. We can spell them a week on the Buckjump Billabong and that'll give the crowd that's coming up at the end of the month an opportunity of seeing them before they go out to the coast. I'm going into the homestead to-morrow . . .' He hesitated, then turned to Sara. 'I'd like you to come in with me, if you will. There'll be arrears of correspondence on the office table. In less than three weeks we'll have sixty visitors on Ransome.'

'Yes, of course,' Sara said.

She was sorry to leave the camp, but on the other hand looked forward to getting on with her work with Greg. Somehow Greg in the homestead would drive away the loneliness she had felt when she had been left there alone with Mrs Camden and Mrs Whittle.

'I hope I haven't left too much to Mrs Whittle,' she added contritely.

Greg said nothing. Jack Brownrigg threw a small log on to the fire with some energy.

'I might come in with you, Greg,' he said.

'No need to do that, Jack. I'm sorry I had a bit of a liver the day you came. I'd take it kindly if you'd stay on a bit. The boys like having you around.'

This was in the nature of a handsome apology from Greg, and Jack could only accept it by accepting the invitation to stay on longer at the camp. Only Marion and Julia noticed he did not seem so anxious to stay after all.

Greg, Sara, a stockman and a black boy left the camp at

dawn while the others were still rolling their swags. Sara had no opportunity to say good-bye to Clifford Camden or Jack Brownrigg, but she did not think anything much of this. They would all be together in the homestead in a few days' time.

The return journey was made by an easier staging because Greg called two stop-offs, each of an hour's duration. They boiled the billy, ate damper and tinned meat which they carried in saddle-bags, and dozed a little under the shade of trees. It was blistering hot but by this time Sara was used to it. Greg and the stockman took it in turns to ride along-side Sara, and because of the heat conversation was desultory. It confined itself to pointing out occasional points of interest.

Greg in his manner to Sara was much easier. It was more like that of a host formally taking a polite interest in the welfare of his guest.

Sara was content, except that she felt something fore-boding in the atmosphere. In spite of Marion's opinion of what Greg intended where Sara was concerned, Sara could not help wondering, a little anxiously now, whether he was going to take her to task or, worse, dispense with her services altogether. The cattle camp had proved a lure Sara could not resist and she knew that in her heart of hearts she had perhaps *wanted* to stay on Ransome all the time. It had only been common sense and not the heart that had made her hesitate.

She had altogether forgotten her anger with Greg because he was a man who thought of women in one of two classes . . . the decorative or the chattel. His chivalrous attitude about betting on women had mitigated this somewhat and more-over Sara had reconciled herself to her place in affairs at Ransome. She was there to work. She was paid to work. How else could she appear in Greg's eyes? It was no good hankering to be a lily of the field. Who wanted to be idle, anyway?

Sara remembered Mrs Camden's accusation and a smile curved her lips. Her eyes took on that gleam of merriment that so pleased Andy Patterson. Four days in the open air had scarified Sara's wounds. She felt healthy and happy . . . and oh, so braced by the riding and the camp life. The homestead, she thought, would never intimidate her again.

They had crossed the river below the homestead and Greg had stopped and dismounted to feel for the moisture, if any, in the long rustling grasses.

Evidently what he felt gratified him, and as he straightened up to say something he caught Sara's eyes watching him idly but what struck him was her smile and the warm glow of something that was almost fun in her eyes.

Her horse took a side-step and Greg put his hand on the bridle to steady it.

'What's making you laugh, Sara?' he asked, puzzled.

Sara shook her head to shake her thoughts back to the present. She looked down at Greg where he stood, one hand on her bridle and one hand still holding a tuft of grass. It was the first time he had ever said anything personal to her . . . touching on her personal appearance.

'I was just thinking how lovely it all is . . . the homestead up there, and the camp miles back there. And right in front that long waving grass.'

Then her eyes rested on his face. She noticed the firm lines of his brow and his chin, the sculptured strength of his mouth, the fine lines at the corners of his eyes, and for the first time the few white hairs intruding in the dark brown of his hair at the temples. For some inscrutable reason those several white hairs stirred her. They were like trophies of battle. Greg had a lonely and strong hand to play in managing this great station and all the warring factions of his family.

She wanted to stay, not only because she was beginning to love the life, but because she wanted to help him. Something went out of her towards him. She wanted to help him.

Perhaps he felt it because he dropped his hand from the bridle. He shook the soil from the roots of the tuft of grass, fingered it and then strewed it into the wind.

'Yes,' he said quietly. 'When a breeze comes from the south it stirs the grasses like waves . . . waves in a mill pond.'

Sara thought that Greg's request for her to stay on at Ransome had been like that. It had been a wind that had stirred her in a troubled way. She had no idea of the next request that he was to make to her. That was to be like a cyclone that would alter the whole course of her life!

'It's nice to come home to the homestead,' Sara said. 'The north doesn't seem so vast after all.'

Greg shaded his hand at the brim of his hat and looked up to the westering sun. Then turned round, he put his foot in his horse's stirrup and swung himself into the saddle.

They rode, without saying any more, up to the homestead.

Sara had committed a grave error in her stewardship of Greg's affairs when she left to go out to the cattle camp. In the morning of her day of departure she had closed the filing cabinet, put papers away in the drawers, and everything in order. She had then gone out of the room and had not returned to it before she rode out with the men that evening. She had spent the greater part of the day washing out her jeans and three blouses and resting in anticipation of the night ride.

For none of these things did Sara reproach herself, but she was bitterly angry with herself for not having gone back into the office before she left.

The door of the office was never locked, in fact rarely closed, and she had not thought it necessary to lock it. There was only Mrs Whittle in the homestead, and Mrs Camden had left in the utility in the middle of the morning. It had not occurred to Sara that Mrs Camden would visit the office, or that she had not any right to do so.

It was after dinner that Greg discovered the mess of scattered papers there.

He and Sara had dined with Mrs Whittle and Sam Benson. Most of the time, while they ate, Greg told Sam of the state of affairs with the mustering and Sara discussed with Mrs Whittle the plans for the housing and feeding of the multitude expected to arrive within the fortnight.

Immediately after dinner Greg had gone to his office and Sara had gone to put on a light cotton cardigan. The breeze had brought a cool draught of air with it.

Sara added another dab of powder to her nose and repaired her lipstick without asking herself why she did it. She patted her hair in place and then went down the long passage, across the hall into the short passage and the office.

Greg stood behind his table looking at a pile of untidy papers scattered over it. Sara, astonished, noticed that her new filing cabinet had drawers open and files tip-tilted half out of them.

Greg lifted his eyes and looked at her. To her surprise she did not see anger so much as despair.

'Sara! What did you do with that list of guests?'

She went to the filing cabinet but knew with a sinking heart she would not find it. She searched for a brief minute and, turning, shook her head.

'It's not here,' she said. 'Perhaps it's there on the table.'
'Did you leave it on the table?'
'No, Greg. I left nothing on the table.'

She felt unhappy as she said the words. Perhaps it would have been more a gesture of *noblesse oblige* to have said nothing and taken the blame for carelessness on herself. But if she did this it might hide the truth . . . that Mrs Camden had taken it. And if Mrs Camden was going to alter or add to that list, then the whole homestead would be involved in a mess. It meant reorganisation.

Greg drummed his fingers on the table. They were both standing facing one another. He looked suddenly tired.

'I should have stayed here,' Sara said. She wondered helplessly if, when Greg got over his tiredness and got angry, he would dismiss her.

He walked to the window and stood, arms folded, looking out into the night. Over his shoulder Sara could see the paddocks bright in the moonlight and through the open window hear the wind rustling in the pandanus.

He spoke without turning round.

'I suppose you know it will mean chaos for the house-party. We won't know how many . . . or who's who.'

Sara couldn't answer. The whole object of her coming to Ransome had been to assist in the smooth running of the arrangements for the house-party. Now by her selfishness in going out to the cattle camp, by not having set a permanent vigil in the office, she had allowed poor inconsequential Mrs Camden to run amok with the guest list. And neither she nor Greg could say one word about Mrs Camden.

'I'm sorry,' she said at length. 'I would offer to dismiss myself . . . only . . . I think I could still help somehow. I want to help. I must do something to make up for . . . for leaving the homestead.'

Greg was silent. His back was still turned to her.

After another long heavy silence Sara spoke again.

'Would you prefer I went, Greg?'

He turned round now and faced her across the room.

'No, I prefer you to stay.' He walked slowly to his table. 'Sit down, Sara. I want to say something to you.'

She felt the blood pulsing through the arteries in her neck. She had seen a touch of his anger out at the cattle camp. She was prepared to take that and a great deal more on her own head.

'I need someone to manage this homestead,' he said unexpectedly. 'And this family.'

He stopped short. Sara looked at him in surprise. She had bared her head, as it were, for his anger but it didn't seem to be there any more. There was a bitter coldness in his voice. Then it was suddenly tired. He sat down. He picked up a paper knife, then let it fall to the table. He took a cigarette from the box and lit it. He put both hands down on the table, the one holding the cigarette letting the spiral of smoke rise into his eyes. He seemed like a man making a harassing decision.

At last he lifted his eyes to Sara. They were like marbles that had no light in them.

'Would you consider marrying me, Sara?'

Before he could read her astonishment for himself he got up abruptly and began pacing backwards and forwards under the window.

'You can see what it's like. You understand the business arrangements by which this property is run. Everything I do has to be done with a velvet glove on my hand. And my hand has to be as strong as steel.'

He stopped and faced her.

'There it is, Sara. I'm sorry to put it all that way. It's a business proposition. I wish I could make it more. I wish I knew the right kind of words to say. I like you and I trust you. I know you could handle the homestead as most of the station owners' wives do. I don't feel as if I'm being unjust to my cousin Clifford. He would never offer you this . . . offer you Ransome. A man who bets on women is not a good acquaintance in life, Sara.'

Then he sat down as suddenly as he had stood up and leaned his head on his hand.

'Go away, Sara, and think about it. Don't answer me. Just go.'

As she stood up, white-faced and feeling as if something in her stomach had caved in, he looked up at her again.

'I wish I had the right words, Sara. It is not fair to you to offer you . . . well . . . myself on these terms. But if you will accept . . . and if you will accept the responsibility of the homestead for me . . . I will see that you are not unhappy.'

Sara felt her lips were dry and her tongue clove to the roof of her mouth.

'Don't answer me. I know I've shocked you. Just go away. I want to think.'

CHAPTER TEN

The following morning Sara, rather pale-faced, made her way to the office after she had had a breakfast of grapefruit and half a cup of tea. Even these she could barely swallow. She had not spent a sleepless night but she had spent long hours thinking about Greg's proposal.

First there had been the shock of surprise. She hadn't known Greg had any kind of opinion of her at all . . . except that she had got her work done. Secondly, one recurring name kept leaping in amongst her thoughts. Julia!

Where was Julia in all this?

Greg, she convinced herself, was making a bargain for Ransome. He hadn't been as blind about Julia as Sara had thought. Whatever her attraction for him, romantic or physical, he had been shrewd enough to know that Julia as chatelaine would do no good to Ransome.

Did his proposed bargain with Sara mean a renunciation of *everything* for Ransome? Was it a renunciation he *had* to make in order to let Ransome survive the disintegrating forces of a foolish family?

The office door was, for once, closed.

Sara took in a deep breath, tried to still the restlessness of her hands and knocked.

Greg's voice said, 'Come in.'

When she went into the room he stood up and faced her. He was very serious and his 'Good morning!' came unevenly.

'Good morning,' Sara said. She had never felt as nervous as this even when being faced by mistresses or prefects at school. But she had to go through with it.

Sara's mouth was dry.

'Greg,' she said, looking up at him, 'I know that you spoke to me last night in a moment of great irritation. Perhaps you think differently now, and if so . . .'

'I don't think differently, Sara. I repeat my proposal and I apologise for all that it lacks . . .' He hesitated a moment.

Sara looked up at him and was struck by the fact his face also was pale.

'Sara, I have a problem on my hands. I am offering you a partnership. Come in with me and manage the homestead for me.' He paused. 'There is more than one man can do in the next few weeks. Two of my relatives are arriving here with their solicitors. One of them wants to carve up Ransome into blocks, the other . . . and mind you, he is not a Camden, only married to one . . . wants a complete investigation into the expenses of running the homestead the benefits of which, he claims, his wife does not have or get recompensed for. Added to that, my mother will bring or invite here a host of feather-brained parasites who encourage her in extravagance that irritates the other shareholders. Moreover, I have to endure their company as well as their lack of ethical principles.'

He stopped and went to the window again.

'Mrs Whittle,' he said, 'is a tower of strength. She will always be that. But a Camden, any Camden, is inviolate to her. Therefore, by standing aloof from any of their foolish ideas and conduct she is silently condoning much that individuals do that is wrong in the interests of the unity of the Company.' He turned round. 'Do you see the problem, Sara?'

'Yes, I do.'

'You could help me. But I don't want to press you to do something that would make you unhappy . . . or that would be . . .' He hesitated. '. . . distasteful to you. But I need you.'

Sara lifted her eyes.

'You, Greg? Or Ransome?'

'Ransome.'

Then he had told the truth. Somehow Sara felt relieved. If he had been dishonest about that she would not have stayed. It was his honesty that mattered. He had said last night that he liked her and trusted her. She in her turn liked and trusted Greg. It was a good foundation. No starry-eyed romance, but who in the world really attained that dream state? Sara did not forgo that, however, without a pang. Nor was she dishonest with herself. It was a good bargain . . . but she was not selling herself. Something about Greg had stirred her ever since she had sat on her horse when they crossed the creek below the river and he had stood, holding the bridle and looking up at her. He had a fine face. It was strong and honourable and she had wanted to help him.

Millions of people all over the world, from the Australian aborigine to the civilised French, entered arranged marriages and found not only happiness but also love.

Deep in her heart, before she had spent hours thrashing

89

out the pros and cons, Sara had known she would accept Greg. The only thing she would not let herself know . . . would not let herself investigate . . . was some little dancing elf of hope to which she could not at the moment put a name.

They sat in silence a long time. It was not an uncomfortable silence. Each was thinking, for each had much to think about. It was Sara who broke that silence at last.

'Greg, I must ask you a question. You will do anything for Ransome. I know and understand that. You cannot forgo the right to children . . . and heirs . . .?'

She was trying very hard to control the deep flush she felt creeping up from her bosom, over her throat and into her cheeks.

Greg's face softened and he no longer looked so serious or so remote.

'Yes, Sara. I would like children. But . . . that could come in time. The big hurdle is the next few weeks. Later . . . well, who knows?' There was actually a smile there now. 'I think we could manage that, don't you?'

The awful question was out and answered. Sara took a deep breath.

'Yes,' and she, too, smiled. 'I'd like a family. Quite a family . . . but one kept strictly under control.'

They both laughed for they both knew that though their children might be Camdens in much they were not to be Camdens in all. There was trouble enough in the present generation.

Greg stood up.

'It's very early in the morning, Sara, but I think we'll drink to that. And it's going to be champagne.'

He walked to the door and his step seemed light. Sara too felt suddenly light-hearted. Could it be possible he felt the same as she did?

Well . . . the omens were good. They liked and trusted one another. They were both willing to keep faith with a bargain with Ransome. And one day . . . never mind when . . . they would have children.

Greg came back into the study. He had a bottle of champagne in a bowl of ice cubes from the refrigerator. He popped the cork and poured out two glasses of the lovely dancing bubbly.

He touched Sara's glass.

'What sort of a toast shall it be, Sara?'

'To Ransome,' she said.

'To Ransome,' he added and they both sipped their wine. He put his glass down on the table.

'Would you ask Mrs Whittle . . .' He stopped, then looked momentarily embarrassed. 'I don't give you instructions any more, do I, Sara? I'll go and get Mrs Whittle myself.'

'I'd rather you spoke to Mrs Whittle alone, Greg. I think she would prefer it that way.'

'I think you're right. I've got a half-caste stockman down at the quarters almost doubled up with fibrositis. I asked for a Flying Doctor service last night over the radio. They may send out a plane to-morrow from the Airways. Do you think you could make it? It will take us straight across to the west coast. From there we can catch the mail plane to Perth.'

Sara felt a sudden lurch of the heart.

To-morrow? So soon? But of course it would have to be in the next day or two if they were to be here . . . in the married state . . . before the influx in a fortnight's time. And the men were all out at the camps.

'You weren't thinking of telling the others? I mean Marion . . . and Clifford . . .' She hesitated a fraction of a second before she added 'And Julia.'

'Mrs Whittle will have to break the news, I'm afraid. Of course I wouldn't have dreamed of going without my mother knowing, but we'll find her in Perth.'

'Yes, of course.' Sara finished her champagne and set down the glass. 'I will leave you with Mrs Whittle . . . if you don't mind.'

He stood aside for her to precede him out the door. Sara turned down the little-used part of the passage that led immediately on to the veranda and to the same aspect of the garden that one could see from the study window. She knew that Greg's own bedroom lay off the study on the other side and, bidden by some new instinct of inquiry, Sara stopped at the other door, on the far side of the office. She turned the handle and looked in the room. The blinds were drawn and it was an unused room but furnished as a spare bedroom. It was a big square room and there was a connecting door leading into the study. Sara remembered a bookcase stood in front of it in the office and she had forgotten about the door behind the bookcase.

'Quite a suite of rooms,' she said. 'I suppose the best way to adjust ourselves is to use all three.'

She went on down the passage and passed through the door on to the veranda.

Beyond the garden stretched Ransome, a thousand square miles of it. Sara stood looking at it for a long time.

'For Ransome . . .' she said to herself and wondered if she was really speaking the truth.

At midday the following day she and Greg flew out of Ransome in company with the sick half-caste in the plane chartered by the Flying Doctor Service.

As they flew over the home paddocks Sara noticed that by the hangar that housed the station Anson was a small glittering Dove plane. For the first time she realised Jack Brownrigg must have flown Clifford Camden and himself in one of his own Airways planes. How easy might pursuit be, she thought. The others were due in at the homestead to-night. Supposing there was a family revolt at the marriage! Supposing they followed! Could they stop it?

She stole a glance under her lashes at Greg. He was looking through the small buttressed window and frowning as if in deep contemplation of his domain.

Then Sara looked away and caught the half-caste's eyes looking at her curiously. Sara smiled and the half-caste smiled back.

'Nice day,' he said.

Sara thought how much he would love to know the secret news this plane was carrying. What gossip for the hospital on the coast! Her eyes sparkled with merriment at the thought. Greg, turning, caught the look in her eyes.

'What are you laughing at, Sara?'

'This plane's secret cargo,' she said. 'A bride and a bridegroom. It's supposed to carry only the sick, isn't it?'

'Most times it carries the sick who are going to get cured,' he said. He looked into Sara's eyes and then, slightly embarrassed, turned away.

For the rest of the journey Sara talked to the half-caste and the nurse who was accompanying him.

They had no difficulty in getting on the night plane for Perth, and in the early hours of next morning found themselves at Perth Airport.

A radio sent to Mrs Camden from Port Hedland had brought a waiting message for Greg at the Air Office.

HAVE SUITE AT ADELPHI WILL WAIT UP FOR YOU
MAMA

'Then to the Adelphi it is,' said Greg.

He ordered a taxi and a few minutes later they were on their half-hour journey into the city.

They had no difficulty in entering the big hotel nor in finding Mrs Camden's suite. The corridor lights were on though the lift staff were not yet on duty.

Mrs Camden, on their entry, rose majestically from a couch in the small sitting-room. She was draped in a silk kimono and her make-up and hair-do were as immaculate as if she had not spent the greater part of the night on the sofa. The only thing missing was the necklace.

'Darling,' she said, kissing Greg and then patting his cheek. 'What are you doing? Not hunting me, I hope. And Sara? Sara dear, what are *you* doing? Have you thrown in your job at Ransome? But come in and sit down. I had iced coffee and sandwiches left for you. I could rouse up a maid, I expect . . . only . . . well, Greg darling, you know what hotels are like these days. Even if you're prepared to *pay* they don't like to get the maids out of bed.'

'They'll be up in an hour anyway, Mother.'

Then he told her why he and Sara had come to Perth.

A curious smile spread from Mrs Camden's eyes to her lips. She sat down on the sofa and said, 'Well, isn't that the loveliest joke played on everybody? Mind you, Greg . . . you had to run away to do it. No one would have let you. A dear little typist from the town! Sara darling, I'm so glad for you. And oh!' Here she threw back her head and laughed. 'Just serve Julia right,' she said. 'Just serve her right.'

Sara flushed but Greg took no notice of any of this.

'How many rooms have you in the suite, Mother?'

'This room and two bedrooms, darling. And a bathroom, of course.'

'Then let Sara have a rest in one of the rooms, will you? I'm going down to the Palace Hotel. Then I've a host of things to do, including finding a special licence and a best man.'

'Oh yes, darling. Put Sara's case in that room there. And if you're going to get a special licence make sure you get married in a church. You'd better find a clergyman, too.'

Greg's eyes caught Sara's.

'Yes, please, Greg,' Sara said. 'I would like a church.'

'Not to take away with you, darling. Just to get married in,' Mrs Camden said and went off into a laughter that sounded like the peal of silvery bells.

Greg put Sara's case in the second bedroom.

'Good night,' he said. 'Or is it good morning?'

'Good morning, I think.' Her voice quivered a minute because she nearly added, 'My wedding morning.'

Greg hesitated in the door. Then he took a step back into the room and held out his hand to Sara.

She stared at it a moment. For a fleeting unaccountable second there came back to her the memory of Greg standing in the horse yard at Ransome, his hand outstretched to a beautiful frightened colt.

Sara moved the few paces towards Greg, her eyes on his hand. It was so strong. She hadn't noticed Greg's hands before. She put her own hand out slowly and when he took it his hand was strong and firm and drew her towards him.

'Good morning, Sara!' and he kissed her on the forehead.

Sara closed her eyes. When she opened them he had dropped her hand and gone out the door.

Sara put her hand to her forehead. Then suddenly her eyes filled with tears. She had wanted starry-eyed romance, after all.

CHAPTER ELEVEN

They were married in a tiny little suburban church at five o'clock the following afternoon.

'Isn't it fortunate we can get married in Australia at any time of the day?' said Mrs Camden. 'I don't suppose you two would have been able to wait.'

She insisted on putting the 'passionate runaway' aspect on the marriage. Moreover, Sara guessed that her barely concealed delight at the marriage was not so much for Greg's sake as for a touch of malicious pleasure at the expense of the rest of the Camden family.

'Oh, I'm going to love this!' she kept saying. 'Just wait till the family comes to Ransome. It will be such fun.' And her eyes would crinkle up with laughter.

Poor Greg, Sara thought. The Camdens would go to any extreme to take a rise out of one another. They didn't see beyond that, and Sara was quite certain Mrs Camden was not looking into the future to see what effect Greg's marriage might have on her own way of doing things.

Sara, being under twenty-one, had to get permission to marry from a Justice of the Peace since her parents were not present to consent.

Greg had arranged the special licence, found a fellow-pastoralist at the Palace Hotel to act as best man, and found a church and a clergyman.

Sara had not seen him in the morning but he sent a message to the Adelphi that he would call at lunch-time.

Sara went into the city and bought herself a wedding frock. It was a white, hand-embroidered linen and she bought, to go with it, a pale pink hat swathed with a paler shade of chiffon.

She sent a cable to her parents. It was long and cost a lot of money but she didn't mind. She still had some of her travelling allowance and Sam Benson had given her her bust-cheque.

When Greg came at lunch-time he was able to tell Sara and his mother of the arrangements he had made.

'Mrs Richards, the clergyman's wife, would like to act as the other witness for you, Sara,' he said. 'They've only been recently married themselves and are a little romantic about it.' A small ironic smile hovered at the corners of Greg's mouth. 'She would also like to give you some roses from her own garden.'

His eyes met Sara's. Was there a hint of apology in them that he himself was not giving her roses?

It was better this way. Sara was deeply touched with the kindness of the unknown Mrs Richards. She didn't feel quite so alone in the world. There was someone who cared about her and yet had never met her. If they'd been married in Adelaide now, there would have been the girls from the office.

Greg's eyes dropped to Sara's hands.

'One has to have a wedding ring,' he said.

'Have mine,' said Mrs Camden gaily, proceeding to take off two jewelled rings to get down to the level of the plain gold band. 'You'll be the third Camden to wear that and I don't really need it any more.'

Sara felt almost affronted at the carelessness of the gift but Greg picked it up and looked at it. There was a look of momentary strain on his face.

'My father was the finest man I ever met,' he said quietly.

'Oh, he thought an awful lot of you too, Greg,' Mrs Camden said brightly. 'His very last words were about you and Ransome. Remember? *Take care of Ransome, Greg. It's cost me my life but it was worth it.* Remember? After that he collapsed, and he never spoke again.'

Greg caught Sara's eyes. She held out her hand.

'I hope it fits,' she said. 'I would like to wear it.'

It was a little loose but not enough to matter.

'I would like to have it, Greg,' she said.

Greg left the hotel immediately after lunch, and Sara went into the city again to have her hair shampooed and set.

'I will give you a face massage and make your face up,' the hairdresser said, delighted to find she had a bride on her hands.

'Why, that would be lovely. I hadn't thought of it,' Sara said.

'You come back at four o'clock . . . all dressed up. We can put your things in a spare room and make a really good job of you. We often make-up brides this way, if they're not wearing a long dress and a veil.'

At four o'clock Sara went back to the beauty expert and she found several of the girls all aflutter. They hovered round Sara and her dress and hat and gloves, and even showed curiosity and delight over the new handbag with its lovely fine lace perfumed handkerchief.

'And you don't know anyone in Perth! What a shame! Never mind, you know us. We'll make you look really beautiful.'

And they did. Sara hardly knew herself as they put on her dress again, arranged her hat and then her curls under it. They even dabbed some perfume under her ears and drew on her gloves for her.

Sara felt almost tearful at such kindness. She was a stranger in a strange town yet these girls had made her feel she was something belonging to them . . . and several miles over the other side of the city was waiting a young and happy clergyman's wife with a bouquet of roses for her.

Sara went to the church in a taxi with Mrs Camden. Greg had said he would be waiting for them.

Sara had never seen Greg in a dark tailored suit before. She was suddenly struck by two separate and conflicting thoughts. It smote her heart to see how handsome and well groomed he was. Thank God the girls in the beauty salon had done their best for her too. At the same time Greg like this was an absolute stranger to her. She almost faltered at the terrifying thought of what the future might hold.

Who was this man? What madness had brought her in front of the altar to stand by him and take his name?

What am I doing? What am I doing? Why didn't I think? I've been in a mad daze!

As Greg put the wedding ring on her finger she swayed. He took her hand and held her. Sara felt as if all her strength was seeping out of her and she leaned on Greg's arm. He steadied her and held her firm.

Reassurance began to creep back as the colour was creeping back to her cheeks. His hand was so strong and his arm was so steady.

She had the idiotic thought that this was how the colt felt when Greg had put the halter round its neck.

'To love, honour and obey, in sickness and in health . . .' Sara's low voice repeated the words.

'Please God, *yes*,' she prayed. 'Let love and honour come. I will try. I will *try*.'

The clergyman had said the prayers, the roses were back in Sara's hands and the clergyman was speaking to them in kindly words. Sara looked fully in his face for the first time and she could see that he believed in their love for one another and it was making him happy too.

'Now kiss your bride,' he said to Greg.

Sara turned her face up to Greg and their eyes met.

Except for that light kiss on her forehead they had not kissed. The colour stole abundantly into Sara's cheeks. Greg had been holding her elbow in his hand and now gently he slid it round her waist. He bent his head and very gently his lips met hers. For a fraction of a minute it almost seemed as if their lips clung together. Then Greg lifted his head. They looked into one another's eyes, startled.

And then the clergyman said, 'Follow me. We must sign the register.'

They all returned to the suite in the Adelphi Hotel. Mrs Camden had insisted she would give this little party and then leave it and go to her Club.

'Darlings, I wouldn't miss being there for the world,' she said. 'Just wait till I tell them all. The *gossip*. They'll love it. It will race through the north-west and the Territory like a bush fire. Camdens are known in five States, you know.'

The staff of the Adelphi Hotel also took a romantic interest in weddings for they had made the little sitting-room beautiful with flowers and now proceeded to serve a beautiful meal. They sat over it long but eventually Mr and Mrs Richards and Noel Bautine, Greg's pastoralist friend, made their farewells.

'Well, I'll have to go too,' said Mrs Camden reluctantly. She loved a party and hated to see it breaking up. 'I'll just take some of those flowers with me. The hotel staff won't mind. They know *me* and what a taking person I am.' Her laugh, light, faintly malicious but very clear, rang out. 'Greg, come down with me and get a taxi for me. Good night, Sara darling . . . sleep *well* . . .' Her laugh tinkled out again as Greg took her to the door.

Sara was left alone with the remaining flowers, the empty glasses and the maids now clearing the sitting-room.

Uncertainly she walked to the larger of the two bedrooms. She had seen when she had come in to take off her hat and gloves that all the cases were there. Her own and Greg's.

She sat a moment on the edge of the bed.

What do I do now? she thought, looking with embarrassment at the cases. Then she got up and opened her own case and took out her night attire and the pretty new dressing-gown she had bought that day. I've just got to carry it off . . . somehow. . . .

Greg was a long time coming back into the suite. Perhaps he had gone with his mother. The Club was only a few yards up the street. She, Sara, could not remain for ever sitting on the edge of her bed waiting for instructions from her husband. She took off her dress and put on the dressing-gown over her petticoat. She creamed her face, but not liking the look of its shining smoothness she put on it the faintest dusting of powder. The lipstick she had worn in the afternoon still left its faint glow of red.

When she heard Greg's footstep she involuntarily stood up. When he knocked and then came in she was standing in the middle of the room, her right hand nervously twisting the gold wedding ring.

'There are my cases!' said Greg. 'I'd better put them in the other room.'

He picked his cases up, carried them through the sitting-room into the room Sara had used earlier.

Sara put out her hand to steady herself against the dressing-table and Greg came back. Sara had half turned away and she could not bring herself to look at him. He was a stranger. He would have to get back into those north-west clothes to look like the Greg Camden she knew. But would she feel any different?

Greg came across to her. He put his hands on her shoulders and turning her towards him looked at her.

'I think it will be all right, Sara,' he said quietly.

The colour ebbed and flowed in her cheeks. He bent his head and kissed her lips. His arms slipped round her and he held her against him.

'Sara . . . shall I stay with you?'

For a long moment there was silence. Sara could hear his heart pounding against her cheek. At last the words came out in a whisper.

'Yes, Greg. Stay with me, please.'

Greg was gone to the Midland cattle sales all the following day. He had risen and bathed, shaved and dressed before Sara was properly awake. Then he came back into the room, dressed now like his old self, and sat on the side of the bed. He took Sara's hand and held it in his own.

'The maid is just bringing you some breakfast,' he said. 'I'm sorry I have to leave you . . . but I must. There's business I must do since I am down here. I've got a booking on to-morrow morning's plane. It leaves at 4 a.m. I think you had better rest as much as possible. It will probably be dinner time to-night before I'm back.' He paused, then he smiled at her. There was everything friendly but nothing intimate in his smile.

'Are you all right, Sara?'

She nodded. How could she say that she would have given Ransome and all the world for him to put his arms around her?

He bent and kissed her on the forehead.

'So long, partner,' he said gently. 'I'll see you at sun-down.'

He got up and went quickly through the door. Sara let the back of her hand lie across her eyes as she listened to his footsteps receding down the corridor.

Perhaps it was better this way. He had been infinitely kind and tender to her in the night, but except for calling her 'dear' no word of love had passed his lips. How could it? People don't love as suddenly as all that. At least not people who aren't called Sara. And the Greg Camdens of the world don't love the Saras, who aren't very tall and whose noses have a tiny tip-tilt.

What had Mrs Camden called her . . . *the little typist from the town.* And Greg . . . tall, handsome, rich, autocratic, king of the million acres he surveyed, would not *love* Sara. He would need her and be good and kind to her. But he would not love her. She hadn't the distinction of beauty or the power of money or the prestige of name.

But he had been infinitely kind to her.

It was better this way. She had for him this new burgeoning feeling and her great trust in him.

We like one another and we trust one another. It is better this way!

Greg came into the hotel, hot, weary and incredibly dusty from the cattle sales, just before dinner. In spite of his weariness which a cold shower and a stiff whisky seemed soon to dispel, he was in good spirits. He seemed almost light-hearted.

Sara hadn't seen him like this before either. Her own heart lifted correspondingly. Perhaps Greg, too, was going to be happy in this marriage. Something had made him happy and had seemed to lift the care from his brow.

He was very nice to Sara. He had not offered to kiss her but then he'd been very dusty when he came in and had shot through to the bathroom at record speed. When he had come back, immaculate and damped down about the head, the drinks steward had been in the room waiting to pour drinks for them both. Greg had sat down in an easy-chair, lit a cigarette, and accepted his drink.

Sara did not wait for him to inquire how she had spent the day but instead began to ask him about the cattle sales.

'Had to see what was fetching top prices,' Greg explained. 'Some of the cattle we overland down the Canning Route is skin and bone when it gets here. I think we'll concentrate on the air-lift and the Wyndham track in future.'

Sara listened. He had called her 'partner.' Well, she would learn all about cattle now.

They had dinner with Mrs Camden in the main dining-room downstairs, and Mrs Camden broke the news to them she was not coming north with them in the morning.

'I'm having a lovely time at the Club,' she said. 'Why, I'm the talk of the town. At least you two are. You've set the whole place by the ears.'

Greg took no notice of this.

'Mother, just how many people have you invited to Ransome and who are they?'

100

Mrs Camden affected to look bewildered.

'Greg darling, I don't *invite* anybody. You do all that. You know you do. Of course Ransome's always had a name for open house and there are always a lot of people who drop in when there's a big muster or races on. You know that. People passing through . . .'

'People loaded down with cases carrying dinner frocks and party clothes,' said Greg, but without more than a tinge of bitterness. 'Oh well, Mother, I suppose I'll never get it out of you at this stage. You've been just airing an open invitation, I expect.'

'Greg, how could you?' said his mother petulantly.

After dinner they walked back to the Club with Mrs Camden and then back to the hotel.

'We'll have to leave here at 3 a.m. to catch the plane at four,' Greg said. 'I've ordered a taxi.'

They were back in the sitting-room now and Greg had ordered some coffee and a liqueur.

'We ought to go to bed forthwith if we want a reasonable night's sleep. . . .'

He was interrupted by the telephone. He went across the room and lifted the receiver to his ear.

'Yes?'

Sara noticed a sudden change in Greg's manner. He straightened himself and his mouth became a hard line. The contours of his face altered. They were sharper and therefore forbidding.

'No, certainly not,' he barked. 'I don't want anyone brought up here to-night. I'll come down. Tell them to wait, please. I'll be down at once.'

He put down the receiver. His eyes seemed to have become darker. His mouth was set in a hard line.

'I'll have to leave you, Sara. I hope I won't be more than a few minutes. I'd go to bed if I were you, Sara. You'll need rest.' He spoke absently as he stubbed out his cigarette. He stood irresolute for a minute. 'I have to see someone on business.' He turned and walked abruptly out of the room.

Sara felt taken aback. How quickly Greg's manner had changed. Not only his manner, but his manners. He had left her as if he had forgotten she existed.

Sara hoped it wasn't more Camden trouble. At the worst she thought it was probably an agent who had arrived to say he had bought Mrs Camden's yacht for her. Well, Greg would soon get rid of *him*.

Sara took a long time having a deep plunge bath. She slipped her dressing-gown on, powdered her nose and set about packing her clothes and squeezing in her new possessions. Then she packed Greg's clothes, taking a new wifely and somewhat tender interest in the chore.

She looked in every drawer and cupboard to see they had left nothing. Only Greg's pyjamas and their morning clothes were left out unpacked.

Then Sara sat down on the sofa in the sitting-room and picked up the evening paper.

What a long time Greg was! She hoped he hadn't found that Mrs Camden had committed herself irrevocably to something impossible.

Her eyes wandered over the paper hardly reading what she saw. Once again her heart was fluttering and her fingers trembled slightly as she turned the leaves. It seemed he was never coming back. Waiting for someone . . . listening for footsteps! Wasn't that the hardest thing in the world!

Someone had once written, 'He also serves who only stands and waits.'

Sara laughed at herself. *One would think this was a war,* she thought.

Three familiar names sprang out of the printed page before her. *Northern Airways . . . Mr Jack Brownrigg . . . Miss Julia Camden.*

Sara started. She folded back the paper and read the paragraph carefully.

Time and distance have been defeated in the present generation of Australian pastoralists. Mr Jack Brownrigg, partner in Northern Airways, flew his own Dove aircraft from the far north to Perth Airport in record time last night. He took twelve hours to bring his passenger, Miss Julia Camden, from a station which Miss Camden's forebears had taken four months to reach from the north-west coast.

Sara was filled with apprehension. Julia became instantly something more than a too beautiful moneyed young woman who was spoilt and capricious. She became a woman ignored. Aroused. In pursuit. What damage could or would she do to Sara, and how would Sara stand up to it?

Sara threw the newspaper down on the sofa. She got up and walked to the table where the steward had left the drinks earlier in the evening. She did something she had never done in her life before. She poured herself a whisky. Her eyes fell on Greg's glass.

'Oh, *Greg*!' The cry was almost wrung from her. 'Without Julia I could manage. Don't . . . don't let her make trouble.' In her heart she admitted it was not Julia but Julia's beauty and those undulating contours that would defeat her. It would undermine her own confidence. And Sara needed confidence badly.

Looking at Greg's glass again, a dreadful thought assailed her. *Who* was with Greg now? How terse he had become when that telephone message came through. It was the same way that his face and mouth had become when he had found on his table the impossible demands made from time to time by his family. But it was not the way his face had been when she, Sara, had first seen him. He had been standing by the window in the billiard room, one foot resting on a chair and Julia leaning against his shoulder. His face then had been easy, half amused, affectionate.

Well, supposing *they* were down there talking to Greg? Supposing they were down there rebelling against what they would consider an impossible marriage? Perhaps Clifford was there too. Perhaps Mrs Camden, easily swung over to the other side of the fence, was there!

Well, what of it? Greg had renounced everything for Ransome . . . even then. And he had strength and pride. He would repel them once and for all. He was trustworthy, utterly trustworthy. His father had shown that in his last words.

Still trembling, Sara tried to compose herself. Greg would tell her when he came up and together they would face the tide of family opinion. They were partners, and a partnership had to stand up to everything and stand together . . . for better or for worse. Last night . . .

Sara brushed her hands across her eyes.

'I'm mad,' she said. 'They're probably not there at all.'

Sara unlatched the double windows looking out over the street. How innocent it looked in the bright street lights with its taxis and motor cars keeping up an endless procession of traffic past the hotel. The air was fresh and dry and clean.

Did *they* have a car down there somewhere, she wondered. She leaned over the window-sill the better to see the pavement beyond the shop verandas. Her heart lurched when she saw Greg walk out to the edge of the pavement and hail a taxi. When it came alongside he held open the door and turned his head back as if speaking to someone still under cover of the veranda.

Julia came out of the shadows and prepared to step into the taxi. Then she drew back her foot and turned to Greg. She said something and suddenly her arm went round Greg's neck. Greg stood there stiffly a moment, then he bent his head and kissed Julia on the cheek.

Sara could bear no more.

She shut the window and went back, through the sitting-room, to the bedroom. She sat on the edge of the bed and fingered her wedding ring. She turned a little and caught sight of Greg's pyjamas. She picked them up and held them against her cheek.

'Perhaps he couldn't help it. He'll tell me when he comes up. He'll tell me what happened.'

The tears were hard and not to be shed . . . but they were behind her eyes. She didn't have to pretend to herself any more about Greg. She was in love with him. It had started ages ago . . . she couldn't remember when, but she had known it without recognising it the day they stopped after crossing the creek on their way home from the cattle camp, the day he had held the bridle of her horse and she had looked down and something had stirred in her heart. That was the elfin something that had been lying repressed in her heart when Greg had proposed this marriage. And sprung to life standing there in the church on her wedding day and lying here in Greg's arms on her wedding night.

She heard his footsteps coming along the corridor. He went into the sitting-room and then after a light knock on the door came into the bedroom.

'I'm sorry,' he said.

Yes, his face looked tired again, and drawn.

'I . . . I waited,' said Sara. 'You were a long time.'

Greg walked over to the dressing-table and stubbed out his cigarette in an ash-tray. His back was to Sara but she could see his face in the mirror as he looked down at the ash-tray. It was troubled. Deeply troubled.

'I had to see someone on business. It was a business acquaintance,' he said harshly.

Sara felt as if her world exploded around her ears. For a moment she could not see.

He had lied to her.

No; her heart cried. *Julia is a business acquaintance. Yes, but she is much more. He has lied to me. If he puts his arms round me he will be putting them round Julia. He lied to me. And I trusted him. Nothing mattered so long as I trusted him.*

She looked down at the pyjamas in her hand, at the pattern on the carpet. She expected to see her world lying shattered there like a broken vase.

She stood up unsteadily.

Greg turned round.

'You are tired, Sara. . . .'

She began to walk towards the adjoining room. Greg's pyjamas were still in her hand.

'Where are you taking them, Sara?'

'To your room,' she said. 'I *am* tired.' She paused at the door. 'And we have to get up at three o'clock, don't we?'

Greg's eyes met hers across the room.

'Very well, Sara,' he said evenly. 'I understand.'

CHAPTER TWELVE

Sara and Greg had finished their last-minute packing in the morning when there was a knock at the door.

'Come in,' Greg said without looking up.

Sara did not turn round because she expected a servant on special shift with the tea and toast.

The door opened and a male voice said, 'And a fine pair you are! I've come to drive you out to the airport.'

They both turned round in surprise. Jack Brownrigg stood there, holding his hat and a parcel with one hand and brushing his fingers through his hair with the other.

'Come in, Jack,' Greg said. 'That's kind of you, but I've ordered a taxi.'

'And I've dismissed it. You're not going to dodge me both coming and going.'

He walked into the room and put his parcel on the table. There was something rueful about his smile as he turned to Sara.

'That's your wedding present, Sara. I got to Perth in time to get that anyway. I had to ask the girl behind the counter what a man buys for the wedding present of the girl he intended to marry himself. I hope she's got good taste.' Jack grinned. 'Of course I explained to her the girl had run away with another man.'

Sara's eyes widened.

'Oh, Jack . . .' she said. He was joking, of course.

Greg looked from one to the other, startled.

'I didn't know you'd staked a claim, Jack. . . .'

'I didn't know about you either. Never mind, old chap. The best man always wins.'

Sara felt as if her breath had been taken away. What a strange world it was! Only a few weeks ago she had been sitting behind a typewriter in the Company office wondering if ever any young man would come her way. And here she was now, a married woman with another very pleasant young man declaring, only in fun of course, that he too had wanted to marry her.

'Jack, you're only joking.'

'By golly, I'm not.' There was real rue in his eyes as he looked at Sara. 'Three days at a cattle camp with the nicest girl that had ever landed on Ransome? What do you think I am? A woman-hater? I'd have to have been that, Sara, to resist those smiles. Never mind. . . . You've got a wonderful bloke in Greg.'

He smiled sheepishly at Greg.

'Now I know why you kicked up so much dust over that bet. She was your girl all the time. Why didn't you tell a fellow?'

Greg had had a look of surprise on his face. Suddenly he bent over a case, turned the key in the clasp and, straightening up, put the key in his pocket.

'For the same reason that you didn't tell me, Jack. I'm sorry. I wish I had known.'

'Don't take him seriously, Greg,' said Sara. 'He's just being nice to me. Am I allowed to look at my wedding present now?'

'You've got just five minutes,' said Jack. He came over to the table and stood by Sara as she untied the wrappings. 'Tell me if the girl behind the counter knows what the second-best fellow really feels like.'

Sara uncovered a beautiful silver plate entrée dish.

'Oh, Jack . . . it's beautiful.' Her fingers lovingly touched the embossed edges. 'It's really beautiful.'

Her eyes were quite starry. As usual, unexpected kindness, like that of the girls in the beauty salon and the romantic clergyman's wife, moved Sara to a suspicious shine behind the eyes.

'My first wedding present.' To herself she added just a little sadly. 'My only wedding present!'

She held the dish up so that the light reflected across its smooth rounded surfaces.

'Jack, thank you so much.'

She put the dish down and turned impulsively towards him. She stood on tip-toe and kissed him on the cheek.

'That's my prerogative,' said Jack. He turned Sara's head and kissed her on the other cheek. 'That's for luck,' he said. Then turning to Greg, 'Well, come on, old chap. If you don't come now I'll clear out with Sara altogether. I'm bound for Alice Springs as soon as I get a clearing from the airport.'

Greg picked up his bag and Jack took hold of Sara's two cases. At that moment the maid with the tea knocked at the door.

'We're not in such a hurry as all that, Jack,' Greg said. 'We've got time for tea first . . . and we'll need it.'

'Shucks, they'll give it to you on the plane. Oh well . . . if you must. I'll carry these bags down while you get on with it.'

Sara sat down by the table and poured out the tea. With a piece of toast half-way to her mouth she stopped and looked, her head tilted a little on one side, at her beautiful silver dish. She felt sad. Very sad.

She had spent a wretched night. She had tossed about from side to side, longing for Greg . . . longing to clear up the misunderstanding, longing to feel her great trust in him again, fearing she had been stupid and blundering and had created a situation between them that she had dreaded and which her wedding night had dispelled. Yet all the time knowing that she could not have borne his arms around her while she herself thought of Julia . . . whether he did or not.

When Greg had come in in the early hours to call her he had been pleasant to her, but quite formal and very aloof.

Had he minded the lonely night too? she wondered.

Somehow all the sadness and frustration of that night seemed to pale and die away in the shine of the beautiful silver dish.

'My wedding present,' she said and smiled half shyly, half eagerly at Greg.

'It's very nice,' he said. He was silent a minute. 'Actually it is not your first wedding present, Sara. I'm sorry I hadn't mentioned it before but I arranged a marriage settlement the day before yesterday. It awaits your signature. That's all.'

'Thank you, Greg,' Sara said, embarrassed. 'I didn't want anything like that, you know. It didn't occur to me . . .'

'It did to me. This partnership might not work out. You were entitled to some kind of security if you changed your mind at any time.'

So he didn't really anticipate a hundred per cent success! Sara put down her teacup. She swallowed the lump in her throat. Greg's voice was the voice of a business man discussing the details of business. Had he ever been any different or had she dreamed it? Greg kissing her in the church? Greg holding her against his heart and saying . . . 'Sara, shall I stay?' They were dreams. They were phantoms. They had never existed.

'I've finished my tea, Greg. I think I'd like to carry my wedding present myself.'

She picked up her handbag and the entrée dish, scrappily covered in its former wrappings. She held it close to her. She felt as she once had felt when a very small child and she had been unjustly punished for an offence her sister had committed. She had taken her doll and held it close to her, drawing comfort from it.

So now she took the silver dish and drew comfort from it.

In Jack's car, in the airport waiting-rooms, in the aeroplane itself she sat with the parcel on her lap, occasionally letting her fingers stray over it, occasionally letting her eyes rest lovingly on it.

If Greg noticed she did not know. There was a wall of ice between them. She did not look at him except when she had to, because she couldn't bear to see his eyes like marbles without light in them. She couldn't bear to see his mouth and remember him kissing her.

So she turned away, one hand caressing her silver dish and her eyes gazing out over the vast incredible distances that were sometimes desert, sometimes dried-out watercourses, sometimes forest and mountain and billabong.

By mid-afternoon she was exhausted. She had not got over her basic fear of travelling in an aeroplane. All through the morning she had been disciplining herself to take notice of what was spread out on the earth beneath. She had stared with concentration at the mat of grey bush, the banana plantations, the curve of sea-line, the yellow desert, the red and blue mountains, the dark forest of the gorges. She had tried to tell herself, as she had on the journey south, that this was one of the world's wonders, and a great experience.

By mid-afternoon she gave up trying. *It's no good,* she thought. *I'm nervous in an aeroplane and I can't fight it any more.*

Greg, in the seat beside her, was dozing. She supposed that people like Greg and Julia and Jack Brownrigg felt no anxiety because they were as much used to aeroplanes, big and small, as they were to a saddle on a thoroughbred horse.

It was near midnight when they arrived at Ransome. They had changed the Dakota for the station Anson some time after dark at Derby and they had made the last hop with Sara in something little short of a daze. When the utility dropped them at the garden gate of the homestead she was almost swaying where she stood. She barely heard what was said and barely noticed that Greg took her arm as they walked up the path to the open door.

Lights were streaming from the veranda and the whole house. Mrs Whittle and Marion were waiting at the top of the steps for them.

Sara braced herself anxiously but Mrs Whittle's manner was impeccable. She spoke to Greg first, however.

'Welcome home, Mr Greg.'

Marion, Sara saw with intense relief, was no different from what she always was. Her manner was friendly and her smile the old amused, ironical one, as if the by-play of personalities on Ransome was a slightly salacious joke.

'There's supper in the drawing-room,' she said. 'We thought we'd better play mother's part and welcome the new member of the family in the proper style. Witty's even got out the silver tea service.'

Someone carried the bags away and Sara found herself walking unsteadily into the hall of Ransome . . . the virtual mistress of it.

She was unaware of the drama of the moment. She had not thought of this aspect of things before, and the altitude when flying had made her ears thrum. She could barely hear what was said. She found herself concentrating to understand what Mrs Whittle was saying about their rooms.

'We had no instructions, Mr Greg, so I prepared the end room beyond the office. I've had the bookcase in the office removed so that the three rooms now connect. I thought perhaps this might do until you care to make suggestions. The main front room off the hall could be renovated, in time.'

'That's all right, Mrs Whittle,' Greg was saying. 'The arrangements you have made are admirable for the time being.'

'I've moved your things, Miss Sara. I hope I did right.'

'Yes, thank you,' said Sara.

She felt relieved. She remembered having thought herself that those three rooms down the short passage would make a kind of private suite, with the office between two bedrooms.

'Do you want to do things to your face before you have supper, Sara?' Marion asked.

'Yes, I think perhaps I do.'

She was bewildered and went to turn down the long passage where her old room was. Marion laughed.

'Not that way, goose. You're Mrs Camden now.'

Sara blushed. Her eyes involuntarily went to Greg but he had turned away to speak to Mrs Whittle.

Sara turned down the short passage with Marion following her. The doors to all three rooms were wide open as was always the case in order to let the free flow of air cool down the house at night. Greg's room was as it always had been, the office seemed untouched, but the third room, the one that was now hers, had been altered beyond recognition.

Fresh muslin curtains stirred in the faint movement of air by the window. There were two beds covered with gay chintz covers. The dressing-table was impressive and Sara was certain it had not been here before. The other big furniture consisted of built-in cupboards the width of the south wall behind the door and a beautiful round table set under the window with two small simple easy-chairs beside it. On the small table between the two beds was a pretty ruched organdie lamp.

The whole was soft and pretty. Sara felt touched. Marion and Mrs Whittle must have worked hard to achieve this. They had made, in so short a time, as much of the room as could gladden anyone's heart. Sara felt there could be no enmity in *their* hearts, at least.

She turned to Marion.

'Oh, how lovely! Marion, you are kind.'

'Don't thank me,' said Marion unexpectedly and still wearing her odd smile. 'Thank Witty. Nothing's too good for a Camden where Witty is concerned. It nearly broke her heart not to get the big room in the front of the house ready. I stopped her on that one. It's hideously old-fashioned, Sara. And a double bed. How the heck do you know if they want to sleep in a double bed in this climate, I asked her.'

'This is very nice,' said Sara lamely. 'It is all that I could wish for the time being, anyway.'

'Oh, Greg might have other ideas. You never can tell with Greg. He's a past-master at vetoing and using the blue pencil without reference to other people. You probably know that by this time. Now stop blushing and do something to your face, Sara.'

'Yes, I think I will,' said Sara, bracing herself. Marion was being kind, but Sara wasn't going to get any nearer to her than she had been before.

'I think I'll have to wash properly,' Sara added. 'I'm covered in dust.'

'The bathroom's off Greg's room. You can see the door in his far wall through the office.'

The light was on in Greg's room and Sara could see the bathroom across the darkened office.

Marion left Sara in order to attend to the supper in the drawing-room, and Sara drew her dress over her shoulders. She kicked off her shoes and, still in a daze of weariness, fumbled for her dressing-gown in her case. She felt as if the journey across the office and through Greg's room to the bathroom was one she had hardly the energy to make. She still felt the lurch of the aeroplane in the air pockets.

When she came out of the bathroom Greg was in the office, bending over the table and sorting out the the mail.

'Bathroom's free,' Sara said, hesitating by the table.

Greg looked up. Whether something touched him in Sara's tired figure or whether her fatigue was greater in her appearance than in her legs and back, she did not know. He suddenly looked concerned for her. He dropped the packet of letters he had in his hand and came round the table to her.

'Sara!' He took her hand. 'Sara . . . I'm sorry. I didn't think about the ordeal of homecoming.' For one moment he looked as he had looked in the church.

But Sara dropped his hand. It was no good. If he kissed her she would be afraid he was holding Julia in his arms. Julia after all-day air travelling had been unblemished by dust and tiredness; had gone riding at five in the morning the following day.

Sara had lost confidence, but not pride. She was not going to have Greg kiss her because he was sorry for her.

'I'll be all right when I've had some tea,' she said. And she walked back into her room.

She heard Greg's door close softly as he himself went into his room.

She had done it again! She had banished him! Her heart cried out against herself. But what else could she do? What else could she do?

She sat on one of the beds and then lay back against the pillow. Greg would be some minutes in the bathroom anyway. She would rest . . . just a few minutes. . . . It didn't matter what dress she put on . . . there was that pretty pale primrose one she had bought in Perth. . . . Had Greg been going to kiss her? . . . Oh, Greg!

The back of Sara's hand lay across her eyes. She was asleep.

The next thing Sara knew Greg was leaning over her and beyond him, in the doorway, was Mrs Whittle.

'I think she's exhausted.' Greg was speaking over his shoulder.

Mrs Whittle came into the room. Then Greg looked at Sara again and saw that her eyes were open. He straightened up.

'Would you like some tea brought to you, Sara? I think it's too much to expect you to go to the drawing-room for a formal reception.'

Sara was making a move to sit up but Mrs Whittle, who had now come into the room, gently pushed her back with her hand.

'We'll bring a tray in, Miss Sara,' she said. Then she looked at Greg somewhat sternly. 'I really thought she was going to faint in the hall, Mr Greg.'

'I'm sorry. I hadn't realised.' He looked thoughtfully at Sara. 'Stay there, Sara. I'll bring you a tray.'

He turned away and left the room in the same abrupt manner that he had left the sitting-room in their suite at the hotel when he had gone downstairs to meet Julia.

Mrs Whittle stayed by the bed, looking down at Sara.

'Is there anything I can do to help you, Miss Sara?' Her manner was carefully correct but Sara knew that she knew there was something wrong with Sara other than mere fatigue.

'It's the aeroplane journey,' Sara said lamely. 'I'm afraid I'm an awful coward, Mrs Whittle.'

'So am I,' said Mrs Whittle unexpectedly. Her hand rested

112

a minute on Sara's forehead. Then she smiled. 'You'll be all right to-morrow, my dear. You should have told Mr Greg. He's not as hard-hearted as all that, you know.'

She adjusted the lamp and turned out the main light in the centre of the room.

'There you are. That will rest your eyes. Greg will be back in a minute. We'll have our little celebration to-morrow. There was only Marion and me. The men thought they'd rather wait till dinnertime to-morrow to wish you both luck.'

She went out of the room with her noiseless tread.

Somehow Sara felt comforted. Mrs Whittle was kindly disposed to her and that was something. It was probably because Sara now had the word *Camden* tacked on her name . . . but it meant she had a friend and not an enemy in the homestead. A resistant housekeeper would have made life dreadful.

Greg came back carrying a tray which he placed on the round table near the window. He poured two cups of tea and carried one over to Sara. He brought her some turkey and cucumber sandwiches.

'There's a great quantity of food to eat outside,' he said. 'Do you feel like it, Sara?'

'No, thank you. This will be lovely. It's all I could possibly take.'

Sara expected him to sit down by the table to drink his tea, but he brought it over and sat down on the side of the other bed. He stirred his tea thoughtfully a minute.

'Why didn't you tell me you were nervous in the plane, Sara?'

'I was nervous when going down to Perth too. Somehow it didn't seem to matter so much. I had other things to worry about, I suppose. I'm sorry I haven't got more stuffing in me. It makes me feel ashamed when I realise how hardy everyone on Ransome is.'

'You're hardier than you think. That horse ride out to the cattle camp was a considerable feat for someone who had only been riding a week or two.'

'It could have been. I didn't really understand what I was undertaking. Then there were the other three. They were so confident.'

'Confident enough to make a bet.'

'Don't hold that against them, Greg. It was my fault.'

He looked at her over his teacup.

'The particular company makes a lot of difference in

113

the things we undertake with a glad heart,' he said. 'Isn't that so?'

Sara didn't quite understand what he meant. A puzzled frown wrinkled her brow.

'Never mind, Sara. Don't worry yourself about it. I understand.'

He put his cup down and lit a cigarette. He smiled rather soberly and his teeth shone white in his brown face as they caught the reflection from the light in the lamp.

'Am I allowed to smoke in a lady's boudoir?'

'Of course.'

Sara ought to have added, 'It's your boudoir too,' but she couldn't. There was a barrier somewhere inside herself that she could not hurdle. She felt vaguely that Greg was trying to do it for her. He was looking at her now. How fine-looking he was, sitting there so easily, one knee crossed over the other, the smoke from his cigarette spiralling into his eyes so that he closed them a little and the fine lines at the corners showed white against the tan of his face. He was looking at her steadily. His eyes were thoughtful and there was a hint of a smile still left on his mouth.

Sara would have given all her youth to have made that gesture that would have put her in his arms. But she couldn't. Perhaps it was because she knew she was in love with him now. Before she had known that, the terms of their bargain had been good enough. They had been amply good enough. Now they were not, and she did not believe in the possibility of his being in love with her.

But why did he persist in looking at her like that?

Sara found it hard to drag her eyes away from his. When this had happened to her before she had thought he was questioning, asking something about herself. Now she knew this was not so. He was asking nothing. He was telling her something. Could it be . . . there was a sort of gentle but relentless command in his eyes? And did he know he was doing it?

Sara sat up and put her teacup on the table between the two beds. When she looked back at Greg he wasn't looking at her any more. He was looking at the last of his cigarette.

'Don't worry, Sara,' he said quietly. 'I understand how you feel. I won't trouble you any more. We've both got rather heavy going in the next few weeks. Together, if we can face them, we might be able to face other things later. If not . . . there is your marriage settlement. I don't want you ever to worry about money.'

He stood up and carried both teacups to the tray on the round table. He picked the tray up.

'I'll leave both the doors open,' he said. 'If you want anything in the night you have only to call. Would you like aspirin? Or a relaxing tablet?'

'No thank you. All I'd like is sleep. I'll be better in the morning.'

He was at the door now.

'Good night, Sara.'

'Good night, Greg.' And to the closing door she added, 'And take your horrid marriage settlement with you. And Julia. And the wretched colts in the yard that you break by talking to them with your eyes.'

She turned her face into her pillow.

CHAPTER THIRTEEN

Sara slept dreamlessly and until eight o'clock the following morning. She had no sooner begun to stir, however, when the lubra knocked at her door.

'You want 'um tea, Missis Sara?' The black girl was all giggles and smiles.

'I'll have a shower first and then come along to the dining-room. Have you got some of that chilled grapefruit, Nellie?'

'Plenty fella grapefruit. I get 'um chop too. Andy Patterson bin tell Blue-Bag kill 'um fat lamb for you an' Greg. That fella Greg plenty eat much 'um. Him hungry that fella.'

'Yes, I'm sure he is . . . was. I suppose he's had his breakfast, Nellie?'

'Oh, him bin go longa Sam Benson. Then him bin go longa Andy to horse yards.'

Sara had her dressing-gown on now.

'Nellie, while I'm in the shower you look in that small grey case. Plenty little boxes for you and Mary and all the other girls. You take them.'

'Oh yes, Sara.' Nellie had dropped the 'Missis' and Sara knew it was gone for all time. 'I gib it other girl.'

Nellie, still laughing, stooped to open the case and Sara

went through the adjoining rooms to the bathroom.

Things seemed easier now. Except for the fact she had woken in the wrong room life was just the same at Ransome as it had been before. Greg was gone out on the run. There was an absence of people around the living-rooms of the house. Breakfast was there in the dining-room for those who came, when they came, as ever, except for the fact the lamb chops were the most delicious Sara had ever tasted. A tribute from Andy! Sara smiled and then realised she felt almost happy.

She and Greg were not going to quarrel. There were going to be no scenes between them. They would go on as they had gone on before with mutual respect and mutual good manners.

Sara would, of course, fall in gladly with this. It was an easy explanation. Sara accepted it because the morning and the sameness of things on Ransome had lightened her heart. It did not occur to her that Greg might have given this instruction to Mrs Whittle because he understood the embarrassment of Sara's changed status and he wanted to make things as easy as possible for her.

She was therefore in the office and leafing through the correspondence before Mrs Whittle came in.

'Mr Greg was too tired last night for me to consult him about the menus,' Mrs Whittle said. 'Perhaps you would look this over for him, Miss Sara.'

Sara glanced quickly at Mrs Whittle. Was this the housekeeper's way of making it easy for Sara to make the domestic decisions that Mrs Camden or Marion should have made in the past but which Greg had had to do?

'I think between us we could save Greg that trouble,' Sara said. 'But your menus are always good, Mrs Whittle.'

'There's too much sameness about them, Miss Sara. I'm hoping you might have a few ideas and be able to dress them up so that the men will accept them readily. Actually it is feeding so many men at the homestead that is the problem. They don't like fancy or what they call "titivated" things. That's why Mrs Camden and Miss Marion gave up interest.'

'Goodness! You've set me a problem,' laughed Sara. 'Maybe I'd better send for some cookery books.'

'Even if dishes are titivated up they mustn't *look* like it,' said Mrs Whittle with a smile. 'I'm afraid the men will all be on guard for a while.'

'Supposing we wear them out with patience,' said Sara,

'We'll just give them what they're used to until they forget all about it. Then we'll slip an odd dish in when they're not looking.'

'I think you're very wise,' Mrs Whittle said. She got as far as the door and then turned. 'I think it is because you are very wise that you made a hit with Mr Greg, Miss Sara. I hope you'll forgive me saying so.'

Sara blushed with pleasure.

'Thank you so much for saying so, Mrs Whittle. I didn't know I showed any particular flair for wisdom. It wouldn't have occurred to me. I'm not very old. . . .'

'Wise people don't know they're wise because they're usually very natural. Foolish people don't know they're foolish . . . for the same reason. Everybody is nearly always . . . just themselves.' Mrs Whittle paused thoughtfully a minute and then added brusquely, 'Well, I must get on with the day's work,' and she left the room before Sara could think of something more to say.

Sara walked over to the window and stood looking out in the same characteristic way that Greg always stood when he was thinking.

Wise? Had she been wise harbouring those bitter doubts the last two days? Was that wisdom? Feelings, Sara thought, had nothing to do with wisdom. They were irrational and often incomprehensible. They obeyed some deeper inner instinct that was beyond understanding or the reasoning of common sense.

Perhaps she had acted with unconscious wisdom in the homestead matters before her marriage to Greg because she had had no deep feelings about the people. She must keep it that way.

Sara, looking out the window as Greg so often did, made her first marriage resolution. 'I will have no "feelings" towards people. Even Greg. I will be myself . . . and let them be themselves.'

And Julia? asked the ugly imp of doubt. Yes, Julia too, when she comes back.

Sam Benson was coming across the garden towards the house and he saw Sara standing at the window. He took off his wide-brimmed ancient hat and bowed low from the waist.

'Welcome home, young 'un. I don't have to call you "Missis," do I?' he called.

'I hope I'll stay young enough long enough for you always

to call me young 'un, Sam,' said Sara, stepping out on to the veranda. 'It will sound funny when I'm old and grey-haired, won't it?'

'I'll be under the coolibah tree then, and I won't care who calls you what, if I'm not there to hear it.'

Sara had stepped off the veranda and she had come up to him. Sam's smile eased away and he held out his hand. His face was serious.

'You know,' he said as Sara put her hand in his, 'I never knew Greg do a stupid thing in his life . . . and he hasn't done it now, you be good to him, young 'un. His kind is the salt of the earth . . . and you'll cop it from every man jack on the place if you do him wrong, even in the little things.'

'I won't, Sam.'

The rotund book-keeper closed his eyes to slits and looked hard at Sara.

'You love him?'

Strangely, Sara did not feel taken aback. She felt more as if she were on a witness stand with a bible in her hand.

'Yes,' she said simply. 'I love him.'

'Good. Well, let's go up and have a cup of tea on it.' His manner was jocund again. 'You've got your hands full, young 'un, with that mob coming up the end of next week. Any idea how mad a city crowd goes when they get out in the Never-Never?'

'Tell me, Sam, how to keep them all occupied.'

'Let 'em catch an old man crocodile or two. Give 'em plenty of picnics, flies and ants and all. Round-up an easy-going mob every second day. Crack plenty of stockwhips. They'll think they're in a wild western film.'

'Except that it's real. I'll have to go into it with Greg to-night. If we plan a sort of itinerary beforehand, the stockmen will co-operate, won't they, Sam?'

'They'll co-operate all right. Stockmen will pull legs like nobody's business . . . and a good time'll be had by all.'

The only alteration in the routine of life in the homestead was that Greg accompanied Marion and Sara on their sun-down ride.

He produced an alternative mount for Sara, a mettle-some mare who went by the name of Stella. 'Because,' as Andy explained, 'she's the star of Greg's constellation. She's the best hoss Greg ever broke in. Had so much spirit every man on the place bet he'd have to take the iron hand to her. But not Greg. He just took that much longer walking round the yard before he tried the halter on her. And took three days before he got her sniffing his hand. Patience ... that's what Greg's got. Result ... a mare with the same spirit she was born with but real co-operation. That's what this hoss has got, Sara. Real co-operation. She'll carry you like the wind, but you handle her right and she'll never let you down. A real little lady is Stella.'

Sara was pleased and flattered that Greg had produced Stella as her mount. When she thanked him he had looked at her with a smile.

'I think you'll learn to manage Stella, Sara. You're a born horsewoman ... not just a taught one. And my wife rides the best I can give her. That is her right.'

Sara had felt a little fire shoot through her when Greg had said 'my wife.' It was the first time. But she averted her eyes quickly. This sort of thing, she thought, was properly consistent with his attitude that she should not suffer indignity because of the odd nature of their marriage. An indignity to Sara would have been an indignity to himself.

Moreover, as the days of that first week back at Ransome passed, Sara could not help noticing Greg's tightening of the rein on Ransome's affairs. There was no mistaking now that under the velvet glove there was a hand of steel. Every man on the place was conscious of Greg's will ... quiet, commanding, implacable in every little detail of the management of the station and the preparations for the big events.

Clifford Camden had come in from the cattle camp and Greg, with a curt instruction to Mrs Whittle, had altered the place positions at the long dining-table.

'Mrs Whittle,' he said, 'my wife and I will be pleased if you will continue at the end of the table and assist me to serve, during ordinary seasons and when we have only routine visitors here. If, and when, we have distinguished visitors I think it is a greater compliment to them if my wife takes your place and you move round to the left in order to assist her. In the meantime my wife will sit on my right and my mother on my left. Marion will move down two places. We will follow that order when the members of the family arrive next week, except for the initial dinner party.'

'But your mother ...' Sara had begun uneasily.

'My mother is a shareholder in Ransome but the homestead is mine, Sara. I am merely following protocol in placing her on my left.'

This was the first time Sara had known that the actual homestead itself was Greg's property. Perhaps that was one of the reasons why he had kept a control over the internal running of it. Mrs Camden and Marion had never had that fundamental interest. Perhaps, too, it was Greg who ruled that the meals should be in conformity with what the men in the inside dining-room liked and wanted. The homestead was primarily for the domestic ease of the men running the station.

Sara could not help wondering where Greg would place Julia when the latter returned to Ransome. She was therefore, surprised when Greg referred it to her.

Mrs Camden and Julia returned together a week later.

'I think perhaps you had better arrange the table for the future,' Greg said to Sara. 'Except for you and my mother I have no particular wishes. When the others arrive I think you had better place the family in order of seniority of age.'

'With visitors alternately between them?'

Greg smiled.

'When the visitors arrive I'm afraid you'd better start the meals buffet style from the first arrival. As a matter of expediency we'll have to wipe the family meal idea.'

After that Sara did not trouble Greg any more with domestic details. As Mrs Camden and Julia were the first of the families to arrive, Sara placed Julia one down from herself, opposite Marion, who was one down from her mother. In the intervening seats she put Sam Benson in one and the oldest of the jackaroos in the other.

Nobody made any comment except Julia.

'The old order changeth . . .' she said coldly.

'Yielding place to new.' Marion finished the quotation for her. 'Julia, do you have to smoke a cigarette with the soup?'

Julia had taken out her long amber holder and was fitting a cigarette to it.

'I'm merely getting it ready. I shall smoke with the dessert. That is, of course, with Sara's permission.'

Her tone was challenging and it was the first time she had mentioned Sara's name since her arrival a few hours earlier. Sara's heart sank but Sam came to the rescue.

'You needn't worry about Sara's permission,' he said to Julia with a grin. 'Smoking yourself to death would be the shortest cut to peace round this place.'

'Meaning what?' asked Julia haughtily.

'When you turn out in a dress like that, Julia, you don't expect any of us to have any peace, do you?'

He had turned his hard words into a compliment, for Julia wore a beautiful dress of primrose silk. With her fair colouring and blue eyes she looked very much the 'golden lady.' And knew it. She was as fresh as if she'd slept all day instead of having passed it in an aeroplane.

Sara had what she called a 'waiting' feeling where Julia was concerned. She was waiting for Julia to strike the first blow. She knew it would inevitably come. Julia wouldn't give up Greg easily.

She wondered what she herself would do about it, if there was too much dissonance. She would wait and see Greg's reaction, of course. He had put Sara in this place of seniority in the family to help him keep the peace. She would do her best . . . but not if it put her pride to too big a test. Sara had some respect for her immortal soul.

It was not long, of course, before Julia was fully aware of the circumstances of the marriage between Sara and Greg. The lubras talked about it at length in the kitchen. Because they were housemaids they knew all about the use of the three rooms in the short passage.

It was on the night of the first big family dinner party that Julia showed her mettle.

All the members of the family had arrived. In their train were several of their children in their teens and two solicitors.

Except for the big front bedroom, which was allocated to Mr and Mrs Hunt, the most senior members . . . Mrs Hunt being an aunt of Greg's . . . the men were housed two to a dressing-room, and one wide sweep of veranda for sleeping; and the women two and three to a dressing-room and the veranda adjacent.

Mrs Whittle had already explained to Sara that this was the only practical solution of the accommodation problem and something to which they were all used.

Marion and Julia shared Marion's own room, and Julia's former room was given up to a younger uncle and his solicitor.

Two extra leaves had been put in the dining-room table, and Sara had given up her afternoon siesta to decorating the table with all the old family silver and arranging such flowers as the garden produced and which would be likely to stay open long enough for the meal. Magnolias were too powerfully perfumed and the hibiscus might close its petals before the evening was over. Sara decided to risk the hibiscus and opened the curtains and blinds of one window to let in the light until the last possible moment.

She took great pains in dressing that night. She had to make *some* impression on the family. She wore a lovely soft midnight blue dress with a photo-frame neckline that she had bought before her original visit to Ransome and which had not yet been worn. It had been kept for a special occasion . . . and Sara thought this night to be special enough.

Greg had been showing his uncle, with the two solicitors in train, the horse yards, and they were all in late.

There was some scrambling between Greg and Sara for their bathroom, and many last-minute decisions to make. All the connecting doors were open as they dressed and they talked through them to one another.

At one stage Sara, in her dressing-gown, while putting on the vanishing cream before powdering her face, walked into the middle of the office to talk to Greg through his door.

'The ducks are all carved ready, Greg. When they're brought in they'll appear to be whole but they will fall apart with a touch. It makes it quicker to serve and keeps it hotter.'

'How did you learn to carve a duck like that?'

'I didn't. Hoh did it.'

'You mean Hoh?' He was amazed.

'Yes. He's a first-class cook as well as gardener, Greg. You didn't know that, did you? I only found out because I wondered why he took so much trouble over his herbs. He told me herbs were the soul of all Oriental cooking and that once he had been chef in a big hotel in Singapore.'

'If you say it will be all right, Sara, I'm sure it will.'

Sara retreated to her room and finished the creaming of her face. She was delicately dabbing the powder puff . . . a piece of lamb's wool that Andy had fashioned into a pad for her . . . in front of the mirror when Greg came in. His chin was well in the air because he was tying his tie.

'Did Mrs Whittle tell you we usually toast the Queen in the billiard room before dinner? Sam Camden and that wretched Hunt man like their cigarettes with the soup.'

Sara had turned to the side to look at him while he spoke. A sudden tender feeling made her long to tie his tie for him.

Greg bent a little and peered into her mirror the better to see how he was going. Standing almost shoulder to shoulder with him, Sara watched his reflection in the mirror. It was fascinating watching a man fiddling with his tie. Greg's tongue was in the corner of his mouth and in unconscious imitation so was Sara's.

Their eyes met in the mirror and they both laughed. Greg turned, took Sara's chin in one hand and kissed her lightly on the mouth. In another minute he was gone out of the room.

Sara's hands trembled as she slipped her dress over her head.

Perhaps I was wrong. I should give in. I should take what he has to offer me—even if it is only second best.

There was a tap on the door from Mrs Whittle.

'There's a cable come over the air for you, Miss Sara.'

A cable! It would be from her parents. She opened it quickly.

MANY HAPPY RETURNS OF THE DAY DARLING HAS YOUR NEW HUSBAND GIVEN YOU A KEY FOR YOUR BIRTHDAY STOP PARCEL FOLLOWING

MOTHER AND DAD

Sara stood looking at the cable aghast, and Greg came back into the doorway.

'Are you ready? Why, what's the matter, Sara?'

'It's . . . it's my birthday. My twenty-first birthday.'

First there was surprise on Greg's face and then something like anger. He strode into the room and took the cable from Sara's hands and read it.

'Why didn't you tell me it was your birthday?'

Sara put her hand up to her head.

'Do you know I forgot what the date was. I never know the dates up here at Ransome. One seems out of the calendar world.'

'You must at least have known the month . . . and that it was near.'

'Yes, I thought about it last week. Then in all the scurry, and so much to do, I forgot.'

'You forgot your twenty-first birthday?'

Sara looked straight in his eyes.

'Yes, Greg, I forgot it. A lot of things have happened to me in the last two and a half weeks. Quite enough to forget,

123

or care about, birthdays.' She turned away from him. 'Anyhow,' she added, 'it was on my marriage certificate.'

He caught her by the shoulder and turned her round.

'I don't know what sort of a monster you think I am, Sara. But I would not have passed your birthday over if I had remembered.'

Sara forced a smile.

'Neither of us remembered. So let's call a truce on the subject of birthdays. I don't know when yours is, either, Greg.'

He dropped his hand and looked down again at the cable.

'I'm sorry,' he said.

He put the cable on her dressing-table and turned back to her. His manner was consciously easier.

'Shall we go and look at the dining-room? This is your first big dinner party, isn't it?'

Sara recognised the truce and so she smiled.

'Yes, let's.'

When they were out in the hall he offered her his arm.

'A birthday as well as a dinner party is worthy of ceremonial,' he said.

They had reached the dining-room. Sara herself was proud of it. To vastness she had added dignity and a feminine softness.

'I think you've done very well,' Greg said.

'Congratulate Mrs Whittle. We did it together.'

'I like to see that old silver centre-piece with the candles in use again on the table,' said Greg. 'What have you put in its place on the small sideboard?'

He walked over to the lesser sideboard on which was standing, in a glorious sheen, Mrs Camden's silver tea and coffee service.

'And this,' said Greg, putting his hand on an entrée dish. 'It seems to have pride of place, and I don't remember it.'

Sara, conscious of a wedding and a birthday without presents, put the tips of her fingers on the scrolling on the entrée dish. A look half sad, half tender, came over her face and she smiled softly.

'That is my wedding present from Jack Brownrigg,' she said.

Greg looked steadily at her and then, turning on his heel, crossed the dining-room to the door.

'I think we'd better join the others in the billiard room,' he said.

He did not offer Sara his arm and she thought now that the urgency of business was on him again, and all ceremony was forgotten.

As usual, Julia had been determined to out-dress them all, but for once Sara did not mind. There were so many fine dresses amongst the womenfolk . . . after all, the Camdens had money . . . that Julia did not stand out as will one lonely, lovely flower in a garden. Marion had, for once, taken pains and wore a beautiful model dress of pale green. Mrs Camden outdid herself in flowing chiffons, necklaces, strings of pearls, bracelets and rings.

Greg asked the youngest jackaroo, just out from England, to give the toast to the Queen, and a few minutes later everyone was holding a frosted glass in one hand and a cigarette in the other. Julia, for the occasion, had produced another amber holder. Two inches longer than her former one. Several of them, including Julia, carried their cigarettes with them into the dining-room. Where an older generation had put finger bowls the present one put ash-trays. Mrs Whittle, who knew the habits of the Camdens, had suggested this to Sara.

The family took their places and Sara, for this occasion, took the place at the far end. Mrs Whittle was beside her to help with the vegetables so that Clifford Camden was placed on her left.

'Well, how's our Miss Brent?' he said slyly. 'You certainly made a success of yourself at Ransome.'

'Sara's my name,' she said quietly to him. 'Miss Brent has gone for ever.'

He took her left hand and made a play of kissing it.

' "Sara" it shall be, now and for ever,' he said. 'Madam . . . your servant!' But he held Sara's hand just a shade too long.

Half-way down the table Julia took note.

'Look at Clifford being gallant,' she said. 'Clifford ought never to be put with the ladies. He's not safe.'

But Sara had retrieved her hand and was speaking to Mr Ashdown, one of the solicitors who had come to the family conclave and who was sitting beyond Mrs Whittle. She did not notice that for a moment all heads were turned to her end of the table.

They had reached the dessert stage before Greg rose to his feet.

'When we meet each year,' he said, 'we join together,

125

irrespective of minor differences, in a toast to Ransome. To-night I want to vary that by a few minutes. My first toast to-night is to my wife.'

Sara dropped her hand from her wine-glass and looked down the length of the table at Greg standing so easily, so much the master of the situation, at the other end of the table. His face, being above the shaded light of the centre-piece, was in shadow, but she could see the white edge of his teeth. He was not smiling.

Everyone lifted a glass . . . some higher than others.

'To my wife,' Greg said slowly. 'It is her twenty-first birth-day!'

There were general exclamations and someone said, 'Good heavens! Two twenty-first birthdays. It's Marion's next week.'

'How about bringing that *what-have-it* in now, Clifford?' asked his uncle from the other end of the table.

'The very psychological moment!' exclaimed Clifford.

He got up from his place and left the dining-room. He came back within a few minutes with the two lubras carrying an enormous silver tea urn.

'The family wedding present!' said Clifford dramatically. 'Where'll you have it, Sara? Greg?'

'Oh, isn't it beautiful!' Sara put her two hands together like a young girl in genuine rapture.

'Perhaps on the lesser sideboard. Between the tea service and the coffee service,' suggested Greg, leaving his place and going to the sideboard to make room.

'Oh no, Greg . . . please,' said Sara. 'They all would dwarf one another. And my entrée dish looks so sweet there, right in the middle. Please let us have the urn on a table to itself. We could use this little serving table. Then it would be on the opposite side of the room and sort of . . . sort of balance the tea and coffee sets.'

'Just as the lady says,' said Clifford, directing operations with the lubras. Then turning to Greg, 'You leave it to your wife, old man. Women always know best about these things.'

The urn was placed on the table. Sara, who had left her place to indicate where she thought the urn would look best, now returned to the table.

'Oh! Isn't it beautiful!' she said again, admiring the lights playing silver and blue on the lovely smooth surface.

'And that's not all,' said Sam Benson. 'Go on . . . Nellie . . . Mary . . . stop that footling giggling and bring in *our* present.'

126

The lubras went out and came back with a vast silver tray.

'From the boys and me. Mrs Whittle taking first place, of course,' said Sam grandiosely.

It was his turn to direct the lubras, and this time the tray was placed without query upright against the wall behind the urn.

Sara's eyes were shining.

'It's a lovely birthday,' she said.

'And a lovely wedding day?' asked Julia. 'After all, these are your *wedding presents*.'

I won't let her spoil it for me, thought Sara. But Julia's voice went on:

'Quite a success altogether is our Sara. Out at the cattle camp Marion and I were tossing up whether it would be Clifford or Jack Brownrigg who was to be conquered. Good job we didn't bet on it, isn't it, Marion?'

There was a momentary and awful silence, for Julia was not joking. There was no fun or laughter in her voice.

It was Sam Benson, back in his place, who broke the silence.

'Sara had conquered us all, Julia,' he said in a voice now rather fruity with a number of drinks. 'There's not a man on the place who isn't eating out of Sara's hand. Don't see why Clifford and Jack should get off scot-free . . . even if they do wear clothes made by a London tailor.'

A burst of laughter met this sally, and Sara found Mrs Whittle's eyes resting on her. Mrs Whittle's eyes said that no Camden . . . not even one recently married into the family . . . would behave at such a moment with anything but dignity.

Sara felt her back straightening.

'Thank you for the compliment, Sam,' she said. 'It is always nice to be paid a compliment, isn't it? Even one as nicely coloured as yours.'

'The more the colour the more the compliment,' said Sam. 'I ever only paid one before. And she was a beautiful young woman too.'

There were cries of 'Who? Tell us who, Sam.'

Julia, ousted in this battle of words, took no apparent interest in Sam's personal story which he was now telling at length. She cracked nuts noisily.

'When do we toast Ransome, Greg?' she asked in her clear compelling voice. 'That is what we all came for, isn't it? I'm dying for my coffee, strictly laced with brandy.'

Sara met Greg's eyes to see if now was the moment to rise. He nodded to her but there was no smile on his face.

Julia, in leaving her place, passed by the lesser sideboard. She picked up the entrée dish, yawned, and replaced it carelessly. Sara, as she passed Greg, glanced at him, but he was watching Julia. Sara saw with dismay that his mouth was in that straight line that was so forbidding. Then suddenly he looked older, and very tired.

CHAPTER FOURTEEN

There was no time in the next few days for Sara to worry about her own, or Julia's, relations with Greg. The family bent itself as one to conclave, argument and the overseeing of Ransome. Greg was gone out on the run at dawn, to be back in the dining-room, now given over as the meeting-place of the shareholders during the day-time, for nine o'clock morning tea. Sara, rising at sun-up, was busy first with Mrs Whittle in the nether reaches of the house and then with seeing that Mr Hunt and Mrs Sam Camden were occupied if not entertained. The family, tight and conservative in the matters of its own estate, precluded all those who were not actual shareholders from these meetings.

Sara took her guests round the gardens.

'Trouble with Greg,' Mr Hunt said, 'he's a law unto himself. He doesn't take advice. Now if he listened to me . . .'

'He does, Mr Hunt,' Sara said consolingly. 'You know I was his secretary formerly and each time a letter came from you he set it aside to read when he could give it undivided attention and thought. He was always very interested in comments from you.'

Mr Hunt looked at Sara with suspicion but when he saw the open candour of her face he was mollified.

'One always gets the impression anything Greg doesn't want to hear about he puts in the waste-paper basket,' he said.

Sara laughed and her eyes were merry and charming. Mr Hunt was being won over to this pretty, half serious, half gay little wife without knowing it.

'I think he does occasionally do that . . . but never with

128

any communication from you. After all, he knows you are a man of affairs.'

Sara was not conscious of any attempt at either flattery or peace-making. What she was saying was the actual truth. She liked Mr Hunt to know the truth about Greg.

'They're too remote up here,' Mrs Sam Camden said. 'They don't know what's going on in the world. Now take Marion. She really has a very careless taste in clothes.'

'Marion likes to take life easily in this hot climate,' said Sara. 'But she does like nice clothes. She was admiring that travelling suit you wore when you came up and wondering if she could get one like it.'

Sara was again unconscious of flattery although she knew this time her words were intended to make peace. Marion *had* admired Mrs Camden's clothes and Marion never said anything catty about anyone, though occasionally she was sharp to Julia and impatient with her mother.

Mrs Sam Camden, like Mr Hunt, was mollified.

After two mornings of these little jaunts and Sara's kind-hearted peace-making remarks there seemed to be an easing of the tension between some of the warring Camdens.

On the third night Greg came into the office quickly to leaf through his mail. For three days he had not once been consulted about internal homestead affairs nor had he had to bother about his mail. Sara had put aside magazines, pamphlets, journals, bills and circulars. Only sealed personal letters were left in a neat pile at the right of his blotting pad.

'To-morrow I'm taking the men, including Mr Hunt, out to the No. 9 bore,' he said to Sara. 'Somehow I seem to have convinced them that carving up Ransome won't get anyone anywhere. That neck at the north-east end is what Hunt was after, but he can see now that in spite of the permanent water-holes there he'd have to use Ransome transport and Ransome cattle pads to get anything through. It would work in this generation because I wouldn't stand in anyone's way. But there's no guarantee what the future generations will do.'

'It's the future generation he's worrying about, I think,' said Sara. 'There's his son. . . .'

Greg went on slitting open envelopes.

'It's the future generation we're all worrying about at this stage,' Greg said. 'I might have sons too. We don't want them all at loggerheads with one another.'

Sara was putting something away in the filing cabinet. She paused and her hands rested a minute on the steel trays. She found it hard to turn round for fear that Greg's eyes would be on her.

When she did turn round, however, Greg was reading a long document.

'This is your marriage settlement, Sara,' he said at length. 'I want you to read it, then sign it in the presence of two witnesses. You could use those two stiff-necked solicitors, or Sam Benson and Mrs Whittle.'

He passed the document over to Sara. She sat down and began to read it with concentration. The legal phraseology called for concentration. Greg went on opening letters without looking at her.

The main import of the settlement was that it gave Sara an annuity for life. One last clause held her attention.

'To have the use, rights and privileges of the homestead known as Ransome Main Homestead so long as the said Sara Ruth Camden remains the true and legal wife in fact and deed of Gregory Charles Ransome Camden.'

This last clause was the only qualification in the document. Sara was to have her annuity from the date of her marriage until her death whatever her whereabouts.

She put the document down on the table.

'I'd like you to sign that as soon as possible, Sara,' Greg said. 'I like to get that sort of thing tied up and done with. Then it's out of mind.'

'It's very generous,' Sara said reluctantly. 'I don't really want it, Greg. I'd rather just be your wife in the same terms that other people depend on their husbands.'

'I'm protecting you against the future,' Greg said with an implacable note in his voice. 'I should have got that fixed up before we were married. There wasn't time.'

Sara sat silent. She supposed an annuity was the same thing as the dress allowance that men of means gave to their wives. It simplified the discussion of money matters as between husband and wife. She could not, however, but feel hurt about the proviso in the last clause. It was a right and proper clause, she knew that, and was designed to give her privilege and even authority in the homestead. Moreover, she could see the necessity for the proviso in the event of their marriage not being a success. But it hurt her. It under-

130

lined the possibility of the marriage not being a success.

Greg noticed her hesitation and unbent a little.

'Sign it, please, Sara.'

She noticed the tiredness in him now. He'd been contending with his family unremittingly for three days. She wasn't being any help by humming and hawing.

She picked up the fountain pen.

'Very well, Greg. I'll go and find Mrs Whittle. It's just that you are generous.'

She went to the door and turned round to speak to him.

'I hope the proviso in the last clause won't ever take effect . . . that is . . . that I will forgo my privileges in the homestead.'

She went out and as she did so she quietly shut the door behind her. Her heart was beating rapidly for she felt she had said something that should convey a world of meaning to Greg.

She did not see him standing looking at the closed door. He stood thus for a few minutes and then walked quietly into Sara's room. He stood hesitant in the middle of the room and then walked slowly over to her dressing-table. He picked up her crystal powder bowl and looked at it. He picked up a fragment of lace handkerchief and lifted it to his nose. Then he picked up her perfume, loosened the stopper and sniffed it. For the first time in days he smiled.

He replaced the perfume bottle and noticed it was Chanel No. 5. What, he wondered, were Chanel 1, 2, 3 and 4? He bent and straightened Sara's slippers and then decided he liked them best the way they were before. He moved them so that they stood under her dressing-table at an angle, their toes pointing in towards one another. This time there was a real smile on his face. He bent and looked at himself in the mirror and brushed his hand through his hair.

Then he went quietly out of the room.

In the passage he met Marion.

'If you're looking for Sara she's in the kitchen regions,' he said. 'But have you got five minutes, Marion?'

'All the time in the world,' said Marion. 'As you well know.'

'Then come into the dining-room and have a drink with me. I deserve a drink.'

'I think you do, Greg. I don't, of course, but then I can always help someone else after six o'clock at night.'

They went into the dining-room and Greg unstoppered a

131

decanter on the main sideboard. He poured the light yellow wine into two glasses.

'What do Chanel No. 1, 2, 3, 4 and 5 mean, Marion?' he said over his glass.

'I don't know. Ask Julia. She's an authority on perfumes,' said Marion. She walked to the end of the room and stood looking at the array of silver on the other sideboard. 'Why does Sara set so much store by that silly entrée dish?' Marion asked.

Greg followed her and picked it up.

'I don't know,' he said. 'Supposing we put it in a less distinguished position. Do you think she'd notice it?'

Marion looked at Greg with amusement.

'What's happened to you to-night, Greg? You sound as you used to sound years ago. Before you had the weight of Ransome on your shoulders.'

Greg smiled.

'I think I'll move the entrée dish,' he said. 'We used to do that years ago when we were kids. Remember? Move mother's silver all round the place.'

'Yes. And it was weeks before she noticed it. Then she thought the bunyips had been in the homestead.'

Greg picked up the dish and carried it to the small table on which rested the tea urn and the silver tray.

'Among the wedding presents . . .' said Greg absently. And he put it down, but in the shadow of the tea urn. 'What's this?' he asked, picking up a silver hot-water jug.

'That's from Clifford. He gave it to Sara this morning. Had it sent up on the plane.'

'But he came in in the family tea urn, didn't he?'

'Oh yes. Quite big-hearted he was. But this is a special one for Sara. Quite a hit with the boys . . . is Sara.'

But Greg was not going to have his mood spoiled. He poured himself another wine and half filled Marion's glass for her.

'Greg, you look as if you might bowl hoops down the path any moment.'

'Two glasses of wine won't do that to me, young Marion.'

'No. It's your mood. What's happened?'

'I don't know. Perhaps it's perfume. It sort of stirs one's memory. One remembers that one was once young and did behave as if one was young.'

'Hey, steady on, Greg. You're married now. Chanel 5 belongs to the days of Julia.'

Julia was passing the door and heard her name. She came in. She was looking particularly beautiful to-night in a tight swathed black dress, her fair hair brushed back so that one could see her fine square forehead unblemished and smooth as alabaster.

'Talking about me?' she asked. 'And do I have a glass of wine too?'

'Certainly,' said Greg. 'Which wine-glass will you have, Julia?'

'The cut-glass one,' said Julia. 'I always have the best.'

'That's just what we were saying,' said Marion. 'Greg said Chanel 5 was his favourite perfume.'

'Did I say that?' asked Greg, surprised.

Julia opened her mouth to say something, then suddenly closed it. A little gleam came into her eyes. She stared thoughtfully into her wine-glass.

'Chanel 5 . . .' she murmured.

Then she shrugged and walked around the dining-room. The undulation was marked because her dress was so tight, but Greg and Marion could only stand and admire her . . . both with something of their old youthful smiles.

Julia paused at the small table. She picked up Clifford's jug and pushed Jack's entrée dish another inch into the shadow of the tea urn.

'Sara's conquests!' she said. 'Oh, well. They did know her first, didn't they?'

'Yes, but she didn't choose them,' said Marion suddenly.

'Perhaps she made a mistake. We all do sometimes.' She came back to the sideboard and poured some more wine into her glass. She looked at Greg in a tantalising way. 'As long as she doesn't regret it . . .' she said lazily.

Sara came into the dining-room. She had the legal document rolled around the fountain pen.

'Family conclave?' she asked with a smile.

'It is now,' said Greg.

His eyes did not leave her face. Once again Sara had that odd feeling that Greg's eyes were looking into hers. Seeking? Or telling?

Marion, standing beside Greg, and Julia, leaning against the sideboard, watched her. Sara dragged her eyes away from Greg and to hide her feelings glanced round the room.

'Oh!' she said, going over to the small table. 'Who put my dish there? I'm really going to growl at Nellie.'

She picked up the dish and returned it to its former place.

Julia looked at Greg and cocked one supercilious eyebrow. 'What did I tell you?' was what that eyebrow and the imperceptible movements of her lips said.

Greg put his wine-glass down on the sideboard.

'I'm not bossy, am I, Greg?' Sara said gently. 'But I can have my own way about my entrée dish, can't I?'

'Yes,' said Greg quietly. 'You can have your own way about that. Is that document signed, Sara?'

'Yes. It's complete.' She gave it to him.

'If you would like a glass of wine I'm sure Marion will keep you company. I want to put this thing in Sam's safe.'

He quietly left the room.

That night when Sara was preparing to go to bed Greg was still sitting behind his table in the office.

'I'm going to work late to-night,' Greg said. 'I think you'd better shut your door.' Then he added pleasantly, 'I'm going to try out the typewriter . . . with two fingers.'

'Can I help you?'

'No. I feel like struggling on my own. Do you mind?'

Sara said good night, and when she went into her room she quietly shut the door behind her. For the first time there was a shut door between them. Sara put her hand to her head.

Greg had been in the dining-room laughing and talking with Julia and Marion. Now he was quiet, polite . . . and wished to be alone. Somehow, Sara thought, Julia was behind Greg's mood to-night.

One day, she thought, when she had time, and when she could gain the confidence, she would fight Julia with her own weapons.

She went to her dressing-table and, catching sight of the perfume bottle, she picked it up.

'And not with Chanel 5,' she added.

She put the scent away in the back of a cupboard. She hadn't much confidence yet, she knew. But one day, if she hung on, who knows?

She undressed, creamed her face and went to the bathroom she had formerly used in the long passage. She got into bed and lay staring at the crack of light under the office door.

She felt like a small girl shut out and in the cold.

And I did it myself, she thought, remembering the night after her wedding night when she had put Greg's pyjamas in the other room. *But would I do different now?*

Did Greg still sometimes think of Julia? What would his thoughts be? The same as hers were for Greg?

The back of Sara's hand rested on her eyes. Her heart longed for Greg, but her head rebelled against Julia. It was like her eyes and her mouth—they argued with one another.

CHAPTER FIFTEEN

For days now there was no time for thought and no time for futile longing. People were beginning to converge on Ransome from far and near. Visitors arrived in ones, twos and threes. Stockmen from other stations on their way to 'bust their cheques' stopped off at Ransome to see some of the fun. Fringe-land natives, spears, nulla-nullas and all, were camping in an area of bush behind the ordinary abodes of the station blacks. The caterers plus all their equipment arrived and had to be installed in one of the galvanised iron cottages that had been cleared out and set aside for them.

A specially chartered plane came through from Adelaide, along the Alice Springs air route, to bring food supplies.

Sara was so busy she didn't know what day it was or where she was herself.

'Don't know Thursday from Swanston Street,' said Sam Benson as he sent an S O S up to the homestead for Sara to come and help him dole out the government stores to the fringe-land natives. 'Most of that stuff,' he said morosely as he handed out flour, sugar and tobacco, 'will go out to the myalls in the Never-Never. Then these fellows will be back for more for themselves. They share everything they've got.'

Up in the homestead Mrs Camden was creating her own diversions. Her friends, the officially uninvited ones, were arriving and Mrs Camden was busy re-allocating bedrooms and sleeping quarters and sending Mrs Whittle and her staff scattering through old cupboards and pantries to bring out long-forgotten treasures that Mrs Camden might display them to her friends.

In the evening there were so many people in the homestead, and so many up from the camps recently erected in the cadgebutt trees, that at least Sara did not have to worry who was who. There were too many people and

135

they all were strangers to her. All Sara had to do was keep smiling and leave them to themselves. They all knew one another, or knew about one another, and there was many a party within the party especially down in the camps. There the fires glowed all night and the mouth organ and concertina competed with the human voice for noise and gaiety.

'How are you wearing, young 'un?' Sam asked her.

'All right, but as you said, Sam, I don't know Thursday from Swanston Street. By the way, where is Swanston Street?'

'Crikey! Where you been all your life? Swanston is the holy of holies. Melbourne.'

'Oh! I only know Sydney and Adelaide. And now Perth, of course.'

'Well, you better know that Saturday's Marion's birthday. And that's the day of the big party. Don't go and forget what day of the week that is.'

'I won't. Did you know that Julia is putting about the idea that nobody dresses until after dinner . . . and that then it is to be a masked dance?'

Sam scratched his stomach with the stem of his pipe.

'Now I don't know whether that's a good idea or not. Some of those stockmen will have heavy going round the barrel and might take advantage of those masks.'

'Oh, Sam, I hope not.'

'Well, now that you've warned me I'll see the overseer and we'll keep a good watch out for any shinanigens. Our own men'll be all right. It's some of those strangers about I'm doubting.'

Sam wheezed and rolled away towards his own office.

'And young Julia too,' he added to himself. 'Now I wonder what she's up to!'

Mrs Camden, in disposing of some of her 'unchartered' guests, had suggested to Greg that a suite of three rooms was a very selfish claim for him and Sara to stake. But Greg had come down with his veto on Mrs Camden's ideas with his old firm way of dealing with an idea to which he did not take.

'Those three rooms stay the way they are, Mother,' he said. 'They're the administrative headquarters while the invasion's on. Turn the drawing-room into a dormitory, if you must.'

But Mrs Camden held up her hands in horror.

'Really, such selfishness!' she said and went away calling

for Mrs Whittle.

Greg looked at Sara with a grin. She couldn't remember when she had last seen him. It must have been days ago. They were no more married 'in fact' than they had been the first day she came to Ransome. He was all day looking after his visitors and inquisitors out on the run, and half the night talking to and entertaining them in either the billiard room or the office.

The door between Sara's room and the office seemed to be permanently closed now, and she was really more relieved than anything else. She fell into bed at night exhausted and slept dreamlessly and deeply until the first sound of galloping horses at daybreak brought her back to another day's organising.

One morning she woke shocked to find that the bed next to her had been slept in. When she went through the office to shower in Greg's bathroom she discovered the reason why. Greg's own bed was full of two very young men who evidently had had to be put to bed the night before.

It seemed strange to Sara that Greg, her own husband, could have slept in the bed next to her and she never to have known he was there.

When he spoke to her for a fleeting moment that night he made no mention of it, so Sara, too, remained silent.

'It seems we've all got to wear masks to-morrow night, Sara,' he said. 'The saddler's shed has been busy making them all day. I told Blue-Bag to bring one up to the homestead for you. This is some new idea of Marion's and as it is her birthday I expect we'd better humour her.'

Sara agreed, but she wondered if Greg would have been so sanguine if he had known the idea originated with Julia. Greg, being a man, probably did not know that some women were schemers.

To-night was not the night to worry Greg about the domestic or social problems of the homestead. He had Mrs Camden's yacht again on his hands. She talked to all her friends about it and it was quite clear that a number of them were already angling for invitations for what Mrs Camden promised to be a 'fabulous' cruise.

'The thing's gone too far,' Greg told Sara. 'We'll have to bring the matter up with the family. Do you know what we can buy a Fairmile for? Because that's what it would have to be?'

Sara shook her head.

'Twenty thousand pounds . . . equipped.'

Sara shook her head again. She would like to have humoured Mrs Camden in her idea of a yacht. But twenty thousand pounds? Sara felt sorry for the reception Mrs Camden would get from her fellow-shareholders. She wrinkled her brow to try and think of a way of diverting Mrs Camden's interest.

If Marion would only take to one of those MacKensies from Turra station, that might do it. Mrs Camden's second obsession was to marry Marion off to a fellow station-owner. If this could come off then perhaps Mrs Camden could be diverted into running a fabulous wedding instead of a fabulous cruise.

The following day brought more restraint to the outside activities of the house-party. Nearly all the fairer sex preferred to restore their batteries in readiness for the dance that night. They stayed around the homestead, creaming the sunburn off their faces, washing and setting their own and other people's hair, and shaking out the folds of evening dresses.

There was much laughter and secrecy about evening dresses. Everyone had taken to the idea of a masked dance and that meant that evening dresses had to remain a secret. No use to hide the fair face if the fair robe could be recognised.

In spite of her former doubts Sara began to look forward with something of secret hope and anticipation to dancing with masked and unknown partners. There was an element of adventure thus with Greg. She banished from her thoughts the idea that this also was at the back of Julia's mind.

In the afternoon Jack Brownrigg arrived.

'Why, Jack!' Sara said. 'We had given up all hope of you. Where have you been all this week?'

'Two pilots off,' he said glumly. 'One with 'flu and the other's getting married. Had to do the night runs myself. Shouldn't be here to-day but I couldn't miss Marion's birthday.' He looked at Sara quizzically. 'Or seeing if the new mistress of Ransome was shaking down all right. You want anybody's nose punched in, Sara? If so, I'm your man.'

Sara laughed.

'Everybody's very docile,' she said. 'Why, I'm having no difficulty at all.'

'You don't say? You got Greg under your thumb too?'

'Not Greg,' Sara said, shaking her head. 'I don't think Greg will ever be under anybody's thumb. And who would want it?'

'Some women,' said Jack knowingly. 'You know what, Sara, there's some women aren't happy unless they're conquering someone. Not some *thing,* mind you, but some*one*.'

'I suppose there are,' Sara said hastily. Was Jack thinking of Julia as she, Sara, thought of her?

'Well, never mind,' Sara added. 'Come and have some tea, and then I'm going to pack you down to the quarters. They've got a veranda sleep-out built on there for latecomers like you. I'm afraid all the men are there most of the time anyway. Do you know what they do down there every night, Jack?'

'Tell crocodile yarns. Who's shot the biggest so far?'

'I don't know. I haven't had time to ask. But they all seem to have shot whopping big crocodiles some time or other in their lives.'

Dinner, buffet style, was like the hors d'œuvre before the feast. It had been decided that the toast to Marion and the family present-giving should be made at supper-time, just before midnight.

As soon as the meal was over Sara did not wait to see the dining-room and billiard room cleared but went quickly to her own room. She wanted to shower and use the right-of-way through Greg's room before she saw what suit he would be wearing, though she guessed it would be the classic uniform of the men outback . . . black tailored trousers and white sharkskin coat with a black bow tie on a soft linen shirt . . . but she just didn't want to see it. She felt almost like Cinderella who might meet her Prince Charming to-night, and she didn't want to spoil the mystery of it.

Through her own window she could see the floor that had been put down in the garden, and the lights swinging from the trees so that all was half light and half shadows. Already some of the staff were using the giant sprays that were to keep mosquitoes and other plagues away for a few hours. Fortunately the night was still and the spray would be effective under the trees and shrubs where the bomber mosquitoes loved most to linger.

Overhead the stars shone like brilliant lamps in the dark velvet blue of the sky. Silhouetted against the skyline were the palms and, farther away, the clump of cadgebutt trees.

It was a heavenly night with all the mystery of the tropical scents in the air.

Sara put on the make-up sparingly and gently over her face and neck and shoulders and arms. Then she slipped into her pearl-pale satin dress. For once she had something of Julia's style in the swathed skirt. Gone were the full pleats and curving flares of her usual dresses. This was more sophisticated, as becomes a young matron, Sara had said to herself when she ordered it.

She went to the cupboard where she had put her perfume and took it out. She unstoppered it, and then hesitated. She was aware that her new dress was more Julia's style than her own, and to use an exotic perfume might be emulating Julia too far. She put the stopper back and the perfume on her dressing-table. Instead she took from a drawer a small bottle of Old Lavender. She sprinkled a few drops on her handkerchief and dabbed some behind the ears.

'That's more like me,' she said.

She picked up her mask and went through the office to Greg's door. She tapped on the door.

'If you want to use the long mirror in my room I'm going out now, Greg,' she said. 'Don't forget to put on your mask, will you?'

'Thanks, Sara.' His voice came gruffly as if he had his studs in his mouth.

Sara smiled to herself and went out of the office door into the passage. She adjusted her mask and went towards the veranda.

She had a tremendous sense of relief. She was just a masked lady to-night. No looking after other people. No hastening to see that all was well in the kitchen, dining-room or drawing-room. Any hint of overseeing and she would have given her identity away.

To her amazement some of the party had carried the intent of their anonymity so far that they had washed their hair in strange colours. There emerged far more brunettes than had been present in the homestead two hours earlier. One almost luscious-looking girl might well have been Julia except that her hair was dark. When Sara looked at it closely she could see the hair was still damp and there was a tiny smudge of coloured rinse just below the hair line. Could it be Julia, she wondered? The full skirt did not look like Julia but the hibiscus behind the ear did. So did the dangling ear-rings . . . and the all-pervading scent of Chanel 5.

140

Everybody was at the same game of guessing, but no one seemed to recognise Sara. She had not touched her hair but no one gave her the credit for it.

'Don't think you're a blonde,' someone said. 'Who's a blonde we haven't accounted for. Oh, I know who you are, that red-headed girl from Brisbane, what's her name . . . Myra Pennyfeather!'

Sara shook her head but would not commit herself to speak. So many of them gave themselves away by their voices. The girl in the hibiscus and Chanel 5 didn't give herself away by speaking either. She merely sipped her cocktail, laughed, and smoked a cigarette out of a short dark holder.

The men who had been strolling round the garden now began to join the ladies. They, too, peered in the dimmed lights from the garden at their fair companions, and tried guessing.

'No guessing,' someone said. 'That will spoil it. And you can't tell by the hair either. We've all dyed our hair.'

'Not all,' a voice said at Sara's elbow.

Sara kept her voice very low so as not to give herself away with it. Oddly enough, Jack Brownrigg had given himself away by his.

'I'm a raving redhead on week-days,' said Sara.

'Come and dance with me and I'll tell you who you are.'

'I'm Julia!'

'No, you're not. Julia doesn't smile the way you do. When you smile a couple of pixies dance in your eyes. Julia's eyes never smile.'

'You've never looked in her eyes. I recommend it. She would find it quite diverting.'

'This is diverting enough for me. I just hope Greg will take all night finding you . . . then I can have you to myself.'

Sara laughed.

'Greg?' she said loftily. 'Who's Greg? Oh, you mean that tall striking-looking man who runs the place?'

'All right,' said Jack. 'If we have to pretend . . . then let's pretend. I'm still going to dance with you as often as I get in first.'

This was a promise he carried out, for Sara found herself dancing for the third time with Jack before the evening was half over.

Several times as tall men had come towards her Sara had looked searchingly through her mask to see if it was Greg. So many of these outback men were tall, bronzed and laconic in their speech. It wasn't till she was in their arms that she knew it wasn't Greg. Would he know . . . if and when he danced with her . . . just as Jack Brownrigg had done? She must remember to keep her eyes downcast, if it was her eyes that gave her away. She just wanted the thrill of dancing in Greg's arms . . . unknown by him.

But as the evening wore on no Greg came her way. Despairingly she began to search the tall men with her eyes. There was one who had danced three times with the girl in the hibiscus and Chanel 5. Sara edged her partner near them. She looked at the back of the man's head. She was sure that was the back of Greg's head. Didn't she know it off by heart? Then reluctantly, for she felt she was cheating, she looked at his feet. No one else in the world wore the beautiful fine leather, hand-sewn shoes that Greg wore, she would recognise them anywhere. Yes, it was he. Did he know with whom he was dancing? And was the hibiscus-wearing girl Julia?

Sara and her partner were dancing near them now. The girl, dressed somewhat Spanish fashion, was affecting a slight foreign accent, but Sara noticed that neither of them spoke very much. Each seemed quiet and content just to dance, well, not quite heart to heart. But very nearly.

Sara felt a pang of distress. She had meant to play that part herself to-night, but Greg, this tall masked man in the fine leather shoes, had not come her way.

Greg for his part had taken rather slowly to this idea of seeking out a masked partner. He had first seen that most other people had partners before he approached, rather shyly . . . for this man, so little embarrassed when with men or out on the run or doing business with men or women, had a touch of reserve about him when it came to parties and dances.

He had danced first with a little woman with greying hair, and this was pleasant enough. After that he adjourned with two of the men to the billiard room and had two stiff whiskies.

Thereafter he went back to the dance floor.

Before he had gone out into the garden he had gone into Sara's room to tie his tie in front of the long mirror. He was a man without vanity but he liked his clothes to fit properly and sit properly. And so he had stood in front of the long mirror to adjust his belt and see the cuffs of his trousers rested just exactly on the instep of his shoes.

He had stopped by Sara's dressing-table and picked up the bottle of Chanel 5 she had left there but not used. He lifted out the stopper and sniffed it. He smiled and put the bottle back in its place. He looked under the dressing-table and saw Sara's slippers standing neatly side by side. He bent down and moved them, turning the toes into one another so they stood at a tizzy angle. This time he was smiling broadly, and when he left the room he closed the door silently behind him.

Out in the garden he had had two dances and two whiskies. He felt like smiling again and was doing just this when the girl with the hibiscus touched his arm.

He peered at her a minute and then quietly took her in his arms. He did not speak for he fancied he was still anonymous. It didn't occur to him that to one young lady his smile would give him away just as to another his shoes would tell the story. He just danced quietly and firmly, listening with a smile and his head bent slightly on one side while the girl spoke a few sentences in an affected foreign accent. Thereafter they danced in silence, Greg holding the girl tightly in his arms, the girl relaxing her body against his and knowing full well the hint of Chanel 5 in the air was filling his nostrils. She could tell by the way the man against whom she rested her body was dancing that he was content.

It was the last dance before supper . . . and the unmasking.

Sara was once again in Jack Brownrigg's arms. The hibiscus girl was once again in Greg's.

'I zink,' said the hibiscus girl, who had hardly uttered a word since they first met, 'zat the tall man wiz ze girl in the pearl satin dress is Jack Brownrigg.'

Greg looked over his shoulder.

'I think I could tell that figure anywhere,' he said softly. 'Couldn't you?'

His partner shook her head.

'I haf vondered all night because he haf danced with zat girl all night. Now I know.'

'Good old Jack,' was all Greg said.

There were only a few minutes to go now. The imported orchestra was entering into the spirit of the occasion. Many couples had taken advantage of the masks to play a part they would have been too shy or too well brought up to do bare-faced. There was romance in the air, which is, after all, the main business of a masked dance.

The lights winked out one by one and the orchestra had muted its tones to something dreamy and sweet and just a little poignant with old melody.

The dancers, some of whom knew who their partners were but were discreetly pretending not to, danced cheek to cheek. The moon and the stars washed them all in pale silver and dark shadow.

Jack and Sara did not dance cheek to cheek but each knew who the other was. For the last minute Jack gathered Sara just a little more closely in his arms.

'This is good-bye, Sara,' he said in her ear. 'I'm off at sun-up. Be good . . . and be happy. Promise me you'll let me know if you ever want anybody's nose punched?'

Sara was touched. She knew now that Jack did have some deep feeling for her. But he had observed the proprieties and he was saying good-bye. She kissed the tip of her finger and placed it on his mouth.

'I'll always remember you carry a good punch, Jack.'

Next to them . . . surely not coincidence . . . Greg was dancing with the girl in the hibiscus. Sara was trying to keep her head averted. The girl seemed crushed in Greg's arms and her head was resting on his shoulder.

There was a sudden chord of music. The lights sprang up. Masks were being torn from faces and the air was full of laughter and shrill protests.

Greg and the girl in the hibiscus had each quietly taken their masks off, as had Sara and Jack. It was Julia. Sara had been almost certain of it. And Julia continued to lean against Greg, looking up in his face.

'I told you zat was Jack Brownrigg,' Julia said. 'And Sara? Why, Sara! What a clever girl you are! I don't believe anybody knew you all ze night long. And you, Jack? Did you know who the girl in the zo pretty dress was?'

Greg was utterly silent. His eyes slid over Sara's satin dress and the smooth swathed skirt with the so sophisticated line.

He didn't recognise me . . . but he doesn't like my dress, Sara thought. But that was a thought impinged in a shallow way on top of her pain. Julia was still leaning against Greg's shoulder.

He did not smile but quite gently he put his hands on Julia and released himself. He held out one hand to Sara.

'Shall we go in?' he said. 'I think we must receive the guests together. In the hall. They will be expecting it.'

CHAPTER SIXTEEN

Sara wondered how much wiser she was after the events of the masked dance than she had been before. She was sure now that Julia had some irresistible appeal for Greg. She was equally sure that Greg was guided in his affairs more by his head than his heart. How much was this a good thing? His hard business head had told him that Julia was no good for Ransome. At least not as its mistress. She would not have bent herself to its responsibilities nor would she have bothered to get on with the other relatives or with the men in the homestead or down at the quarters.

Therefore Greg had, when he married, decided for Ransome. He had married someone who would care for all those aspects. Yet he could not rid from his heart the mirage of Julia's appeal and Julia's beauty.

The girl he had married, Sara, he would honour with the proper dignities of her position. She would receive his guests with him. She would ride the best mount on the station.

Sara had no fear that Greg, in this respect, would let her dignity down. Perhaps he hoped that some day Julia would go away for good, would marry and have children somewhere the other side of the vast continent. Then perhaps he could forget her and settle down to a normal life with Sara, the Martha of Ransome.

Never, felt Sara, was the story of Martha and Mary more truly enacted in real life than as at present on Ransome.

However much Sara loved Greg, and she did, she could not and would not suffer the thought of him touching her while in his heart he was still conscious of Julia. The idea shrivelled the very roots of Sara's being.

Apart from the problem of Julia, Sara was angry with Greg.

The day following the masked dance Sara had gone down to the horse yards with other members of the house-party.

This time the horse-breaking was being done by a renowned stockman come out of the interior. His was the broncho-riding, break-in-a-day kind of work. It was fierce and spectacular and was carried on to a hullabaloo of cries, shouts and general barracking from the gallery.

Sara thought it went without saying that Greg did not give

this man one of his blood colts to break. At the moment the stockman was working on a wild mountain colt that would later be used for mustering cattle in the wild country.

'He only understands the jungle law, that fella,' Andy Patterson said of the colt. 'He'll be a better horse for it but he'll always love the free rein and a battle with a dodger better than the home paddocks of Ransome. He'll be a friend to no man but the man who'll ride him for the rest of his life.'

'But what if the stockman who rides him leaves the station?'

'He'll take that hoss with him. That's the way of it with Greg. Man and hoss go together.'

Yes, Sara thought, that was typical of Greg. There were two ways of bringing a horse into the discipline of Ransome. The one was the intellectual persuasion that this was a better life; the other was a destruction of will, and the giving in to bondage.

For the life of her Sara could not help reading Greg's own character into this attitude of his. It was consistent with the iron way he ruled the people in the homestead. To herself he had made the appeal to the intelligence. This was a good way of life. There was work to be done, and she, Sara, could do it.

The other approach was that of his way with his mother and sister. The ruthless use of the veto or, alternatively, and to mix the metaphor, giving the green light when he thought fit, and no consulting them about it.

Perhaps Greg has lived too many years of his life with animals, she thought. Then knew at once she was not altogether doing him justice. He also lived with his stockmen and rouseabouts and there was no question about their respect for him. Well, maybe the mountain brumbies respected their ultimate owners too!

Sara let her thoughts flow along these bitter channels because she was hurt, and because her confidence was shaken. When she had left England to come to Australia with a Board of Trade Commission she had had plenty of confidence. She had had plenty of confidence about remaining in this country of sunlight and opportunity.

It was only after she had seen Julia on Ransome and then looked in the mirror and seen that she herself was not very big, that her face was round except for the little pointed chin and her nose was not long and aristocratic, that her self-confidence had been shaken.

Even then it would not have mattered except that she had fallen in love with her husband and he was a man of distinguished relatives and distinguished acquaintances.

Out of her pain she saw Greg as a man who grazed cattle and reared horses, and sooner or later everyone, the human beings, came into that category. All except those women who were decorations. She was back to the division of people . . . the decorative and the chattel.

So she was angry with him.

The stockman had finished with the horse, now alternately sweating and shivering in its corner, and there was a general scattering from off the top of fences, the sheds and the branches of the coolibahs. It was tea-time and already the men's tongues were loosed on reminiscence.

'Remember that grey-haired stock-rider came out of Queensland in the thirties? Broke more horses between Alice Springs and Darwin than's been broke in the whole country since.'

Or:

'There was a colt up there at Turra station there was bets on from one end of the north to the other. They reckoned there wouldn't be a white stockman who'd ride him.'

Greg came across to the group with whom Sara was standing. He had with him the stockman, covered in dust, and here and there the blood-tinted foam of the colt smudging his own sweat-damp clothes.

'Jake,' Greg said quietly. 'I want you to meet my wife.'

My wife!

The words raced through Sara like a thrill of fire. She couldn't help feeling a surge of belonging, almost of possession. She could not help feeling a rearing pride. She was his wife, in fact and name. Though they had exchanged no caress since the first twenty-four hours of their marriage, there had been that marriage and there had been that twenty-four hours. No one could take any of that away from her. She was his wife and neither the Camdens nor the law could alter it.

After a few minutes' polite conversation Sara left the group, and on the pretext that she had things to attend to in the homestead she mounted her own horse and rode back up the slope.

Except for Mrs Camden and a few of the older ladies and one or two still getting over the 'night before,' the homestead was empty. It was unexpectedly quiet, and once inside it was cool in the rooms darkened against the fierce beat of the morning sun.

Sara went into the hall. She could hear voices from the drawing-room where Mrs Camden sat with her friends. Sara did not want to go in and join them. It might take time to get away from them and she wanted to be alone. So she hesitated in the hall, wondering if she should see if they had all they wanted. Fans, cool drinks and magazines.

It was Mrs Collins's voice she heard. It was cool and clear yet with the hint of sympathetic understanding that the true social climber or parasite manages to introduce into her voice like some cloy.

'Of course one had *heard* they didn't really live together. Everyone seems to know about it. Must be the bush telegraph. Wonderful how everything gets around. They say the natives send smoke signals.'

'I don't see why you should all know about things I don't know about,' Mrs Camden said fretfully. 'If it wasn't for Julia saying she was really in love with Jack Brownrigg I would have heard nothing. And in my very own home too. I always thought myself it was Clifford she liked. I must say Clifford doesn't seem to mind. But then he's got so many girls. Here, there and everywhere. . . .'

Sara had no doubt in her mind they were talking about her. She felt the affront like a blow to the heart.

So! Instead of the dignified hostess and helpmate she had thought herself to be, she was, in fact, no more than the object of common and not very charitable gossip in the drawing-room. Gone like a bubble was that sense of security.

Shaking with a mixture of confusion and agitation, Sara turned hurriedly away. Anything to escape them and their tarnishing words.

She crossed the hall quickly and found herself in the dining-room. The blinds were drawn against the sun and it was cool and dark. A sanctuary.

She walked round the table, touching the old-fashioned green baize cloth with fingers that didn't know they were touching anything.

She paused in front of the sideboard and put the decanters of wine in the cupboard without ever knowing she had done so. She stopped in front of the little table on which stood her wedding presents. She picked up the jug Clifford had given her and the entrée dish Jack Brownrigg had given her. She touched them gently, then crossed the room again and put them in the cupboard in which she had already put the wine decanters. She closed the door.

Then she went into the darkened corner of the room by the western wall and sank down into the old leather-covered arm-chair.

Then she wept.

For a long time she sat there, huddled in the arm-chair. The tears exhausted her, and she had had a late night, so she buried her face in her arms and fell into a sad little sleep.

Once she woke because she wasn't very comfortable.

'Do I stay? Or do I go?' she asked herself. 'What is the right thing to do? What am I? Just a cause for idle and unkind chatter. I have no other meaning.'

She moved herself and now her head was resting back on the gentle roll of the head-rest. Both hands lay listless along the cool surface of the leather arms. She closed her eyes and because the room was darkened by the drawn blinds, fell into a worn-out sleep again.

It was someone moving in the room that aroused her. She had not heard him come because the door had been ajar and the floor was too thickly carpeted. She could hear him well enough now because he was opening one cupboard after another in an exasperated way.

'Where the devil . . .?'

It was Greg.

Sara opened her eyes and looked at him. She did not move . . . just lay there in the chair, looking at him.

'Oh, here they are! What in the name of fortune . . .'

Greg had one decanter of wine out and on top of the sideboard. Now he brought out the silver jug Clifford had given as his wedding present. Greg bent down and peered into the cupboard. He brought out a decanter of whisky and then the entrée dish. He put them on top of the sideboard and stood looking at them.

He shut the cupboard door with his knee and picked up the two decanters and walked to the door.

'Nellie!' he shouted. His voice was like the cracking of a stockwhip.

'Yes'm, Greg. What you want?' The lubra was padding up the passage from the nether regions. 'What for you call like that, Greg? You plenty mad you sing-out all-a same stockman.'

Greg pointed to the sideboard.

'Polish those two things and put them on the table with the tea urn. And don't take them off. *Ever.* My wife likes them there and you damn well leave them there.'

'Ar right, Greg. Some other bad fella take 'um off.'

Then as Greg looked as if he would explode again, Nellie said placatingly, 'Ar right. Ar right, Greg. You make 'um too much big fella noise. I fix 'em.'

'See that you damn well do.'

Greg was gone and Nellie chuckled gaily after him.

'Him all-a same bad in the head, that fella. Too much grog las' ni', maybe.'

She picked up the silver pieces and was rubbing them with her apron as she left the room.

Mrs Whittle was just outside the door as Nellie emerged.

'What's the trouble, Nellie?'

'That fella Greg. Him plenty mad. Never mind. I fix 'um up proper. Him sing out plenty good to-night when him bin go sleep. Him plenty tired, that fella.'

Nellie's and Mrs Whittle's voices were lost to Sara as they went down the passage.

Sara had not moved. Neither her arms nor her legs nor her head seemed capable of movement.

What had Greg meant by restoring her favourite pieces of silver to their former places?

There was a kindness in it, perhaps, and a certain justice. She, Sara, was to have her rights. But why had he been so angry?

Sara thought gently of Nellie. Even Greg's vitriolic anger had not taken the chuckle out of Nellie's voice or the smile from her shining, good-natured face.

How tolerant they were of Greg, even when he was in the wrong. They must like and respect him. Even love him.

Sara straightened herself. What the lubras could take with stoic good humour, surely she, Sara, could take. They didn't give in so easily. She, Sara, wouldn't give in either.

She would have to think of a way of carrying on.

But her heart dropped again when she thought of that clear, cool drawing-room voice. 'Everyone seems to know about it. The bush telegraph, I suppose.'

Even Greg would be, as Nellie had said, 'plenty mad' if he knew his wife was the talk of drawing-rooms, and maybe of stockmen's quarters. Even Greg had wanted to invest his wife with dignity. Even Greg, with his blood tingling when Julia leaned so intimately against his shoulder, had remembered that it was Sara, his wife, who must stand beside him when he received the guests to Marion's birthday feast!

This thought gave Sara courage. After all, the bargain had been for Ransome. Neither more nor less. Greg was maintaining protocol where the young mistress of Ransome was concerned. Sara must forget everything but this.

Sara went out into the hall, and Marion was just coming in, slightly dishevelled, in her jeans and wide straw hat. Sara thanked heaven for the cool darkness of the house so that Marion would not see the signs of tears and strain that must be still on Sara's face.

'Hallo,' said Marion. 'What happened to you? Too hot?'

'There were things to do . . .'

Nellie came into the hall with the silver jug and dish now highly polished. She was on her way to the dining-room.

'Oh! They get an extra polish, do they?' laughed Marion. 'You like to keep us reminded of your gallery, Sara. How many broken hearts have you left behind elsewhere?'

'I didn't think I was the heart-breaking kind,' said Sara quietly.

'Oh yes,' said Marion, looking at her with her slightly quizzical smile. 'A dash of aplomb and a pinch of sophistication and you probably could bring even Greg to heel. That's how Julia does it, you know.'

Sara felt her small hands clenching.

Marion's voice altered slightly as if she had an afterthought.

'Not that Julia's got what you've got, all the same.'

'Meaning?' asked Sara evenly.

Marion was turning away.

'Oh, the thing that beats and pumps blood all over the body.'

In another minute she had gone down the long passage, swinging her hat in one hand.

Sara gazed after her.

Was Marion kind or unkind? Or was she plain indifferent, a disinterested onlooker?

CHAPTER SEVENTEEN

Sara felt the affairs of the morning were all just a little much for her to bear and maintain the cheerful calm that should be part of the hostess role.

Lunch each day since the house-party had commenced had been served buffet style both in the dining-room and in an open marquee just below the side veranda. It had been Sara's wont to wander between the two, seeing to the well-being of all her guests but particularly to that of the Hunt family and the Sam Camden family.

She had begun to see that already there was a change in their attitude. She thought they were beginning to show a pride in the unity of the family and the oneness of Ransome. Their doubts and fears had been allayed and they were now ready to concede that Greg was not working for himself but for the well-being of the whole.

It made Sara a little cross with Greg that he had never bothered to justify himself as a person. There was a sort of stiff-necked pride in him and he thought the other members of the family ought to have been intelligent enough to see from the books and their various bank statements that all was well in the management of Ransome. This, Sara thought, was an attitude too rigid by far. Couldn't Greg see for himself in his daily life that Mrs Camden and Marion, for instance, did not use intelligence, no matter how much of it they had? They were the lilies of the field, the decorative women, and didn't want to put forward the effort of intelligence. Greg, Sara thought, should have made an effort to win confidence in himself as well as in Ransome.

This he would not do, so Sara did it for him. Already results were showing in the easier attitude of the Hunts and the Sam Camdens.

I'm keeping my bargain by Ransome, Sara thought.

Because she was still disturbed from her bout of tears in the dining-room and the odd behaviour of Greg in the matter of the wedding presents and the odder behaviour of Marion, who appeared to say something catty and something kind in the one breath, Sara decided she would leave the lunch party to fend for itself. No one would miss her. The inside group would think she was with the outside group, and vice versa.

She would take her hat and escape them all. She would go and ask Sam Benson if she might lunch with him down at the main office.

She took the precaution of carrying a large piece of iced melon and some sandwiches in a nest of lettuce leaves, just in case Sam didn't have enough for two.

When she arrived at the office she saw that she needn't have worried. Sam was doing very well for himself with a specially installed refrigerator and an impressive array of bottles.

'Come in, come in,' said Sam. 'What? Brought your lunch with you? What goes on? Didn't you think old Sam was capable of doing a spot of entertaining himself?'

'I might have guessed, Sam. We haven't seen you much up at the homestead and I thought you must be anti-social. I see I was wrong. You're just very choosey.'

'It's not me that's choosey, young 'un. It's some of those fellers you've got up there at the homestead. A good yarn and a neat drop of Scotch with old Sam is more to the liking of some than gambols with the girls on the veranda.'

'Are you expecting anyone to join you to-day?'

'You never can tell. I just sit here like a spider in his parlour and see who walks in.'

'So far it's only me,' said Sara, sitting herself down in the most comfortable chair that wasn't Sam's. She put her melon and the sandwiches on the table.

Sam looked at her through half closed eyelids. He relaxed into his own chair and leaned back. He packed his pipe down with a new load of tobacco and looked up again at Sara. His eyes were still no more than slits in his face.

'Young 'un,' he said at length. 'Don't let me ever hear you make a statement like that again.'

'Like what?' asked Sara in surprise.

'A statement that includes those words "*only me*." Who do you think you are, that you talk of yourself as "*only me*"? You're the Missis of Ransome. An' even without Ransome you're Greg's wife. You notice, mebbe, I left off the word Camden. Even without the Camden it's something to be Greg's wife. Supposin' he was no more than a stockman on the north-west beat, he's still worth being married to.'

Sara looked at Sam thoughtfully.

'You love him, don't you, Sam? Why do you love him?'

'Same reason you do. He's the finest man north of twenty-six. *And . . .*' He leaned forward and pointed the stem of his pipe at Sara. 'From a young lady's point of view he's not such a bad-looking fella, either. You ask Julia.'

'Yes,' said Sara slowly. 'Ask Julia.'

Sam leaned back in his chair.

'Now we've come to the crux of it,' he said. 'That why you came down to have lunch with a fat old book-keeper?'

'Yes. I think it was.' She looked up. 'I've no one else to

talk to but you, Sam.'

'Not Greg?'

'Greg is always out and about. I don't see him very much, you know.'

'You could if you tried. Julia chases him all over the run.' Sara's eyes were angry.

'Is that what you would have me do?'

Sam sucked on his pipe.

'No,' he said after a minute. 'I don't think I would.'

They were silent for a few minutes.

'Tell you what,' said Sam. 'Let's eat, and mebbe have a drink, eh? On full stomachs we can really loosen up.'

Out of the refrigerator Sam produced some cold turkey and tomatoes. Sara opened the sandwiches from their packing of lettuce leaves.

'Tell you what,' said Sam. 'Hidden away here in my safe I've got a bottle of real Irish whisky. I think twice before I give anyone else but myself a nip of that.'

Sara laughed.

'You can put a teaspoonful in the bottom of a glass and fill it up with water, Sam. I won't despise your precious Irish whisky. But I'd rather have a long drink than anything else.'

Sam looked grieved. He did as Sara asked but looked sorrowfully at the glass he put on the table in front of her.

'Drowned!' he said. 'Terrible waste. My father would turn in his grave to see it.'

When they had eaten a little and sipped their respective drinks Sam asked Sara what it was that was troubling her.

'I couldn't help overhearing a conversation between the ladies in the drawing-room. It depressed me. Somehow I suddenly wished I had someone to talk to. I wonder if one would have talked over these things with parents if one had had them at hand. Do young married people do that, do you think, Sam?'

'So I'm to be Father? All right, give, Sara. What did you hear and when do you want me to hang 'em all out on the fence and beat 'em like carpets?'

Sara laughed.

'You sound like Jack Brownrigg. He offered to punch anybody's nose for me.'

Sam was serious again.

'Let's leave Jack Brownrigg out of this. He complicates things more than you think, young 'un. Now what did you overhear?'

'The ladies think that Greg and I don't live close enough to one another. It isn't very easy, Sam. Greg is so terribly busy, and how much we see of one another is our business. But I couldn't help feeling miserable that I was the subject of gossip. I had felt I was helping very hard with the success of the party. All the time I was just somebody to be talked about.'

'You'll always be talked about. Everybody always is. Whatever kind of a person you are, good, bad or indifferent, you will be the subject of conversation between your friends and acquaintances. Why, we talk about you down here. Want to know what we say about you?'

Sara looked at Sam in surprise.

'We reckon you're the best thing that ever hit Ransome. We reckon those bright eyes of yours and that clever peacemaking tongue of yours has done more for keeping the family together this muster than all the totals at the bottom of my books have done. Moreover, we like your pert little face and there isn't a stockman on the station who wouldn't put you in his pocket and ride off with you across the border, if it wasn't for Greg already having a halter good and fast round your neck.'

'Oh, Sam!' Sara blushed. 'You're a flatterer.'

'Not on your life, I'm not. Never flattered anyone in my life. Now let's get back to the ladies in the drawing-room. Maybe you and Greg aren't close enough together. He's busy. It's a terribly hard time for him with nearly a hundred people on the place as guests and the place to run too. Moreover, he's got Lucifer's pride. He wouldn't eat out of your hand. . . .'

'Unless I ate out of his first?' put in Sara quickly.

'Now, I wasn't going to say that. What I was going to say is this. Greg does things his own way, and in his own time. Give him time, Sara. You just carry on. You're doing all right. But I'd clear that baggage Julia out of the place. Mind you, Julia can't harm you. But she's irritating.' He paused.

'She doesn't irritate everybody. She doesn't irritate Greg. She's his cousin and he's entitled to have her here if he wishes it.'

'Ever seen Greg show irritation or what he's feeling for anyone? Very close, Greg is, about his feelings. But he's got 'em. You'll be surprised one of these days. He'll kick the whole works overboard when he's good and ready.

155

You'll know all about it then, young 'un. Sparks'll fly.'

Yes, Sara thought. She'd nearly seen sparks fly to-day when Greg had roared at Nellie over the silver dishes. She did sense that Greg had the capacity for a blow-up in him. She wondered what it would be like if he blew up at her, Sara. Well, Sara had some spirit too. It ought to be a good fireworks show when they both blew up.

Sara could not help smiling at this idea of histrionics. Surely she and Greg were much too much disciplined for such foolishness.

But Sam saw the smile and the little lights in her eyes, and he leaned back in his chair.

'That's the girl,' he said. 'Stick that chin out . . . and to so-and-so with the ladies in the drawing-room.'

'I'll take your advice, Sam, and keep going. It's done me good to have this talk with you. And now will you do something else for me?'

'Fire away. You've only to ask.'

Sara took a scrap of paper from her pocket.

'You're doing the session when the air opens up for Ransome, aren't you, Sam? Would you send an order for me. I took these numbers from David Jones' catalogue and I'd like them sent through as soon as possible. Will I get the things quickest if I get them to send them by ordinary air-mail delivery or do you think it might be a good idea to get them to deliver them to Jack Brownrigg's Airways office and then send him a wire? He'd know on his route what plane might be detouring for Ransome. He'd look after them for me, and see that I got them.'

'What's the hurry, young 'un? Why don't you let 'em come by ordinary air-mail? Chances are you'd get 'em just as quick as Jack could get 'em through to you. That is unless you think that Jack 'ud take a flying visit to Ransome just to deliver them to you?'

Sam was watching Sara through half closed eyelids again.

'Oh no. I don't want Jack to bring them,' said Sara hastily. 'He wouldn't do anything as silly as that, surely? I just thought he'd contact any private plane coming this way, and they seem to be in and out all the time.'

'I'd leave Jack Brownrigg out of it,' Sam said evenly.

Sara caught the note of seriousness in Sam's voice.

'Why, Sam . . .' Then she broke off. Surely Sam, too, didn't think the way the ladies in the drawing-room thought. A little flush of anger dyed her cheeks.

'Then by ordinary air-mail, thank you, Sam. They aren't as important as all that. If you really want to know, they're ear-rings . . . dangling ones. Nice long dangling ones. To make my face look longer. There'll be another evening dress party before everyone goes back and I want them to go with my new pearl satin dress.'

Sara was looking at Sam with her chin well in the air.

'Any objections to the improving of my appearance with a pair of dangling ear-rings?' she asked.

Sam took his pipe out and wiped his mouth with the back of his hand to hide a smile. So young Sara was on her mettle, was she? She was going to see what a pair of dangling ear-rings would do to bolster up her confidence!

'You know more about those things than I'll ever know,' he said at length. 'If that's what you want, young 'un, I'll see you get 'em. And in record time.'

There was the sound of footsteps outside and a sharp knock on the fly-screen door.

'What's been doing something in record time?' It was Julia. 'Are those stockmen from the Territory racing again?'

'They never stop, Julia,' said Sam, slowly rising from his chair. 'Come in and cool us all down with that icy smile of yours. There's a nice comfortable chair over there. Now what can Sara and I do for you?'

Julia looked at the array of lunch remains and the empty glasses.

'You two look as if you've been enjoying yourselves,' she said.

'We have,' said Sam simply. 'And now you're here we'll enjoy it better.'

'I want guns, Sam,' said Julia. 'What sort of guns have you got in the store?'

'Who you going to shoot first?'

'It isn't a "who." It's a "what." I'm going to shoot crocodiles with the men to-morrow night.'

'First I heard of a crocodile shoot to-morrow night,' said Sam, looking at Sara.

Sara shook her head in equal ignorance.

'Greg's rounding up two boatloads,' said Julia, 'I'm going too.'

'Then you'd better ask Greg for a gun. He's got a rack up there behind the office door.'

'Greg doesn't know yet. I'm simply going to be there at the crucial moment. When Greg finds me there he won't say no. He never does.'

Julia shot a sidelong glance at Sam. Sam did not miss it.

'He always takes extra guns with him. You'll have to have one of those. I can't let those things out of the store without registering them with the police. You know that, Julia.'

'Were you thinking of going, Sara?' asked Julia.

Sara was at a loss. Greg had made plans of which she knew nothing, and yet he had evidently told Julia. Sara didn't want to admit Julia knew more of Greg's movements than she did herself. Sara took the simple way out.

'I'm not going, Julia. I can't shoot and I imagine that women'll be in the way. I think the men want a night out and I wouldn't spoil it for them.'

'That's where you're wrong,' said Julia with a supercilious smile. 'Women, the right kind of women, never spoil things for men. There's nothing they like more than pleasant female company when in a boat on the river.'

She stood up.

'Oh well, I'll have to seek elsewhere,' she added. 'Probably Marion can raise a gun for me.'

Sam let her out the screen door and stood watching her a minute as she walked slowly and gracefully towards the homestead gate.

When he turned round his and Sara's eyes met. He shook his head slightly.

'All the same, there's a lot of things about Julia I admire,' said Sara, anticipating his next remark. 'She always looks beautiful. She never looks ruffled. Her skin is never burnt and she can ride and shoot and face the desert and crocodiles without flinching.'

'True,' said Sam. 'But then there's an awful lot at stake, isn't there?'

His eyes looked searchingly into Sara's. He said nothing and neither did she, but each knew what the other meant.

The lateness of the night before and the activities of the morning had induced a soporific laziness in everybody that evening. Everybody, even the younger people, voted an early night, and so it was barely eight-thirty when Sara found herself in the office looking through the papers that had come in by a friendly traveller who had picked them up at the airport.

She was standing by the table leafing through the papers

when Greg came in.

'Have you had some tea, Sara?' he asked. 'Or would you like a port wine and biscuit? I suppose, like everyone else, you're going to bed too?'

'Yes, I'm going to bed. I'm very tired. I don't think I'll have any supper. You look tired too, Greg. Do you have to work in here to-night?'

'Not to-night. I'm going to bed. I'm taking some of the lads out on a crocodile hunt to-morrow night, and that will mean no sleep at all.'

'Yes, I heard about it.'

Greg, who by this time was looking through the mail, did not appear to notice the curious note in Sara's voice. Nor did he appear to notice that she had heard already about the crocodile hunt. And not from him.

He threw the bundle of mail on the table.

'That can wait,' he said. 'I'm off to bed. You'll probably be thankful to leave the office doors open to-night. It must have been rather airless for you these last few nights. I'm sorry.'

'My windows are wide and let in plenty of air. All the same I'd rather have the doors open. I don't feel so cut off then.'

Greg looked at Sara quizzically.

'Well, my room was darned airless,' he said. 'Sara, shall you and I go for an early ride to-morrow morning? I don't seem to have seen much of you.'

'I've been so busy.'

'Splendidly busy,' he said gently. 'I ought to thank you.'

'Don't thank me. It was all part of the bargain, wasn't it? Besides, I have liked doing it.'

She turned away to bite her tongue and prevent herself from saying too much. She had no right to have any feelings because the bargain had been that and no more. She had no right to have any feelings because Greg was a man wrapped up in his work and the only time he had to give to human relationships was in order to pigeon-hole people into the decorative or the useful.

'You didn't say whether you would like an early morning ride, Sara.'

'Yes, I would, Greg. Very much. Thank you for thinking of it. Well . . .' She hesitated in her own doorway. 'Good night, Greg. I'll see you in the morning.'

'It will be very early. Before the others stir, I think. I'll

159

call you. I'll just get Dave to go down to the stables and tell them to bring in Stella and my own horse. Good night, sleep well.'

It was barely dawn when Sara and Greg went down to the stables. Blue-Bag had the horses saddled and Andy Patterson was standing by with steaming mugs of tea.

'You know, Sara,' Andy said with a grin, 'the first time you went up on a hoss I said to myself, "That girl's a born rider. She'll be out on a thoroughbred before the drovers hit the Wyndham track." And I was right.'

There was a third horse in a stall and Sara recognised it as the roan Julia used. With a pang of misgiving she wondered if Julia was coming too. Had Greg included her in the invitation? She felt that in going out early in the morning with Greg she had reached a certain mile-stone in their relations. She remembered the first morning at Ransome when she had seen Greg and Julia galloping up the rise on their return from a similar excursion. It had seemed to underline a relationship that must be close. Now here she was herself in the same role. She felt as petulant as a small child at the sight of Julia's roan.

However, Greg took no notice of the other horse, and presently held the stirrup to help Sara mount. He swung up into his own saddle and led the way out of the yard.

'Now you got Greg with you, you can go play with the crocodiles, Sara,' said Andy with a grin.

Sara's momentary depression dropped from her and she smiled back at Andy.

'With Greg on hand,' she said, 'I can go play with anyone I like.' She stole a glance at her husband from under a fringe of eyelashes but Greg showed no signs of having heard.

'We'll canter down to the creek crossing,' he said. 'I want to see how far along the pad they've brought the mob in from the Hiding camp.'

Sara often thought about the strange names of the water-holes on the station. Some were just called 'bores' in numerical order. This was where wells had been sunk to reach the water underground. But the natural water-holes all had names that had something to do with their first finding. There was Deadman's Camp, Hell's Own, One Tree, You-and-Me, Love's Lurking . . . and a host of others. To-day they were to look at the cattle coming in from Hiding. Who, Sara wondered, had they found hiding at this water-hole in the early days? She would ask Greg some other time. At the moment he was cantering effortlessly down the ant-hill slope and some distance from her.

Once across the creek the cattle pad was so wide it now allowed for them to ride side by side, and Greg reined back his horse.

He pointed with his whip to the country ahead of them.

'It is eerie in this grey early morning light,' he said. 'No wonder the blacks believe in bunyips and ghingis. It's not hard to believe in them living in those ant-hills.'

The sun was not yet up. The plain stretched away from the timbered country in a forlorn grey light. The sparse, thin reed-like trees and the great mountains of ant-hills made one think they were not on the earth but perhaps on the surface of the moon or some other remote planet.

'It's very old, this country,' Sara said quietly.

'Old?' said Greg. 'It began in what the natives call the dream-time.' He turned his face to Sara and she saw there was something thoughtful and even tender in his face. 'One wonders what the dream-time was like? And was it a better world?'

They had ridden a few yards off the pad and Greg pulled up his horse beside an ant-hill that was as high as his mount. He threw his reins over the pummel, swung his leg over the saddle and slid off his horse.

He held up his hand to Sara.

'Come and look at this,' he said.

Sara got off her horse and joined him on the ground. They stooped before the ant-hill, looking into a great burnt cavern in its side.

'An oven,' Greg said. 'Somebody cooked their damper and possibly a kangaroo here.' He pointed into the burnt-out interior of the ant-hill.

'The rottings from the termites at the base make a wonderful tinder,' he said. 'And then the whole glows and heats like coals. The perfect oven.'

Stooping there beside Greg, Sara felt a soothing peace stealing over her. Now there were no conflicts between them. Greg, his mind and perhaps his heart, were thinking only of the strange ways of nature and of man and he was imparting that knowledge to Sara. It drew them together. The things of the heart hurt but the things of the earth brought only wonder.

Sara straightened herself and looked around.

'It would be frightening to be lost here, Greg,' she said.

'Yes,' he said soberly. 'More so, I think, than in the Red Ranges farther south. Though once I was lost there.'

'I can't imagine you lost,' said Sara.

'Yes. We came down in a plane. In the early days. They're magnetic ironstone, those ranges, and though we tried to land short of them we came down on a plateau dead in the middle. The blacks found us and got us out, but it was eerie.'

He said no more.

She wondered if she was as much a stranger to Greg as he was to her.

Perhaps early morning rides, when they were alone together in the vast spirit-dreaming country, might dispel some of that strangeness and bring them closer.

Somehow Sara respected Greg for the hint of deep feeling that he had shown when he had spoken of the oldness of the country and of the fear of the Red Ranges.

He held her stirrup for her while she mounted.

Once again she found herself looking down at his face the same way she had done the day they had crossed the creek on the way home from the cattle camp. The day Greg had proposed his strange bargain to Sara.

Once again she read that something in Greg's face she had read then but not fully understood.

It was a face no longer withdrawn and preoccupied. His eyes were no longer hard or thoughtful. They were eyes that looked at her now as if recognising her and speaking to her. His face was gentle. And there was something else in it. What was it? Could it be a hint of sadness?

Greg put her reins in her hand. Then he looked up and smiled right into her eyes.

'The sun is coming up over your right shoulder,' he said. 'Good morning, Sara!'

Sara turned round to see a patch of startling, shimmering gold on the eastern horizons. The trees and ant-hills stood black against it.

Movement farther round behind her caught her eyes. Two horses were coming up the slope from the creek. They carried Julia and Marion.

CHAPTER EIGHTEEN

The members of the house-party had nearly all dispersed. Stockmen had ridden out as they had ridden in, unannounced, to disappear from whence they came into the vast anonymity of the continent. Fringe-land natives were drifting back into the hinterland and from the smoke signals, pointing like fingers in the distant skies, one knew the myalls and tribal natives had receded again into unknown territories.

The crocodile hunt came and went, with two crocodiles bagged and both of them to Clifford Camden. The station races came and went. Sara's dangling ear-rings came and she had worn them with her pearl grey shimmering gown that was smooth and long and very svelte.

Except for a few strays down at the quarters and one or two swagmen in the bush there was only the family left in the homestead.

It now appeared that the Hunt family and the Sam Camdens were bent on visiting the sheep run down on the Ashburton River. At the present moment in time the big money was coming in to Ransome from the wool clip and the family was bent on seeing it for themselves.

'To see if there aren't more sheep on the run than Greg says there are,' Marion said cryptically after Julia had thrown herself into this notion and insisted it was folly on the part of the shareholders to say all was well with Ransome when they had no knowledge of what went on in the place where the big money was really in grazing.

When the plans had been finally and neatly concluded Mrs Camden and Marion announced they were not going but instead intended paying a three-day visit to Turra station. A three-day visit meant a plane.

Why couldn't the station Anson take them?

This was the sort of thing that exasperated Greg but of his exasperation he gave no sign.

'The Anson could take you up and leave you there,' he said. 'It could fly back and pick you up later. Nobody ever stays on Turra for less than a week.'

'It would be highly indelicate,' Mrs Camden said haughtily. 'We have been invited by the two boys. To stay long would look bad. After all, Marion is not as "eager" as all that.'

Sara had got the impression that it was Mrs Camden more than Marion who had been 'eager' about the Mac-Kensie boys all along. But then one never could tell with Marion. She never spoke of herself or of her interests.

However, if there was something 'in the air,' then Sara agreed with Mrs Camden that a short visit was the diplomatic thing to do at this stage.

'Well, if the Anson won't take us,' Mrs Camden said crossly, 'then I'll send a message to Jack Brownrigg. If he's a few days to spare he won't mind bringing his own Dove plane and helping us out.'

This was another embarrassing suggestion because the plane Greg had already chartered had not been one of Brown-rigg's Northern Airways planes but one of a West Australia company. Greg believed that as they were going to fly over West Australian territory they should use those particular services that had pioneered that state.

'Very well, Mother,' he said at length. 'If Jack's free and can lend us the Dove to make up our party I'll·send the Anson to Turra with you and Marion. We'd better make it an official charter. I'm not going to use Jack without his being reimbursed for it.'

The consequent parties were arranged.

Sara was delighted to hear that Jack Brownrigg was coming. She had not quite made up her mind about going to Ashburton with the family as she dreaded air travel, but Jack and his own Dove gave her greater confidence. She told Greg she would come but instead of travelling in the big plane she preferred to travel with Jack. Sara was ashamed of her cowardice and so she was evasive when she told Greg she would like to go in the Dove. He looked at her troubled face. Sara thought that he guessed her nervousness.

'I . . . I like Jack,' she faltered. She could not bring herself to say, 'I won't be so frightened with him because he knows I'm nervous and he's so chivalrous, he'll be careful.'

She told Sam Benson, however.

'Go with Jack if it makes you happier, Sara,' he said. 'But if you're going to live in the north you'd better get used to plane travelling. Otherwise you'll be cut off. And you can't always have Jack at your beck and call.'

'Actually, Sam, it was Mrs Camden's beck and call. The Dove happens to be going to the Ashburton so I'm just happening along with it.'

'Listen, young 'un,' Sam said. 'Every pilot takes care.

You know what? The best pilot is the chap who thinks of himself and takes care of himself. So long as he's looking after his own neck the passengers don't matter. See what I mean?'

Sara laughed.

'I see,' she said. 'If nothing happens to the pilot then nothing happens to the passengers.'

'Exactly.'

But she gained the impression that Sam wasn't pleased with her. She'd have to grow a lot tougher yet to match up with the careless courage of people who lived in the outback. Sara sighed. Maybe, one day, she would.

In due course Mrs Camden and Marion took off in the Anson for Turra station and the big plane arrived with its front seats removed to carry a big load of freight into Ransome and an equally big one from the cattle station down to the sheep run.

Greg, two of the stockmen and a jackaroo who were changing over with men from the sheep run, and Sara took off in the Dove with Jack Brownrigg. The Hunts, the Sam Camdens, Clifford and Julia took off with the freight in the Airways plane.

Sara was thrilled with the sheep run. The homestead was old, having been built fifty years before by the former owners. It was of timber and galvanised iron and consisted of four living-rooms surrounded by a veranda, which itself was enclosed by net screening against flies, the curse of the sheep country, and mosquitoes.

The formality of the life up at Ransome was gone. Here things were more at the picnic level. The food was brought up from the kitchen, an iron hut twenty-five yards away from the house, and they ate in the biggest of the living-rooms. One of the other rooms was the habitat of the overseer and the other two rooms were given up as dressing-rooms.

For the rest they sat and talked and discussed business affairs on the veranda. In fact it was what Jack called a 'veranda life.'

The cooked food was poor because the station cook had been used only to catering for the men on the place, but the Ransome party had brought with them all their own requirements in fruits, salads, biscuits and cakes.

As the station was run, as far as possible, by jeep, motor-cycle, tractor and truck, there were few good riding horses.

These perforce were left to the men who spent a great deal of time going out to the flocks.

It was Jack Brownrigg, who had taken his plane off for an outing the foregoing afternoon, who suggested a picnic farther up-country. He had spotted a claypan for good landing and within short distance of trees and water-holes.

'When I'm on the ground,' he said, 'I'll be able to see if I can taxi to the north end of the claypan. If so, I'll be within three-quarters of a mile of the gorges. If the water-hole doesn't offer enough to entertain us we might summon up the energy to walk to the gorges.'

The idea was received with delight. The company had already been so much together at Ransome they had ceased to be charmed with the novelty of what each other had to say of his or her affairs. They all wanted to be doing something.

Only Greg was doubtful.

'Picnicking by the plane might sound all right,' he said. 'There's always a hazard by air, though . . . and picnicking . . . well, maybe we could arrange a day to send out a fleet of trucks and take you up-river.'

Julia, sitting relaxed in her chair, her very fine legs showing themselves to advantage as she crossed them negligently, replied by pointing round the room and counting.

'Four to one, Greg. I'm sorry. You've only one vote when it comes to saying how much money we, as a family, will spend on an outing.'

Greg lit a cigarette slowly. The others had chimed in to support Julia's point of view, but both Julia and Greg remained silent. They were like two protagonists between whom some telepathic contest was being enacted but of which nothing was said in words and which didn't really relate to the picnic. Of the others only Sara had nothing to say. She was watching Greg and Julia as one would watch a play on a stage. What would be the end of this duel that Sara had been conscious of since the very first day she landed on Ransome?

It had been there all along. To-day it had come out in the open.

'It is Jack's plane,' Greg said at length, slowly. 'If he chooses to use it as transport for you all, then I won't make any difficulties. Sara and I will remain on the station.'

He got up quietly and walked to the veranda door and looked out over the brown grassy downs. He turned.

'I'm going down to the shearing sheds,' he said. 'Anyone coming?'

There was a silence. Then Sara stood up and brushed her skirt. She tried to be as easy and non-committal in her manner as Greg now was.

'I'll come, Greg,' she said. 'Will you wait till I get my hat.'

'Bring a shady one,' he said. 'The sun has got the wrath of God in it.'

Sara went into the dressing-rooms and reached for her straw hat from a peg driven into the wooden wall.

What did it all mean? She was certain there had been a battle of wills between Julia and Greg and that it was an important one to both of them. It had mattered to her, Sara, too. It had mattered that Julia should not destroy Greg's authority. It had mattered for Ransome's sake. His authority as manager was a tenuous thing based on personality and confidence. As Julia had, not so delicately, pointed out, he did not have a controlling vote on the destinies of the Camdens.

But he had over Sara. Unless she were like Julia and defied it too. Had Greg's flat statement, 'Sara and I will remain,' been *his* challenge to her? If she had defied it, what then? His authority would be broken altogether. Why had he that faith that she would not defy his authority? Her acceptance of it meant that the victory had not been entirely Julia's. If Greg was going to keep *one* in the shadow of his wing, then it was going to be Sara and not Julia.

Greg had gone to the edge of the small enclosure round the homestead by the time Sara joined him.

Sara felt once again that tearing of herself in two. Her duty to Ransome, her bargain, kept her faithful to Greg's commands. But once again it put her in the role of the subservient and not the wilful and decorative.

She expected Greg to say something now to thank her for backing him up but in this she was disappointed.

Because he said nothing at all to her as she joined him she began to feel angry and just a little miserable.

'Why are you going to the shearing sheds?' she asked to break the silence.

'I want to look over those wool presses. The overseer thinks we should employ an extra man for maintenance. The quick changes of temperature rust up the springs.' He paused moodily, then continued: 'If wool prices hold, and that's guesswork, we'll have to extend the sheds. We could employ two carpenters there in the off season.'

'Your guess would at least be an informed guess,' said Sara.

'True,' said Greg. And they continued on in silence.

Sara's spirits sank lower still. How could he walk thus beside her and be no more conscious of her than he would be if it was one of the stockmen? Where were his thoughts really? Were they with the shearing sheds or were they with that current of electrified air that had flowed between himself and Julia on the veranda?

They had reached the shearing sheds and Sara broke the silence again.

'I think I'll wait here in the shade. I'd probably be an encumbrance while you're looking over the presses.'

'If you prefer, Sara,' he said. 'I won't be long,' and he strode on to the first big wool-polished floor.

Sara sat down on a box in the shade on the east side of the shed.

So! He had left her flat. She herself had mentioned the word 'encumbrance' but Greg had not denied it.

Well, it was her own fault, she thought. She could hear Greg's footsteps inside and her heart longed for him. Yet she knew that if he had come, and if he had held out his arms to her, she would have turned away.

If there is any future for us, she thought bitterly, it can never begin to be realised with Julia present. She defies me too. She defies me to capture Greg from her. And I don't know how to fight.

She would not admit to herself that the pearl-grey satin dress and the dangling ear-rings had been like putting on an armour to do battle. She was too angry with the thing in Greg's character that made him differentiate between Julia's type and her own and Mrs Whittle's type to want consciously to do battle to win him.

Greg was a long time, but Sara did not move. She sat and thought long enough to feel she had reached rock bottom of depression, and then, as always happens when one reaches rock bottom, she began to fight back.

She had a right to Ransome because she had a duty to it. One day Julia would go too far. Then for Ransome's sake . . .

Greg, who had gone out of the building into another farther on, now came around the corner.

'I suppose all this means another argument,' he said. 'But

we'll have to extend that far shed. I've been thinking about it for days.'

'The plane picnic is not so important to you then. You are thinking more about improvements on the place than the fact that the others will probably go off to enjoy themselves?'

Greg looked at Sara for the first time since they had left the homestead.

'Why not?' he said curiously. 'I always think of the place first. I thought you knew that, Sara.'

'Yes,' she said slowly. 'I think I did know that. It's myself who gets side-tracked by thinking of people as well as places.'

Greg was still looking at her curiously.

'I think of some people,' he said in some surprise. 'I didn't want you, for instance, to go off on that plane ride.'

Sara's heart leapt unexpectedly.

'I know you don't like plane travel. And you get just a little air-sick, though you don't admit it. But if you really want to go, Sara . . .'

Her heart stopped leaping. So that was it! Oddly enough Sara was now disappointed that he had not ordered her to stay because he had chosen her safety before Julia's. Even if it had only been for Ransome's sake.

'No,' Sara said, bending down and picking up a twig to whisk away the flies. 'I do not want to go. The sun has been rather much for me, Greg. I think I'll have a shower and a rest before we have drinks on the veranda.'

He held open the gate of the enclosure for her to walk through. In silence they approached the homestead and went through the wire door on to the veranda.

'Had fun?' asked Julia. She was still reclining on the chair and her legs were still displayed to advantage.

'Lots,' said Sara shortly. 'I'm now going to have more . . . under the shower.'

The gauntlet, so politely hidden from view before, was now thrown down. Julia must think she was in an advantageous position. Sara wondered why.

CHAPTER NINETEEN

The plan for the picnic by air was finally abandoned. This did not constitute a defeat for Julia, for the decision to give up the idea came in the first place from Jack Brownrigg, too much a friend of Greg's to want to go against his wishes, and in the second place because the Camdens and Hunts, particularly their children, had become truthfully bored. And their boredom was not to be borne any longer since the open session in the air informed them an Airways plane was due to-morrow to pick up a sick child at the station farther up the reaches of the river.

Everybody decided at once it would be just no trouble for that plane to land in the sheep run and transport the now discontented families to Perth. Everyone agreed that a week's holiday on the Swan in the kindlier southern latitudes would be a grand way to finish off the whole business of Ransome. A week later they could get a booking on the Trans-Australia plane and be back in Adelaide in no time. The Hunts would fly straight on to Melbourne where they lived.

From Greg's point of view this folded the party up nicely, though he gave no sign of feeling this way. Only Sara knew it because she saw the little creases of tension disappear from his forehead.

Jack Brownrigg, too, now decided he wanted to get back on his own beat and became suddenly, and a little inexplicably, so anxious to do so it was decided that he, with Greg and Sara, would fly back to Ransome the day before the Airways plane would be able to pick up the rest of the party.

Julia said she would go south for some shopping. Possibly go on to Adelaide to see the Company about 'business affairs,' and fly back to Ransome by the Alice Springs route. Clifford would go with Julia and return to headquarters to take over the management of affairs there.

Both Clifford Camden and Jack Brownrigg seemed to have lacked their usual spirits since they had left Ransome, and Sara wondered if she had been too indolent a hostess. The truth of it was, it was difficult to be a hostess of any kind at the old homestead. The life was too much one long veranda picnic. It was fun in itself but it was every man for himself, and no privacy at all, there was no chance to give the little individual attention to a person that one is able to do when in a big homestead.

On their last night together Sara determined to make some special effort. She found it quite a problem to try and juggle chairs, and who sat in which chair, without drawing attention to what she was doing.

When they sat on the veranda with coffee and cigarettes

after dinner it was hard to prise the overseer out of his chair in order that she, Sara, might sit next to Clifford for a little while. She could only do so by asking if she herself could change places as she wished to discuss something with Clifford.

When they were all arranged, after all the men stood up and helped her arrange the chairs, she found she could not think of what to say to Clifford to justify such a move.

'Heigh-ho, young Sara, what's on your mind?' asked Clifford in a voice that everyone listened to.

'Well, not really anything much. I thought perhaps you might give the girls back in the office my love. Tell them about me, and the kind of things I'm doing. . . .'

'Not on your life. They'd all be cadging favours with me to get a transfer to the station. Then they'd get married and I wouldn't get them back.'

'Who's left on Ransome to get married now you're leaving, Clifford?' Sara laughed.

'I could always come back. And there's Jack. No one goes to Ransome without striking Jack somewhere on the route. And his tongue's fairly hanging out for a bride. Why, you could have had him yourself for tuppence, Sara.'

Clifford's voice belonged more to the city than the great outback. It hadn't the soft muted tones of men who drawled and spoke through half closed lips. It could be heard all along the veranda.

'What nonsense you do talk.' Sara tried to laugh Clifford's words away.

'Nonsense be blowed. You could have had me too. Why didn't you give me the same glad eye you handed Greg?'

'You weren't looking.' Sara tried to meet Clifford's rough attempt at gallantry with one of her own but she didn't like the way her polite intention was turning out to be a conversation piece to which everyone was studiously listening.

She felt it was meant for humour but it wasn't in very good taste. Greg, she thought, by the way he sat back in the shadow, so still that even the lighted cigarette in his hand didn't move, thought this way too. The Greg who had not cared for men who made bets on women would hardly care to hear herself discussed thus, even though it was only in fun.

She worked back to the girls in the office, sending each individual one a message. By this time she was too disheartened to try to get near Jack and be pleasant to him.

It was not until they were all on the point of parting for the night that she found herself near the edge of the veranda with Jack.

'Jack,' she said, 'I haven't had the opportunity of two words with you. I know we'll be with you in the plane to-morrow, but you'll be up in the pilot's seat and I'll hardly be able to talk to you there. I do want to thank you for bringing us down and . . .' she hesitated.

They were standing in the shadow just outside the circle of light.

'And what, Sara?' Jack asked, bending his head a little to try and see Sara's face in the half light.

'And for being with us,' she concluded.

Jack turned his head and looked out through the fly-screen.

'Look!' he said. 'The moon is just rising. It makes the paddocks look like a silver sea.'

They stood side by side looking out to the west where the moon, a great silver and apricot ball, was hanging low on the skyline.

Jack moved to the wire door.

'Let's go out and feel it as well as see it,' he said. 'Ever felt the moonlight, Sara?'

Sara was reluctant to go but felt it was a discourtesy to hang back. Moreover, it would look as if she was putting a construction on Jack's invitation that was something certainly not in his mind.

'Just for a few minutes,' she said. 'We leave at sun-up to-morrow, don't we?'

They were down the short flight of steps and moved towards the wooden fence enclosing the homestead.

'Now you can breathe,' said Jack. His hand was a shadow sweeping in the arc of the heavens. 'Can you believe we are not alone in a world of grass, sky and stars?'

'I think it is very wonderful and I think you put it in a very romantic way. But I'm a married woman now and the beauty alone has to be sufficient for me.'

'And no romance.'

She turned her face to his.

'Yes, there is romance, Jack,' she said quietly. 'But it belongs elsewhere.'

Jack was silent.

'You don't want any noses punched?' he said at length, and quite seriously.

'No thank you, Jack.'

He sighed.

'Then we'd better say good-bye to the moon and the stars. Come on inside. I'll return you to your husband. Is that what you want?'

Sara squeezed his arm.

'Yes, Jack. That's what I want.'

He put his hand on her hand where it rested in the crook of his arm and they returned to the homestead thus.

Greg, hearing them coming, stood up and opened the wire door for them. Neither removed their hands until they were back on the veranda.

'No success,' Jack said, shaking his head lugubriously. 'She is so bemused she can't even see the stars.'

'You've got no technique, Jack,' said Clifford. 'Now let me try . . .'

'Oh, no, thank you,' said Sara quickly. 'If everyone tried to show me the stars I'd be worn out before dawn. I'm off to bed.'

Only Greg, Jack and Clifford were left on the veranda.

'Good night, everybody,' she said. 'I'll see you in the morning.'

'What? No stars, even for Greg?' said Clifford.

Sara hesitated.

'Yes, one star for Greg,' she said. She went up to him. 'A good night kiss before I retire to the female part of the sleeping quarters.'

It seemed as if he would not bend his head, so she stood on her toes.

She kissed him on the mouth.

Then as she slowly drew back their eyes met. The moonlight was shining in Greg's, and her own eyes were in shadow. She swallowed a lump.

'Good night, my dear,' she said.

'Good night, Sara, my dear,' he said. Then he held open the door for her as she went into the dressing-room.

'Greg's was for the gallery,' Sara said to herself. 'But mine wasn't. Mine wasn't.'

It was shortly after sunrise the next morning that the Dove took off, carrying Greg, Sara and some freight from the sheep run. The stockmen who were later to come to Ransome would follow in about ten days' time.

Everyone was up and breakfasted, and those waiting till

the next day for the Airways plane gave the three of them a tumultuous farewell. Now that the party was really over and everyone could see the horizons of home in sight, the old good spirit had returned. It was momentarily forgotten that forty-eight hours before they were so bored with one another it took all their time to keep tempers in check.

Only Julia did not appear and her absence was more notable, as far as Sara was concerned, than her presence would have been.

Sara was thrilled to find herself heading back for Ransome without Julia. Now perhaps life would be different. Not only would she have some respite from Julia, but the house-party would be over. They would be back to the way they were before any stranger set foot on the place. And the strain of impending events would have gone too.

What would it be like? She meant, what would life with Greg be like.

Greg had just been up in the seat next to the pilot and he now stepped down and sat in the seat on the other side of the gangway from Sara. All the seats in the Dove were single seats so he could not sit next to her.

'You feeling all right, Sara?' he asked.

'Quite. I don't even feel very nervous.' She smiled. Her eyes suddenly showed their two pixies. 'That surprises you, doesn't it?'

Greg was thinking the two pixies had been hiding for a long time now and he replied:

'Oh, no. I knew you'd get used to it sooner or later.'

Sara thought ruefully that he didn't give her any credit for *trying*. And she had tried very hard. Her attempts at self-discipline had taken more out of her than anyone guessed.

'You go back and talk to Jack,' Sara said. 'I rather like being here and just *looking*. Besides, I think Jack likes company.'

'I'll come back later,' he said, and went back to join Jack.

They'd been flying for over an hour when Sara heard a bang.

Strange! she thought to herself quite calmly. I always knew this would happen.

She closed her eyes. She was quite certain her pulse was normal. She wondered why.

174

The engine was spluttering badly. She lay back in her seat with eyes closed and thought quite calmly, 'I suppose I might die. I hope it doesn't hurt.'

She was aware that Greg had come back into the seat over the gangway. He was leaning forward over the short distance and pulling at her safety belt.

'Sara,' he said gently, 'I want you to fasten your safety belt.'

She looked down in a dazed way while he adjusted her safety belt.

The engine was spluttering. It seemed to be back-firing and every now and again it cut out. The plane was wobbling.

'Sara?'

She looked up at him now. His eyes were dark pools.

'Are you listening to me?'

'Yes. I'm not frightened, you know.'

'Good girl. Now listen carefully. Keep your right hand near that press clasp. When we land, touch that clasp instantly, but not a minute before. You understand?'

'Yes,' she said. 'But why have the belt on at all?'

'Because the bump can throw you out of your seat and break bones. Don't press until we touch ground. Right?'

She opened her eyes wide at Greg.

'I'm very calm,' she said. 'Don't worry about me.'

Greg was speaking a little more urgently now. The engine cut out for a long time before it seemed to grip again.

'Jack is sending our position by radio. He is going to pancake land when he can find a clear spot. He's jettisoning as much petrol as possible. But the time is short. There'll still be petrol on board. Sometimes there is fire. The moment we land you're to press that clasp and get out through that door. Don't look back or wait for us. You'll be holding us up and every second will count. Every fraction of a second if there is fire. Got that?'

She nodded.

'We'll follow you instantly. If you clear the door we can get through. You can save us all, Sara, by obeying orders.'

'I understand,' she said. 'I'll do exactly what you say.'

They were losing altitude rapidly now. The engine kept cutting out monotonously, almost to a rhythm.

'You've done this before, Greg, haven't you?'

He nodded. She remembered his telling her of the lonely eeriness of the Red Ranges. Were they going to land in the

175

Red Ranges now?

'It's funny,' she said suddenly. 'I feel quite calm.'

Greg put his hand out across the gangway and took her left hand with his left hand. It meant they sat awkwardly but it left their right hands free for the clasp on the safety belts.

'Sara?' he said. There was a deep note in his voice.

But her eyes were closed. She had her hand in his. How warm and strong it was!

'I feel quite calm, quite calm,' she said, as if astonished.

The next moment they struck. The plane hit, then seemed to ricochet off the ground into space. Then it hit again.

'Thank goodness for the safety belt,' Sara said, but she didn't really think the words left her lips.

They struck again.

'*Now!*' said Greg.

Sara's thumb pressed the spring of her safety belt. Greg was leaning back in his seat to give her room to get out into the cramped gangway.

She was in the gangway now and Greg was behind her. He leaned over her shoulder and shifted the bolt on the door.

'Jump, Sara! *Jump!* You're to run for it. Put three hundred yards behind you. *Jump and run.*'

As she jumped she remembered that Jack, in the pilot's seat, had sat humped forward as if he was not going to move.

'Why didn't he look round?' she said, as she hit the ground.

She fell on her face and her nose hurt.

'Perhaps I'll get a straight nose after all. But wouldn't it be awful if it was more turned up than ever. I've got to get up and run. . . .'

She stumbled a few steps and turned round.

Greg was not following her. At any moment the plane might go up in flames.

She stopped.

'I'll stay with him,' she said. 'And furthermore I wish I'd stop talking to myself as if I was Alice in Wonderland.'

She ran back to the plane. From a few yards off she could see Greg struggling with Jack's body inside the plane. He had turned and was trying to wedge Jack around in front of him towards the door. He saw Sara.

'*Run!*' he shouted. '*Run.* In God's name, *run*, Sara.'

He'd got one of Jack's legs through the door, and Sara

came under the plane where Greg could not see her.

She tried to reach up to help Jack but his foot kept escaping her. Then after an interminable age both legs came through and the lower half of his body.

'Drop him, Greg. Drop him,' Sara cried. 'I'll catch.'

Greg probably did not hear, but Jack was suddenly hurtled through the door. A second later Greg leapt after him.

No time for words now. They picked Jack up between them and half dragged, half carried him for fifty yards. Then Sara lost her grip.

'Look . . . get him on my back, Sara. Quick! You push from behind.'

They got Jack's inert body on Greg's shoulder like a sack of flour. They ran on, Sara pushing from behind. She remembered thinking she must keep her footsteps in time with Greg's so that they didn't trip one another up.

They were two hundred yards from the plane when it exploded.

Simultaneously they threw themselves and Jack flat on the ground. They lay thus for a full minute. Then Greg sat up.

'Let's get out. The heat will get us.'

They got up again, this time dragging Jack as before. When they'd gone another fifty yards they hoisted Jack on Greg's back again. Then they ran on. When they ceased to feel the heat they sat down, their heads on their knees, Jack's body lying prone between them.

After a long time Sara straightened herself and looked at him.

'Is he . . . is he dead?'

'No,' Greg said. 'I knocked him out. He has two legs broken as far as I could see. The pain was too great. He couldn't make it.'

He stiffened himself and, without getting up, straightened Jack. The two legs lay crooked, one of them covered with blood, stretched before him.

'Let's get some shade before he comes to,' Greg said. He stood up.

'Cross hands, like we did when we were kids?' said Sara. Greg shook his head.

'You're too little, Sara. Put him on my back again.'

'But it might be miles.'

'Let's go as far as we can.'

They did. They'd been walking in the blazing sun for what

must have been two hours when the tops of green trees appeared above the horizon.

'One more pull, Sara.'

Neither of them said anything about thirst. They couldn't. Their tongues clove to the roofs of their mouths. Sara wondered if the green trees meant water. If not, it might have been better to have died in the plane.

The trees did mean water. Well, not exactly water, but Greg, being a bushman, knew they were on a dried-out watercourse and that if one dug long enough one would find it.

Greg was exhausted beyond measure and dry beyond words, so he did not explain this to Sara. He merely dropped Jack under a tree, straightened Jack's legs and then began to dig with a heavy stick in the middle of the decline.

After ten minutes he came to moist sand, and Sara copied him and dug out a handful and put it on her mouth. It was cool and wet.

They both dug with their bare hands till there was a pool of water in the bottom of the hole. They both drank and then Greg soaked his handkerchief and carried it to Jack and squeezed it in Jack's mouth. Meantime Sara went on digging. She went to the trees and gathered some bark and lined the hole with it so the hole wouldn't cave in.

Greg broke off some small straight sapling branches.

'Have you got a petticoat, Sara?'

'Yes, a nylon one.'

'Good. He's beginning to come to.'

Sara took off her petticoat and Greg slit it into strips with his knife to make bandages for splints.

Jack was stirring and groaning, but when Greg straightened the bones of his legs he stopped because he had fainted again.

Greg bound the legs to the splints and then got more water for Jack. Then he sat down beside him and waited for him to come to.

Sara found a patch of shade and lay down on her stomach, her face in her arms, to avoid the flies. Then she went to sleep.

It was dusk when she woke up to the sound of an aeroplane thrumming overhead. Greg was out from under the trees, waving his shirt. The plane circled, something dropped in two small parachutes, and then it flew away to the south.

Greg went out on to the plain to retrieve the parcels sent by parachute. Both contained tins of water and one had food, the other bandages, ointments, other medical supplies including morphia and a hypodermic syringe.

Greg handed some biscuits, chocolate, and vitamin tablets to Sara, and went over to Jack. Sara could see that Jack's eyes were open but his face was sheet-white and he said nothing. Neither did Greg till he had put the needle in his arm.

'There you are, old chap,' he said. 'You'll have a decent night at any rate.'

In all none of them had said two hundred words since the engine of the plane had finally cut out.

The next morning the plane, the same Airways plane that was to have taken Julia, Clifford and the families to Perth, landed four or five hundred yards away across the plain. Two hours later they were back on the Ashburton sheep run and half an hour later Sara, with two sleeping tablets inside her, was in bed and asleep.

She slept through the heat of the afternoon and well into the night. When she woke up her mouth was dry with thirst. She wondered if that dreadful dryness would ever leave her.

There was a light on in the living-room. Sara got up, put on Julia's silk dressing-gown and went barefooted into the living-room. She would make herself some tea.

As she came through one door, Greg, with a teapot and a jug in his hands, came through the other. He was in pyjamas.

They stood in silence and looked across the width of the room at one another.

Then Greg put the teapot and the jug on the table. He held out one hand.

Wordlessly Sara went to it, took it.

'We made it!' Greg said.

They stared into one another's eyes.

'Yes, we made it!' Sara said simply.

Sara felt her body quivering against Greg's. His hand was on the back of her head, pressing it against his shoulder. His other arm was round her and held her tight.

But Sara could say nothing. The words dried up in

her throat. Greg's hand gently caressed the back of her head.

'Sara . . .' he said softly. 'You were very brave,.'

She shook her head where it rested against his shoulder. At last she looked up.

'We were all very brave,' she said. Suddenly she was so tired she could hardly stand. 'It doesn't mean very much any more, does it? Because one just *is*. Something just acts for one. One doesn't think. You didn't think, did you, Greg?'

'No,' he said. 'I didn't think. Not after you wouldn't run for it. After that it was just a team with work to do . . . against the sun, and against time.'

'And against weariness. We were very tired, weren't we?'

'It was an endurance test.' He took Sara's chin in his hand and looked into her face. He smiled. 'Do you know what, Sara? The tip of your nose is scraped off and you've a lopsided cut near your mouth?'

'And you've got a bruise on your forehead and a long cut on the back of your hand.'

'I wonder how we got them? Do you remember?'

'No. I was only thinking about what we had to do.'

They sat down at the table, she in her dressing-gown and he in his pyjamas, and drank tea. They had nothing more to say. They were too tired.

'Go back to bed, Sara child. To-morrow we'll talk about it.'

'What time is it?'

'Three o'clock. The stars are beginning to fade.'

'The stars?'

He took her pointed chin in his hand and kissed her gently on the lips.

'Good morning, Sara,' he said.

'Good morning, Greg.'

CHAPTER TWENTY

The heat of the morning's sun woke Sara. She felt quite different from what she had felt before. Her body was still tired but the rest of her, her spirit, wasn't. She felt as she had never felt before. She had a purpose. A strong, compulsive purpose and she hadn't any idea what it was about.

All she knew was that she wanted to get up, have a shower, get dressed and be this different person that she now was.

She had confidence. She had faced the thing she most feared in life . . . an aeroplane . . . and had not been afraid. She thought it all had nothing to do with herself but was due to some outside, though unknown, agency, whereas it was in reality her own character which had shone through of its own accord in a moment of extreme trial.

All her clothes had gone up in smoke with the plane, so she found a cotton dress and some underclothes of Julia's and put them on. They fitted, which made her think that Julia had created an illusion of greater height because of her high heels. Sara thought she would get higher heels with her next shoes.

Mrs Hunt and Mrs Sam Camden heard her moving about and they came to see if they could help her.

'I'm quite all right,' said Sara. 'I never felt better in my life. I'd like some hot tea . . . and some hot toast *not* made by that dreadful Chinaman who hashes up those stews. . . .' She paused. 'That reminds me. We've got a very good Chinaman at Ransome. And he can cook. When we get back to Ransome I'm going to see that Hoh *does* cook. And something more than roast mutton or steak every night too.'

Mrs Hunt and Mrs Camden exchanged glances.

'My dear,' said Mrs Hunt, 'the men at Ransome only eat roast mutton or steak.'

'Not from now on,' said Sara, buttoning her frock. Then she smiled. 'What do you think Julia will say when she sees me in this?'

'Does it matter very much what Julia says?' asked Mrs Sam Camden acidly.

'No,' said Sara, 'it doesn't.' And then stopped, astonished at herself.

I must have got a bump on my head when we hit the ground, she thought. *I am different!*

Julia evidently had not concerned herself with Sara's recovery. When Sara had finished her tea and toast, made by the kindly disposed Mrs Hunt, she could see from her seat on the veranda that Julia had presumably been concerning herself with Greg's recovery. They were walking up from the store together. Greg had a pile of cotton goods in his hands so he'd been getting himself, and possibly Sara, a new

181

wardrobe. Yes . . . Sara could see he had on a new open-necked shirt and a pair of brown cotton drill trousers like the stockmen wore when they weren't dressed for the saddle.

Julia was talking to Greg in an animated way but Greg was saying nothing. Now and again he wrinkled up his eyes as if looking out into the distance. And once he lifted up his spare hand and moved the brown stockman's hat to the back of his head.

From the brilliant sunshine outside he could not see on to the fly-screened veranda so it was Julia coming through the door first who saw Sara.

'So,' she said. 'You survived!' Her eyes took in Sara's dress. 'And in my dress by the look of it.'

'Yes, I'm alive,' said Sara pleasantly. 'And in your dress. I hope you don't mind.'

Greg was on the veranda now.

'I brought you one of the ginghams from the store.' He grinned. 'It was really meant for a lubra.'

'When it's time to change out of Julia's dress, I'll put the gingham on. Have you had tea, Greg?'

'Yes. I didn't bring you any. I thought you needed the sleep.'

'Talking about "when it's time to change *my* dress," ' said Julia, sitting in a cane-chair. 'I'm likely to need that dress.'

'But you're going to Perth. You don't need cotton dresses like this in Perth. Or in Adelaide, Melbourne or Sydney. Besides, I only want a loan of it.'

'I need it when I'm at Ransome,' said Julia peevishly.

'But you won't be at Ransome,' said Sara.

Greg, who had put his bundle down on a small table and seated himself in another chair with his hat on the floor beside him, shot a startled glance at Sara. He was in the act of taking out a cigarette and his hands stopped in mid-air.

Sara looked at him steadily.

'Oh, I'll ask Julia quite often,' she said. 'Don't look so startled, Greg. I'm quite hospitable at heart really.'

'*You* ask *me*?' said Julia. Her voice was bored. 'I happen to be a shareholder . . .'

'Not of Ransome homestead,' Sara said quietly. 'Of Ransome leasehold . . . yes. But the homestead was left to Greg in his father's will. And in my marriage settlement Greg gave me the privileges of the homestead.'

Greg had lowered his eyes and was pushing tobacco in

the end of his cigarette with a match. The corners of his mouth twitched.

Julia sat up with a start.

'Greg!' she demanded. 'Do you hear what that girl is talking about?'

Sara had heard of a dead-pan face but she had never seen one before. Greg's face was expressionless.

'I hadn't thought of it before. But that is Sara's legal position.'

'Do you mean to tell me . . .' began Julia with a rising voice.

'I'll have to consult my lawyer,' said Greg. He looked at Julia out of two level blue eyes that were as peaceful as a mill pond. 'I'm sorry to have come at last to the use of the family chorus. But that's about it. Every member of the family says, "I'll have to consult my lawyer." Now I, too, have come to it. All on account of marrying . . .'

'Your secretary!' Julia put in. She jumped up and stared at Sara. 'You were in a sweet position to tie him up that way, weren't you?'

'I suppose I was,' said Sara quietly. 'Though I didn't really think of it at that time.' She turned to Greg. 'When are we going home, Greg?'

The expression on his face did alter now and he looked concerned.

'We could go right away if we were going by plane. The Airways plane is going to take off with Jack and that sick boy from inland about midday. They'll fly them to Port Hedland Hospital. But you . . .'

'I don't mind going by plane,' said Sara. 'You forget, Greg. I'm not frightened any more. I think I was really frightened of fear. Now I know I'm not.'

Greg was watching her face as she spoke.

'Very well then,' he said. 'We can leave at midday. I think I can get the Anson through to Port Hedland to pick us up but we may be a day there. I'll have to get on the air and see. . . .'

'And what about us?' said Julia. 'Have you forgotten that plane originally intended flying to Perth and we were to be its passengers?'

'I imagine it's under the Flying Doctor routine now,' said Greg. 'If it's directed to Port Hedland, then that's where it has to go.'

'Wait till Clifford hears about this,' said Julia, and she

flounced away as if in search of him.

Sara avoided meeting Greg's eyes.

'I don't think I'll ask Julia to Ransome for a long time,' she said. Then she, too, got up and took away the remains of her breakfast of tea and toast.

At midday they left the sheep run in the plane flying the two invalids north. It had been arranged for the rest of the party to go by car to Onslow where they would pick up the ordinary mail plane south.

Jack Brownrigg, who was suffering badly from shock, was still under a soporific so that all that Sara could do for him in the plane was sit beside him.

She brooded over him quietly. He had offered to punch noses for her, but he had done her a better turn than that. He had landed her in the desert and it had taught her to get the spirit of nose-punching herself.

Something had happened between Greg and herself. The experience had drawn them together. She didn't know quite what it all meant but she did know that she, Sara, would stand up to anything the future had in store for her. Greg had something to offer her. She would take that something, and if it was not all she would be philosophic about it. But she wouldn't have Julia, or anyone else, taking him away from her. She knew that much at least.

When they arrived at Port Hedland she was surprised to find herself overwhelmed with that dreadful fatigue again, as if something physical had suddenly collapsed inside her. She was even more surprised to find the Flying Doctor clapping her into hospital for the day and shooting a needle into her arm too.

'You need that, my girl,' he said. 'You're not nearly as hardy as you're cracking. But I admire you for the show.'

The next day the Anson was waiting for them and it took all day to get to Ransome. Sara wasn't at all nervous or air-sick. That was probably due to another soporific they had given her before leaving the hospital.

'They all think I'm suffering from shock,' she said to Greg. 'But I'm not. I'm just tired.'

'It's not you who is suffering from shock, Sara,' Greg said with a smile that could almost have had a hint of fun in it. 'It's the rest of us.'

Now what did he mean by that? Did he know she was different now? Accidents made people lose their memories.

Did they also bring out a latent aggressiveness like shock therapy sometimes did?

Was that what was different about her? Sara's confidence faltered a little. Then she pushed up her chin again.

'I'm going to stay this way,' she said. 'Maybe I could get thrown by a horse now and again to keep me this way. . . .'

Greg had seen her chin go up and the small firm set of her mouth. He looked down at the cigarette he was packing with a match and the corners of his own mouth twitched. But his face was expressionless and his eyes were blue limpid pools when he looked up.

They arrived at Ransome in the late afternoon, and Sara, who had dozed under the soporific for most of the journey, would not allow anyone to suggest she was tired.

Mrs Camden and Marion, except for some concern for Jack Brownrigg, seemed to think the aeroplane crash was something of a joke.

'You both look so fit,' they said.

Mrs Whittle turned to Greg first.

'Mr Greg, are you sure you're all right?' she asked, and then turned to Sara. 'What can I do for you, Miss Sara?'

'Ask Hoh if he'll come and see me,' said Sara. 'I've got a longing for fried rice for dinner. He makes it beautifully. I had some one day . . . in the secrecy of the men's kitchen down by the quarters.'

'Fried rice? Well, of course, my dear. I'm sure Hoh won't mind.'

'Let him make it in the kitchen, please, Mrs Whittle. And ask him to make enough for everybody.'

'Everybody? Well, he could make it by all means. But I expect the men at the table won't eat it.'

'Yes, they will,' said Sara. 'They'll have to eat it, sooner or later. I'm going to have it often. I love it. Specially when it's made with a curry and sweet-and-sour sauce.'

They were all in the billiard room while this conversation was going on, Sam Benson too. There was a stunned silence.

Mrs Camden broke it with something that sounded like a hollow laugh.

'My dear, you won't get away with those ideas for long. Greg always takes the men's part. Doesn't he, Sam?'

Sam nodded his head in agreement.

'He's not going to now,' said Sara. 'Not in the house anyway. He can be master outside, but *inside* . . .' She paused. 'What are you laughing at, Sam?'

'You, young 'un. If you think you're going to tell Greg what to do, inside or out, you've got another think coming.'

Greg, in between blowing smoke-rings, contemplated the toe of his shoe. He said nothing.

'What's more, Clifford and the rest of the family gang like ordinary dinners,' put in Marion.

Sara stood up.

'I don't want to hear you, Marion, or Mrs Camden either, talk about Clifford or Jack Brownrigg any more. They are pleasant persons and I like them. But they bore me. At least the discussion of them bores me. Sam! I don't want any more wise advice from you either. If you don't like my new ear-rings, then please don't say so to me. *I* like them. That's what's important.'

Nobody had their mouths open, but the expressions on all the faces except Greg's looked as if the mouths would open any minute.

Sara walked to the door. Mrs Whittle followed her.

'Are you . . . are you all right, Miss Sara?'

'Do you mean did I get a bump on my head, or something? And that I'm a little mad?'

'No, my dear, of course not.'

'Because I didn't. All that happened was that I got my confidence back. I had to face something pretty bad. And I did it without any effort at all. Now I can face everyone on Ransome. Even . . .' She looked uncertainly at her husband for a moment. 'Even Greg,' she finished with a sweep and left the room.

'I think I'd better go after her, Mr Greg,' Mrs Whittle said anxiously.

'We'll go together,' Greg replied.

They entered the office just as Sara was about to quit it for her own room.

'Is there anything you want, Miss Sara?' Mrs Whittle began lamely.

'Just say, Sara. The whole homestead's yours,' said Greg. His eyes weren't quite such limpid pools now. There was something dark in them. Mrs Whittle, catching a glimpse of them, looked suddenly worried.

'Now, Mr Greg . . .' she began.

He hushed her with a gesture of his hand.

'Say what you want, Sara,' said Greg. 'We're here to please you.'

Sara wasn't sure whether he was making fun of her or

186

not. She drew herself up.

'Yes,' she said. 'I'd like that door between your room and the office closed. All I see from my bed is a vista of doors, particularly the bathroom door which you nearly always leave open, Greg. I'm sorry if it means your room will be airless but it's not unendurable. Mine wasn't when I had to have it closed while the family party was on.'

'But what if I do find it unendurable?' said Greg with an ominous quiet in his voice.

'Why then, Mrs Whittle could fix up that big bedroom at the front of the house for you. There's room for you to sprawl over the bed your own way, Greg. Or put your friends in it when they've drunk too much. And there's three windows, besides the door. Plenty of room and plenty of air, even if it is a little old-fashioned.'

She turned away, half waiting for the repercussions of such a bomb.

Mrs Whittle's eyes flew to Greg's face, where she expected the explosion first to ignite. To her surprise all that Greg did was stand still and blink. Then his eye caught Mrs Whittle's. Something passed between them.

'Yes,' said Greg slowly. 'That's just what I think I'll have. Plenty of room and plenty of air. Perhaps you'll be kind enough to get Nellie or one of the girls to fix that bedroom up, Mrs Whittle?'

'Why yes, Mr Greg. I'll do it right away.'

Mrs Whittle literally hurried away. Sara had never seen her hurry before.

Without a word Greg turned away and went into his own room, the one from which he was to be banished. He closed the door very gently behind him.

Sara sat down suddenly in front of her dressing-table. She looked at herself in the mirror. She put her hand to her forehead.

'I'm mad,' she said. 'I've gone mad. I must have had a bump after all.'

Conversation at dinner was sparse. The company seemed to be constrained, though they all ate fried rice in diminutive helpings. Two of the jackaroos had gone south to the sheep run and Sam, for the first time in history, had absented himself. Sara had lost her aggressiveness, and though she made a few attempts at polite conversation with the other two jackaroos she soon gave up. Every now and again she put her hand to her head.

'Is something wrong with your head?' Greg asked.

'No, thank you,' said Sara. 'I feel quite well.'

Her voice was so docile it startled everyone all over again. Mrs Camden shook her head at Marion, and Marion in her turn shook her head at her mother. As if forcing the conversation, such as it was, in other directions they began to talk of Turra. It seemed as if Marion was, after all, a little interested in the elder of the MacKensie boys. Sara, looking at her, noticed for the first time the irony had gone out of Marion's smile and there was something more of a tender nature in it when she spoke of Turra.

Lucky Marion! She would be marrying for love. What a wonderful thing that was! Moreover, Mrs Camden said they couldn't afford a yacht *and* a big wedding. She supposed it would have to be the wedding. Well, thought Sara, that disposes of the yacht.

For politeness' sake to Marion Sara sat a little with them in the billiard room after dinner. All the time her thoughts kept drifting to that barred room that would be the other side of the office. Why had she done it? Why had she said that? What madness had possessed her?

If she couldn't have Greg beside her she liked him near. She had been miserable when her own door had been closed when he had used the office late at night during the party.

He had been so kind and gentle, almost loving to her, that morning after their rescue! That morning when the stars had been fading and they'd sat drinking tea together at the table in the old homestead! This was the second time she had banished him. Maybe it was a mistake all along. Maybe she should never have done it that night in the Adelphi Hotel. She should have taken what little there was to offer . . . and tried to build on it.

But how could she with Julia?

Julia!

Odd, how Greg had said nothing when she, Sara, had virtually banished Julia from Ransome. It was almost as if he had been glad!

Two hours dragged by while Sara listened without listening to Mrs Camden's prattle and watched Marion's absent-minded fender-gazing.

Sam Benson, who had absented himself from dinner, now came into the billiard room for a night-cap. Sara decided it was time for her to retire with dignity. If Sam was going to be silly enough to be hurt, then it would take more than a late hour appearance to condone his offence in taking offence and staying away from dinner.

'Good night, everybody,' Sara said. 'I'm afraid I *am* rather tired.'

Sam watched her go with a smile. It was not at all the shamefaced smile he should have worn considering he had behaved badly.

He himself thought he had behaved rather well.

After dinner Greg had come down to the main office to find out why Sam had gone dinnerless. Sam had guessed that this was the most effective way of bringing Greg to him in the privacy of Sam's own world.

He had taken the fatherly line with Greg too. The same way he had done with the young 'un. He'd told Greg to treat Sara with great affection and care during this period when she was so obviously suffering from shock.

'She might do and say a few odd things for a while, Greg. But she'll get over it.'

To this Greg listened in a silence due to his respect for old Sam. Whatever his own thoughts were he did not communicate them to Sam. Sam didn't expect he would. He knew Greg too well.

'You see, she's worth salvaging,' Sam went on. 'I'll never forget the day you brought her home to Ransome as your bride. Came right into the garden to see me. She stood there, straight as you like, that chin of hers in the air and eyes like saucers. Pretty, and proud and serious they were. Her heart was shining out of 'em the same way as the devil does when she laughs. *Yes, Sam, I love him.* That's what she said.'

Sam saw the sudden flicker in Greg's eyes. That's got him, Sam thought. That's what I meant to tell him. He couldn't see what that baggage of a Julia was up to.

'So you see,' Sam was saying aloud, 'just treat her carefully.'

'Carefully be blowed!' said Greg suddenly. 'Who do you think is the boss around here that I have to treat anyone carefully?' He pushed back his chair and went to the door. 'Sara sounded to me in the last four hours mighty like looking after herself,' he said over his shoulder. 'I don't think you'll have to worry about her, Sam.' With that he said good night abruptly and went off into the night in the direction of the homestead garden.

It was after that that Sam had gone up to the house for his night-cap.

He had smiled on Sara's retreating back because she had told him to mind his own business and he had gone about minding hers to no mean purpose, he felt.

When Sara had undressed and gone through the now forbidden territory to the bathroom, she saw signs of great upheaval both there and in the bedroom. As a parting gesture Greg seemed to have made more splash on the bathroom floor than usual. And the towels were thrown down wet. In his room his clothes had been taken off and thrown across the bed. He, who had always been scrupulously tidy, had suddenly left his things lying all over the place.

So he had gone to bed!

Not even a polite good night!

He had gone off to the room at the top of the house!

Sara felt she would never see him again. That he had gone out of her life altogether.

She went through the two doors into her own room and stopped dead in the middle of the floor.

Greg, in pyjamas and dressing-gown, was sitting on the stool in front of her dressing-table. One knee was crossed over the other and he was examining from an aloof height the toe of his slipper. On the table beside him was the bottle of Chanel 5 and her new dangling ear-rings.

'What are you doing with those things?' she asked.

'Collecting,' Greg said. 'And I haven't forgotten the dress either.'

'The dress?'

'That grey thing.'

He stubbed out his cigarette, got up slowly and purposefully and walked to her dress cupboard. He pulled aside hangers till he found the pearl grey satin dress she had worn at the masked dance and at the farewell party. He took it off its hanger and dropped it in the middle of the floor. The ear-rings and the bottle of perfume followed.

Sara sat down with a jerk on her bed.

'I didn't dance with that thing at Marion's party,' Greg said, 'because I thought Julia was inside it. And Julia at close quarters is overpowering.'

Sara's eyes opened so wide they seemed to dominate her whole face.

He picked the bundle up from the floor now and tossed it into the shoe cupboard.

'That's where they belong,' he said with satisfaction. He was about to close the cupboard when he caught sight of Sara's old pair of red slippers. He stooped and brought them out. He was like a young boy with a plaything. He carried the slippers over to the dressing-table and put them on the floor. He looked at them with his head sideways and then he bent down and placed them at a tizzy angle to one another, with their toes turned inward. He smiled.

Then he looked at Sara's feet across the room. She had on a new pair of feathery mules. The smile disappeared from his face and he went across the room, bent down and took the slippers off Sara's feet and threw them after the dress and ear-rings into the shoe cupboard. Then he dusted his hands.

'Have you gone mad, Greg?'

'Not at all,' he said, turning round.

'Then what on earth are you doing?'

'Just clearing up a small mistake that's been in your mind all day. I'm demonstrating *who* is the master of Ransome.'

He walked over to the door that led into the passage and opened it. Then he walked back to Sara. He took the towel and soap-bag from her and threw them on the bed. Then he took her hands and pulled her up to the standing position.

Sara was galvanised into life. She tried to push him away with her hands.

'Greg! What are you doing?'

'This!'

He swung her off her feet and up in his arms. He carried her towards the door.

'Greg . . . Greg. What are you doing? Where are you taking me?'

'Where you belong.'

They went down the short passage and into the hall. Greg kicked open the door of the big front bedroom and in three strides had dumped Sara on the bed.

'Where my wife belongs,' Greg said. 'By my side.'

With one hand he pushed Sara back against the pillows and in another minute he was leaning over her, his arms around her and his mouth on hers.

'Sara, you darling little fool. I love you. Now stay there, while I turn out the light.'

He strode over to the door switch and flicked it off. The moonlight flooded the room. Sara was sitting up:

'Oh, Greg . . . Greg darling, I love you too!'

'High time you said so.'

191

He sat on the side of the bed. He was loosening his slippers from his feet. One slipper slid across the floor and hit the wall.

'And I don't want to hear about Clifford or Jack Brownrigg either. They bore me too,' he said.

The other slipper hit the door with a clatter.

'Darling, you didn't think I'd ever thought about *them*?'

'Tell me in the morning. There isn't time to-night.'

'But Julia . . .'

'Damn Julia. She's the biggest nuisance that ever set foot on Ransome. I'll tell you about *her* in the morning.'

He punched his pillows into shape, turned them upside down and punched them again. Greg had blown up . . . but oh! in what a lovely way!

'Greg darling . . .'

'Sara, you sweet, brave little *wretch*. And darling, even if you say you weren't brave, you were. Very, very brave.'

'And you?'

'Me? I was just madly in love with those lights in your eyes and bent on saving your life. I had to save Jack's, which was chivalrous of me, but a nuisance.'

'Oh, Greg! You see, Julia came to the Adelphi . . .'

'Yes, and I pushed her out.'

'I thought . . .'

'Ssh! Say no more. Only sleep.'

His mouth was hard pressed on hers again, his arms around her.

'You're quoting Robert Browning,' she said, muffled because his mouth was in the way.

'Yes, but I'm loving you. That's much more important. Now do you know who's boss round here?'

'Yes, darling.'

'Then don't forget it.'

'I never will. Cross my heart.'

'And you love me?'

'I love you, Greg.'